RETALIATION
(Lex Talionis)

Diana Lainson

RETALIATION
(Lex Talionis)

FICTION4ALL

ACKNOWLEDGEMENTS

I should like to dedicate this book to my dear husband Derek, who stood by me and put up with my moods whilst creating it and urged me on to finish this novel as he cooked meals for us both. Without his help it would be still mouldering away on my laptop. Also to the rest of my family, who spurred me on to finish it, when I almost gave up. Not forgetting of course, Reggie Cous-Cous, Nockie and little Frilly our cats, who kept walking over my laptop and purring in my face trying to fill me with inspiration!

AUTHOR'S NOTES

THE MEANINGS

Lex Talionis - commonly known as

The Law of Retaliation as described in the Bible.
EXODUS XXl Ch. 22 – 25

Ch. 22 – If men strive, and hurt a woman with child, so that her fruit depart from her, and yet no mischief follow: he shall be severely punished, according as the woman's husband will lay upon him: and he shall pay as the judges determine.

Ch. 23 - And if any mischiefs follow, then thou shalt give life for life.

Ch. 24 - Eye for eye, tooth for tooth, hand for hand and foot for foot.

Ch. 25 - Burning for burning, wound for wound, and stripe for stripe.

Always remember things like this can happen in real life, and also

remember, there are times in one's life when it is proper to make common

cause with an enemy, but always be on your guard. **Know thine enemy.**

(**Spanish words**: - Querida - darling, Buenos tardes - good evening, Cojones - balls!)

PROLOGUE

NORTH LONDON 2004

Darkness blanketed the streets. The rain and the cold wind battered cars and houses. The shabby green door of the dingy semi-detached council house swung open and a young man dressed in an old black leather jacket and black denim jeans strode out, shouting obscenities at someone inside as he left.

As he walked down the weed covered pathway, he had a spring in his step; it would seem that he'd obviously had a fix.

He adjusted his well-worn red baseball cap down to cover his face from the stinging rain and walked down the badly lit road. As he moved off in the distance, the smart black BMW car, with black tinted windows that had been following him, overtook him and pulled into the kerb and parked at the roadside. He walked past ignoring it, he was too wrapped up in his own thoughts and making a mental list of whom he could sell some of his recently acquired *crack* to. He felt he was coming up in the world, having that morning met some new clients.

The door of the car slowly opened and a tall slim woman stepped out dressed in black; her red hair covered with a functional PVC rain hat with the brim pulled down fashionably that matched her black raincoat. Her hands were encased in dark mauve surgical latex gloves.

The whole area was poorly lit and offered many shadowy places to move around unseen. Her face was partially hidden in the shadows. She paused and then slowly followed the young man down the gloomy street. She was now filled with a certain calmness as she followed him; her anger from that morning still remained, but was overridden by the satisfying thrill of what was about to happen. To seek revenge for herself and other women who might have suffered in the past.

Suddenly the young man became aware that someone was behind him and he quickly turned to face the person. A chilly shiver ran down his spine and he felt a wash of terror pass over him as he momentarily hesitated in his step. The tall woman pulled out a weapon from the inside of her black raincoat and pointed it at him. It glinted menacingly in the dim street lighting as the rain splashed onto it.

He looked terrified.

She aimed for his groin and pulled the trigger and the projectile smacked into him. It passed almost through him shattering his coccyx and imbedding itself into his right buttock. The impact swung him around and sent him crashing to the ground screaming in agony as he fell to the pavement in his bodily fluids. He clutched wildly at himself both hands cupping his wounded testes, the blood seeping fiercely through his dirty fingers and pouring down his grubby denim-clad legs.

She bent over the fallen man and looked down at him writhing with pain. For a few seconds she stood silent and motionless, smiling contemptuously, then as if he were a piece of dirt in the road she kicked out at him and he rolled into the gutter and then she turned and walked quickly away towards the car, alert to every shadow, every little noise and every hint of movement around her.

The tall woman now back in the black car smiled sardonically and with a great sense of accomplishment. She looked around her ensuring that no one was about that dark and rainy winter evening to witness her deeds. She pulled the plastic hat from her head and the red wig and dropped them behind the front passenger seat and shook out her shoulder length blonde hair.

Then she returned the weapon into the large black leather handbag lying open in the front foot well of the back seats and snapped it firmly shut. Her hands remained there a moment, resting them, savouring the sweetness of her revenge. Starting up the engine, she put the car into drive and drove off at a leisurely pace.

It was all over in a matter of minutes - her deed was done - another had paid the ultimate penalty.

She slept well that night.

***

Three days later bold headlines in several of the leading tabloids read as follows: -

ANOTHER DRUG ADDICT FOUND DEAD IN A POOL OF BLOOD

The papers went on to say that he was a registered heroin addict and a known woman and child abuser living with his current girlfriend and their infant in a dilapidated part of North London on a council estate. Both parents were unemployed. He was the fourth male over a period of eight weeks. So far the police had very few clues as to who the killer was and the other victims might be. Who is the mystery killer? A vigilante? A man hater? Or perhaps an avenging Angel of women, delivering society from scum in a hard and effective style. Is it a man or could it be a woman? Why are the victims always dark-haired young males in their late twenties...is there a **SERIAL KILLER** *on the loose?*

Sarah Lawson picked up the Daily Mail and read the headlines of the article written about the latest victim of the mysterious Serial Killer. As she bit into her toast a paragraph in the article caught her attention:-

The murder enquiry is still under way following the discovery of yet another young man's body, in North London two nights ago. The post-mortem revealed that the twenty-six year old had died as a result of a fatal wound to the lower part of his body. This is the fourth incident and DCI Paul Forrest, who has been leading the investigation, is now convinced that this murder is linked to the three other fatalities that have been discovered over the last two months.

He also commented that at this point in time the police have got no idea who killed these unfortunate young men. It is said that there seems to be no obvious motive for the killings; they have no witnesses and very little forensic evidence at the moment. Further investigations are taking place. Is there a Serial Killer on the loose? DCI Forrest has called in Mr David Myers to help with the case. Mr. Myers the well-known Forensic Psychiatrist and *leading expert on the Psychopathology of Serial Killers was interviewed as he left his West End penthouse apartment yesterday morning. Mr Myers commented that in his opinion the murders are the product of a person under emotional siege, someone who is not necessarily cruel or even bad, but someone who has perhaps suffered in the past from mental as well as physical abuse. This could almost be a case of - **LEX TALIONIS** - commonly known as the Law of Retaliation - as described in the Bible - Exodus XXI. 23 - 25.*

"Yes, you're right, Mr Myers. *Retaliation.* He also deserved it, just like the others," she proclaimed aloud vehemently to the large cat sitting in his favourite Edwardian armchair, enjoying a ray of winter sunshine filtering through the patio windows of her sitting room.

"Yes...he certainly deserved it Picasso, didn't he? Just like the first, fancy beating that poor girl up in the street like that and nearly killing the pretty baby girl. What a devil!"

She closed the newspaper, patted her knees and the big English Blue blinked several times, then looked at her lazily before jumping into her lap. She was glad she had none of those problems anymore, she didn't need a man, she was perfectly happy on her own. Or so she kept trying to convince herself.

BOOK ONE

EXODUS XXI Verse 22: *If men strive, and hurt a woman with child,*
so that her fruit depart from her, and yet no mischief follows:
he shall be severely punished, accordingly the woman's husband
will lay upon him: and he shall pay as the judges determine.

CHAPTER ONE

LONDON - 2004

Just over two months before Sarah Lawson had been driving along a narrow road in a run-down part of North London and seen a filthy, unkept dark-haired young man, in grubby white sportswear, walking along with a pretty blonde girl in fake designer clothes, pushing a beaten up old pushchair with a baby girl in it. Suddenly it seemed, for no reason at all, he had turned on the young woman, swearing loudly and then punching her in the stomach, chest and face. In her panic to defend herself, she put both hands up to shield her face from the blows and as she let go of the buggy it ran down the incline of the pavement, into the road and in the path of an oncoming car.

The driver coming the other way had narrowly missed it. He swerved violently as he jammed on his brakes and nearly crashed into her black BMW before going on his way. The young mother had leapt into the road to save her child, followed by the dark-haired man who was still hurling abuse at her and trying to hit her again.

Sarah had stopped and watched the whole scene through her windscreen and once again it brought back dreadful memories of Julio whom she had lived with in Spain for nearly a year, and the terrible beatings and verbal abuse she had put up with from him, for no reason at all. When he had been stoned or drunk, or both, Julio's character had changed completely and he had become the Devil Incarnate, totally possessed by the poison in his mind and body. The dark haired young man shouting in the street had the same wild look about him. She pressed the switch of the electric window at her side and shouted at him, threatening him with the police.

"Fuck off you bitch," he yelled back at her as he gave her an offensive sign with his middle finger. Then he had run after her car also hurling more abuse at her and waving his fists as she angrily drove away. She would really have liked to have run him down there and then, but that would have been too obvious.

"Oh, fuck off yourself," she had shouted back through the window. "Just you wait; I'll get you for that." She had accelerated hard, shot around a nearby corner and stopped her car.

Her heart was thumping inside of her slight body and she could feel the adrenaline from her anger coursing through her veins. The young man had not bothered to try to follow her. She knew the girl had not heard what she had said; she'd been too far away.

Sarah waited a few minutes before getting out of her car. Then she had walked around the corner and saw the couple making their way towards her. Neither of them recognised her as she bent down and fiddled with an imaginary spot on her shoes. They passed her still bickering loudly. She'd stood up and slowly followed them at a discreet distance. After several moments they had entered a very shabby looking semi-detached house, with one window boarded up and the front gate hanging on one hinge, on a run-down Council estate, backing onto some old railway lines.

She had waited behind some bushes across the road opposite the old house for nearly half an hour. Eventually her patience was rewarded. The young man came out of the dilapidated house, and slammed the shabby green door behind him, but this time he had on a black leather jacket, over a pair of old blue denim jeans. He took out a cigarette from one of his pockets, lit it and walked off with a spring in his step.

He's most probably had a fix, Sarah thought, and he was full of himself. He had even combed back his long greasy dark hair off his gaunt pale face into a small ponytail at the base of his neck. No doubt he couldn't even remember that he had tried to beat the girl up. Pulling out a mobile phone from another pocket he started to key in some numbers. It was now starting to rain.

After a few moments he flagged down a battered old red Vauxhall Cavalier as it came screeching around the corner. It stopped and he exchanged a few quick words with the driver, opened the passenger door and jumped in. They drove off together in a cloud of black smoke, tyres again protesting loudly at the treatment they were receiving.

Several moments later, the young girl came out of the house with her small child in the same shabby pushchair. She looked around nervously and then slowly limped along the street in the opposite direction to where Sarah was hiding. Sarah wondered if she had been beaten up again. The bile had arisen in her throat as she re-lived her own pain and humiliation of the past. She had no need to write down the name of the street or the house number, they were firmly etched in her mind along with a mental picture of the young man; she had things to do. Very quickly she walked back to her parked car and drove off. She would be back.

* * *

The next afternoon when she had arrived back at her house in Richmond, from her voluntary work at the Rehabilitation Centre the first thing she did was to go upstairs to her bedroom and from its hiding place she took out the small custom-made crossbow.

She had found it sometime ago in the attic of her Aunt's house, when she had first moved in after arriving back from Spain. It was presumably a souvenir her Aunt had picked up from one of her holidays abroad. She did not throw it away as she thought it might come in handy one day. It was still in its box, together with six shiny eight-inch stainless steel bolts. The ideal weapon she thought. Very carefully she checked and loaded the small crossbow and made sure the safety catch was on. As she fondled the beautifully crafted weapon, she planned her movements carefully for the rest of that day.

She had spent most of the morning at the Rehab Centre going through the records in the office and pulling out of the computer several names of young men that should be taught a lesson, she had printed them out and brought them home with her and hidden them in the attic as well.

Sarah knew what she had to do and took the mobile phone from her dressing table and made a quick call. Then placing the small crossbow with one of her wigs into her large black leather Gucci handbag, she hung it over the top of an upright chair standing in the corner of her bedroom. Then she walked into her en-suite bathroom to have a shower.

As she felt the hot water running over her lithe body, she ran her soapy hands over her firm breasts. Momentarily she conjured up a vision of Julio, when he had been nice to her and she had been in love with him. Her nipples quickly reacted to her touch and became erect. Her right hand slowly moved down her body and lingered on her mound of Venus and then she started caressing herself and thinking about the good memories of Julio.

Suddenly she snatched her fingers away and she felt intense anger with herself for thinking about him. She stopped, horrified that the memory of him could still make her want him and she forced herself to remember the bad times when he had abused her mentally as well as physically, forcing her to have sex with him against her will. At once the old anger came back to her. She turned off the shower and stepped out of the compartment hastily and grabbed a large white fluffy towel from the heated towel-rail and patted herself dry. She needed the intense anger in her to do what she had to do that rainy evening.

Returning to her bedroom she swiftly dressed in a smart black two piece suit, slipped her black stocking-clad feet into a pair of low heeled black court shoes and applied a light outline of kohl pencil to her eyes and a dusting of translucent powder over her beautiful face. A little touch of pink blusher and finally a touch of lip-gloss to her lips. She twisted her blonde hair into a soft pleat at the back and pinned it into place with a couple of tortoise-shell hairpins. Then she glanced in the mirror and smiled at herself. *She was ready*. She picked up the large black handbag that contained a red wig and a black plastic rain hat, went downstairs, into the kitchen and quickly fed her cat that was brushing himself against her legs, purring loudly.

"Okay, Picasso, I will not be long my darling."

Sarah bent down and caressed his thick blue fur, before setting the alarm system, then locked the front door securely behind her. She double-checked that the door was in fact secured before walking to her car. She told herself that she was getting paranoid about security and must get over her obsessive behaviour of checking everything two or three times. As she walked down the gravel path, she waved to a neighbour across the road who was commenting about the weather. Sarah nodded and smiled in agreement, not really hearing what the woman was saying, as she was so deep in thought. She got into her car and carefully backed it out of the driveway. It had started to rain heavily.

***

When Sarah returned later that winter evening, she put the crossbow and wig away in their hiding place in the attic, showered again, tied her blonde hair back into a ponytail and changed into a pair of comfortable winceyette pyjamas with little Poo bears on them and her old dressing gown and a pair of pink Tote socks and ran downstairs. She entered into the ultra-modern kitchen and poured herself a glass of well-chilled Chardonnay and took some chive-flavoured crisps out of one of the cupboards. Walking through slowly to her elegantly furnished lounge/dining room she put on a comedy DVD, and then sat back on the large comfortable white Italian brocade settee and relaxed.

She sighed deeply, it had been a very busy day and she felt exhilarated and powerful, yet extremely contented, she felt she was at last starting to exorcise Julio out of her system, but she had to be very careful though and make sure that her every move was thoroughly thought through, double checked and checked again, she must make no mistakes. Picasso came over to her and nestled into her lap trying to ease the tension in her body as he started to tread her with his front paws and as he felt her relaxing he flopped down beside her and he too fell into a deep sleep.

BOOK TWO

GENESIS 11 Verse 26: And God said let us make man in our image…

CHAPTER TWO

MARBELLA – SPAIN - 2002

Sarah lay back in her comfortable chaise longue on the big balcony of her apartment in Marbella at the Playa Esmeralda. She was looking across the golden beach in front of her at the sparkling blue Mediterranean Sea, through her large Versace sunglasses that covered her startling blue eyes. Her shoulder length blonde hair was caught up into a knot on the top of her head. She had no make-up on.

She had on a very brief white bikini and was enjoying the last few rays of the September afternoon sun. There was a gentle breeze blowing and windsurfers skilfully skimmed across the light waves, they seemed to be just going nowhere really, only backwards and forwards. A bit like me she thought, her life seemed to be sweeping by and she was not really going anywhere either.

Sarah had enough of Spain. Everything had gone wrong since she'd moved to the Costa del Sol from the UK three years before with her second husband Mark, a tall handsome, arrogant blonde aristocrat, ever since he had taken the job in the Middle East.

Mark Lawson had worked for an American offshore oil company in Saudi Arabia as an Engineering Consultant for nearly twenty-two years before losing his job at the age of forty-five, through his own carelessness. He had been at a party given by one of the young Sheikhs. A party where young women as well as young men, alcohol and plenty of recreational drugs, were prolific.

The Secret Police in Saudi Arabia had been informed about it and had raided the Sheikh's palace and Mark had been deported within twenty-four hours, along with several other Europeans who worked for two of the other oil companies. When he returned to Marbella after *the incident*, as he called it, he spent most of their savings in the bars and clubs that catered for his needs, including a nasty habit he had picked up over the years, Cocaine. As they were getting so short of money, he had decided to go back to England and claim some more of his inheritance from his rich parents and promised her that he would find work and send for her. Shortly after that he left and the new job never materialised. Mark had in fact walked right out of her life, never to be heard of again it would seem.

She didn't know whether he was dead or alive. Even his wealthy, snobbish parents didn't know, or pretended not to know where he was. Maybe one day he would contact her regarding a divorce. She knew it would happen when he found himself the right partner, his preference being - young men. She had found out that Mark was gay two months after their marriage. Sarah was just a trophy wife, the American company he had joined many years ago, preferred married men working for them. But even so, she had never been to Saudi Arabia. She had stayed on in Marbella, as she had nowhere else to go.

For the first three months of their married life they had lived with his parents, in their manor house in Kent, before he was posted to Saudi Arabia and then she had joined him later in Spain, when he was on one of his regular four monthly breaks. Finally they had decided to rent a fully furnished apartment in Marbella, as Spain was more convenient than England for Mark when he took his vacations, or so he said. She knew otherwise, he did not get on with his parents.

Sarah was unaware when she married him that he took drugs. She was also unaware that there was so little money in their bank account when he left her. Another bad shock for her was the fact that he had not paid the rent on the apartment for nearly three months. The bank manager was very sympathetic towards her and allowed her to become overdrawn until such time that her husband returned or sent sufficient funds to pay off the overdraft. He also had recommended her to several of his business friends who needed some confidential correspondence translated into English, her Spanish being fluent, but the steady stream of work had eventually dried up.

Her first husband she had met and married in England, though wealthy, he had been extremely mean and he often subjected her to physical abuse when he had been drinking. One night after a violent argument he had driven off and run head on into an articulated truck and been killed outright. She felt that justice had prevailed. She had inherited most of his money, but even that had dwindled away because of Mark's expensive life-style as well as the meagre savings he had somehow managed to accumulate whilst working in Saudi Arabia.

Sarah had met Mark six months after the death of her first husband, at one of her friend's wedding and they had had a whirlwind marriage a month later. It was only later on that she found out that he had only married her because he needed a wife for show and also that he thought she was rich, and now there was nothing left. She had managed to pay the arrears off the apartment, but she was again a month behind and the letting agent was getting impatient for his money, she'd had a letter from him that morning allowing her another week in which to find the money.

"Oh well..." she exclaimed out aloud, "I'll just have to get enough money together somehow for a one-way ticket back to England and do a moonlight."

That sort of thing though, was entirely against her principles, she had to do something and get away quickly. At least she still had some good jewellery left to sell, if needs be. She sighed deeply and slowly got up from the red-striped sun lounger and went inside to make herself something to eat. She had decided to go down to the little bar beneath the luxury apartment complex where she lived for a drink, as she felt the need for some company that evening.

***

"Buenos tardes, senora," said Manuel, the owner of the little Tapas bar, with a cheery smile on his chubby weather-beaten face. "The usual senora?"

"No thanks Mano, not tonight. I think I'll have a white wine spritzer for a change."

She gave him a dazzling smile, replying back to him in perfect Spanish.

Hope my credit is still good with him she thought, as she carefully perched herself onto one of the high black vinyl covered stainless steel stools alongside the long bar. She pulled at the hem of the little black dress she was wearing, so that she wouldn't show too much of her long tanned shapely legs.

She was thirty-four years old and a stunning tall blonde. Too tall some might say at five foot nine inches in bare feet, with a well-toned figure that many women would die for. Shoulder length blonde hair, incredible blue eyes and a tan that showed her beauty off to its full advantage.

She looked around the already crowded bar, it was only nine in the evening, but being September and the weather still very hot, the popular little place was quickly filling up with the latest influx of tourists and of course, the local handsome, sun-tanned, dark-haired young gigolos, looking for foreign middle-aged women with money to buy them a drink and a meal and no doubt spend the night with them. Also if they stayed with them for the duration of their victim's holiday, they might receive a handsome reward for their favours.

Sarah smiled to herself. When she had first arrived in Marbella, the same thing had happened to her, but she had not been interested as she was a happily married woman, or so she had thought at the time. As she looked around she noticed several sunburnt young European females, no doubt on a shoestring budget holiday for a week, looking for wealthy middle-aged men to buy them a drink or meal. That was one way of getting some money. Perish the thought; she would never do that. Perhaps Manuel and his lovely wife would make her a small loan until she could sell some more of her jewellery, she knew they were very fond of her and she had often helped them out in the bar without payment.

"Good evening, senora."

A soft well-spoken male voice, in slightly accentuated English greeted her.

She swivelled around on her high stool to encounter the speaker. A pair of almost black eyes, surrounded by the longest sweeping black eyelashes she had ever seen on a man, stared back at her. His wide smile displayed perfect dazzling white teeth that gleamed at her from a very handsome bronzed face.

He was dressed in tight black designer jeans, a white T-shirt and wore thonged soft black leather sandals on his feet. She tried at first to ignore the young man and stared straight through him. Not again, she thought, don't they ever give up!

Sarah was well aware of her attractiveness; she looked after herself by keeping fit and monitoring her diet. She had well-shaped breasts that tapered to a slim waist and narrow hips and knew that an attractive blonde woman was always a target for the Mediterranean male. She still had a few good clothes she'd bought after the sale of Mark's Mercedes sports car that he had left behind. She didn't mind being without a car though; there were always taxis and the walking did her figure good.

"I know you are English." He persisted.

He spoke to her again obviously determined to make his presence known to her.

Focusing her bright blue eyes on his dark ones, she replied curtly.

"Yes, I am English, I'm not a tourist, and I live here, okay? I do not need an escort for the evening. I am waiting for my husband!"

She tried very hard to sound annoyed. Perhaps he would go away and pester some other woman.

He stared right back at her and boldly held her gaze with a slight smile playing on his lips for several seconds before replying.

"You are a very beautiful woman, Senora Lawson. But I expect you know that! I also know that you are not waiting for anyone. You live upstairs. Alone."

He grinned knowingly at her, once more showing his even white teeth.

She held his cheeky gaze, curious, how did he know her name and how did he know that she lived alone? And how did he know she lived in one of the apartments upstairs? Damn, she thought, he is attractive, a bit young perhaps, but so what. She felt an intense desire for him sweep through her body. It was over six months since she'd had any sex and that had been a very hurried and dissatisfying session at a very boring party of one of her very boring friends. Tonight could be the night, what did she have to lose anyway? She would be leaving Spain soon. Her lovely face broke into a seductive smile.

"So how do you know so much about me?"

"I have seen you many times on the beach and in this bar. I simply asked Manuel, he is a good friend of mine and knows nearly everything that goes on around here."

The young man held out his hand. "My name is Julio Antonio Gonzales."

He shook her hand firmly, and then let it go slowly. Smiling at her again, as he spoke, the charm oozed out of every pore of his young muscular body.

He was a tall young man, in his late twenties, she reckoned. Broad shoulders and his raven black hair was cut short and swept back over his head without a parting. Clean-shaven, his face was tanned, strong and slightly angular. His large dark eyes glistened, they were deep set and nearly coal black, surrounded by long black lashes and he moved with an air of confidence and assurance.

Sarah felt uncomfortable; he made her feel reckless. She swallowed deeply and cleared her throat, as it always seized up when she was nervous or excited. Warning bells rang in her head, but she chose to ignore them.

That was how they met and that was the reason for her staying on in Spain for several months - months of terror - that would always remain with her...forever. *That was also the biggest mistake she had ever made in her life!*

Julio told her he was twenty-six and came from a very wealthy family. He received a generous allowance from his father, he didn't need to work, but he helped his father with many of his business activities. His father was a high-ranking Spanish Diplomat and travelled a good deal, especially since his English mother had died from a heart attack when he was only 16 years old. His father had married again when he was twenty-one to another English woman and they both lived in London next to the Spanish Embassy.

Julio's family owned a lot of land, many large properties all over Spain and also some bars and restaurants, leased out to foreigners and local people. Manuel being one of his father's tenants and they also owned the luxury apartment block of apartments that Sarah lived in. Julio himself owned a luxury block near Puerto Banus, a twenty-fifth birthday present from his father, where he now lived.

At the beginning of October, Julio asked her to move in with him, as he wanted to look after her. He knew she owed rent on her apartment, but he was quite happy to write it off. He said he would also buy her a small car if she wished.

"I will look after you always," he had told her.

Where had she heard those words before, she thought. Both her first and second husbands had said similar words to her, but she thought this time they were for real.

Somehow over the weeks he seemed to have taken over her life. He sold the contents of her flat, which were hers, to a friend, giving her the money, which she put into her bank account. She had been struggling hard for so long on her own; it was wonderful to have someone so generous to look after her. He didn't demand anything from her sexually at first, just her company. They even slept in separate bedrooms in his large apartment.

Julio pampered and spoilt her; no man she thought had ever focused on her so completely. He took her shopping nearly every day and bought her expensive gifts of clothes, perfumes and red roses by the dozen. In fact anything that took his or her fancy. She had never been looked after so well in her life. The warning bells kept ringing, but she still chose to ignore them. She came to rely on him completely, for her it was so wonderful to be treated as a desirable person once again.

After a couple of weeks she moved into his bed. He was a fantastic lover, in fact the best lover she'd ever had. Sometimes they just spent all day in bed making love, never moving out, and sending out for food. She never did any cooking or housework. Sarah thought she was idyllically happy. A young Spanish girl called Maria came in twice a week to clean the apartment and she also did the washing and ironing.

The first three months of their relationship were perfect, they did not need anyone else and they cut themselves off from everyone. Then suddenly Julio started to go out alone, returning late, sometimes during the early hours of the morning *rent collecting* or so he said, for his father. Of course she believed him at first, she had no reason not to; he had never lied to her before, or so she thought, so she asked no questions and it was nice to have a little space sometimes.

Usually when he returned late he would wake her gently and make passionate love to her. Suddenly it stopped, he was too tired and she had difficulty waking him in the mornings. She wondered what the unlabelled pill bottle that suddenly appeared by their bedside contained. When she had confronted him, vitamin pills, was the reply. She did not question him any further.

CHAPTER THREE

MARBELLA – 2003

In February, the fifth month of their relationship, Julio left one day and did not return for about forty-eight hours. When he came in eventually, around three o'clock in the early morning, Sarah was waiting up for him, needing to confront him. She'd had just about enough of his bad behaviour.

He lurched through the front door, and then slammed it loudly behind him, entering the lounge where she was stretched out on one of the long, low black leather settees, watching a DVD, or at least pretending to.

"What's that stupid film you're watching and why are you waiting up for me, don't you trust me?" He shouted at her and kicked out at the television set, knocking it off its stand and it shattered into several pieces as it fell onto the white marble floor with a deafening sound.

"You're not my mother, what the hell are you waiting up for me for?"

He questioned her again; his face ugly and distorted as he swayed towards her searching frantically for something in one of the pockets of his black leather jacket, with trembling hands.

"No, I am not your mother, thank God," she replied disdainfully, sneering at him. "Are you drunk, or something?"

"No I'm not. I've only had two beers. Can't I drink when I want to, bitch? You don't own me." He shouted back at her in Spanish.

Sarah stared hard at him, recalling an occasion when Mark had acted in a similar manner when he had been using cocaine. Please God no, she prayed silently. She also noticed that Julio's eyes were shining unnaturally, their pupils completely dilated. He seemed angry, but at the same time drunk. She realised then that he was taking some kind of drugs, but not being too familiar about illegal substances, she wasn't quite sure what.

However, over the next few weeks, she was to become very aware of his drug abuse.

She looked intently at him, as if seeing him for the first time. He had finally fished out a mangled Marlboro' Red cigarette from his pocket and was trying to light it with unsteady hands. He had always looked so smart in the past, but now he was a mess she noticed, as she stared at him. He was also in need of a shave and his black hair had become almost shoulder length and greasy, badly in need of a wash. As she scrutinised him she felt nothing but disgust, but at the same time a little scared for her own safety.

"Don't you call me a bitch, you ugly drunken Spanish pig." She spat back at him. "How dare you! No one speaks to me like that."

She was furious and wanted to hit out at him, but did not have the courage to.

He stepped forward and grabbed her, and then drawing back his right hand he hit her across the face sharply. Blood welled up and ran down the side of her mouth as he split her top lip open. From the impact of the blow she fell sideways onto the large square olivewood coffee table and one of the corners caught her between her shoulder blades. Gasping aloud with the acute pain, she fell to the floor in a heap. She screamed and hurled abuse at him in Spanish. Blinking with anger and pain she focused on the big black onyx cigarette box on the top of the table. Unnoticed by him she picked it up with her left hand.

As he bent forward towards her, as if to strike her again, she brought up her arm and with every ounce of strength in her slender body she struck him on the forehead between his eyes, drawing blood.

He was unable to avoid the missile, the blow stunned him and he dropped to the floor beside her, pushing the settee along the shiny white marble floor with his dead weight.

With great satisfaction she noticed the large gash between his eyebrows at the top of his nose was bleeding profusely as he lay unconscious in front of her. She moved away from him, distaste written all over her face. Then she started to shake uncontrollably. She was very frightened, the cigarette box was still in her hand and she placed it back gingerly onto the table-top.

What had she done?

As she eased herself up onto the settee, she wondered if she had in fact killed him and where she had got the strength to hit him so hard. Then Julio started to moan and move slightly, as he gradually regained consciousness. He sat up and suddenly his whole personality changed and he burst into remorseful tears. He crawled over to her and took her in his arms, kissed her gently and started crooning soft words to her in Spanish.

Her flimsy robe had fallen open; she could feel herself automatically responding to his touch. She was nearly naked beneath the silken dressing gown except for a white lace bra and matching thong. He pulled her on top of him; she could feel the hardness of his erection through his jeans. He ripped the tiny pieces of lace from her as Sarah clawed at the zip fastener of his denims and sat astride him.

They had violent sex on the cold floor, their hungry passions grew as their pleasure increased, it was frantic, a base sex, giving them the release they both needed - or was it just uncontrolled lust? She had never experienced anything like it before; it was savage and painful, and yet it satisfied the longing for him inside of her, in a very cruel way. A way that she never thought she was capable of enjoying.

They kissed savagely and she could feel him bruising her tender lips as he gripped her shoulders, his fingers digging into her flesh painfully as he rolled her over onto the hard floor, but she didn't seem to notice the discomfort. Her back arched as she came up to meet his powerful thrusts and she cried out like a wild animal with her release, he too shouted out loudly, as they climaxed together. At that time she didn't know that this was a performance that would be repeated time and time again.

Over the next two weeks, Julio never left the apartment without her. He cleaned himself up and had his long greasy haircut and styled, once more he looked like the young man she had originally fallen in love with, but she was still wary of him. He bought her more presents. One of them was a beautiful black Persian cat that she had fallen in love with in a pet shop in town. He named her Sario, a combination of both of their names.

They took long rides in his new red Ferrari around the lovely Spanish countryside, had picnics and made passionate love in the open air. Spring was upon them and he promised to take her up to the hills to see the big old Spanish hacienda and the very large expanse of land, covered with olive trees, fruit trees and grape vines that his grandparents had left him. He seemed very repentant, very loving, but somewhat nervy and he was smoking heavily again. Then he started drinking in the evenings, at first moderately, then heavier, but he wasn't violent as before. Not for some time!

Sarah watched him carefully over the weeks for any behavioural changes. He kept telling her how sorry he was and that he would never hit her again. He said he was afraid that she would leave him. She noticed he was becoming extremely possessive about her and didn't like any other man looking at her. She told him she would certainly leave him if he ever laid a finger on her again.

"In fact," she said very seriously to him. "I shall kill you if you do."

She recalled the memory of her cousin who had been physically abused by her husband for years and eventually took her own life. Sarah had known nothing about it until her aunt Meg, who lived in Richmond, told her at the funeral five years previously. She had become very close to her Aunt after her own parents had died tragically in a road accident during her teens and had moved in with her until she was old enough to live on her own and even closer after the death of her cousin.

Justice had prevailed though. The cruel, deceitful, lying husband had been killed a few months later in a car crash in Birmingham, with his current girlfriend. There was no way that Sarah intended to become a punch bag for any man as her cousin had. *Or so she had thought at the time.*

BOOK THREE

EXODUS XXI Verse 23: And if any mischief follows, then thou shalt give life for life.

CHAPTER FOUR

LONDON - 2004

David Myers was a professor of Psychiatry and Forensic Psychopathology. He'd been working with the police all over England and in Europe for more than twelve years and had come upon many strange things. He had a good idea that the killer was a woman, his gut feelings were rarely wrong. With his great knowledge of serial killers, he was in great demand and called upon regularly for his services, even though he was an independent Psychiatrist with his own very successful practise in Grosvenor Square.

He had told the police that the killer would probably carry on killing at an even greater rate until he or she was caught. It was almost as if the killer was seeking attention, if not help. Most definitely the killer was someone who had suffered in the past personally, or was avenging someone close to him or her who had been physically or mentally abused. The killer could be a gay person, with a grudge, but he did not think so.

At this point, he was very sure it had to be a woman. The weapon used also pointed to this, easily hidden in a large handbag. Women too, as a rule, were often more careful than men, they usually left less clues as they were more fanatical about details.

*Lex **Talionis,** he had told the reporters of various newspapers - **the law of Retaliation** - **an eye for an eye** - whereby punishment resembles the offence committed in kind and degree, as quoted in the Bible.*

DCI Paul Forrest, David's friend and colleague, who was on the case, had spent many long hours discussing it and together they tried to create a profile of the killer. The victims were all users of hard drugs and living off the immoral earnings of their girlfriends. Maybe it was one of the girlfriends.

The post-mortems had confirmed that the all of the young men had been shot in the testes with an eight inch silver-plated bolt from a small-customised crossbow, tearing the scrotum apart and the victims left to bleed to death. Ballistics verified that the crossbow had been imported or brought in illegally from abroad, either from Spain or Turkey, the only countries where such weapons could be made to order. However, the police had not disclosed to the media yet the type of weapon used. The only information given out to them was that the victims had been shot in the genital area, but not beaten up before the incident. It would seem that they were not sexual killings either, it was not that sort of crime. Could it be ritual or a vendetta he asked himself?

David sat at his computer in his luxury penthouse and fed the data into it.

Victim one: - Yannis Papadopoulos - Greek Cypriot - 25 years old, known drug user, unemployed, 2 years GBH involving his girl-friend and also for assaulting a female police officer whilst resisting arrest. Recently released, last known address Finchley. Shot in testes with an eight-inch crossbow bolt. Unable to identify assassin. DOA.

Victim two: - John Porter - Pimp unemployed - British - 27 years old, known drug user and alcoholic. Shot in testes. Victim found dead 24 hours after the event. Last known address Golders Green living with his girlfriend - prostitute.

Victim three: - Antonio Giordano - Italian - 25 years old, child abuser, reformed alcoholic. Wife returned to Sicily with daughter two years previously. Now working as a part-time waiter in an Italian restaurant in North London, reported missing by employer. Found dead in derelict warehouse in Palmers Green. Shot in testes. Forensic evidence showed that he had crawled there after being shot and bled to death several hours later.

Victim four: - Gary Medway - British - from Newcastle - 26 years old. Known heroin user, unemployed. A woman and child abuser. Shot in testes found on pavement in Palmers Green, alive at scene of crime, ambulance called. Unable to identify assassin. DOA.

No one so far, it seemed, had been able to identify the killer; also there had been no witnesses. This person was very clever; it had all been planned down to the very last little detail.

David stopped for several moments then stood up and ran his left hand through his thick, slightly greying dark hair again. The usual neatness of his hair had been wrecked by the continuous nervous sweeps of his hand. He was unshaven, his clothes crumpled and he was very tired. He closed his eyes waiting for some sort of inspiration. Then he started pacing his study floor slowly; his thoughts turned to some of his patients in the past, his mind searching for clues. Could any of them have done it? His patients were predominantly women, extremely wealthy ones, to be able to afford his fees.

Either their partners or husbands had beaten them up at some time or other under the influence of alcohol or drugs. As far as he was concerned it was one of the most despicable things that a man could do to a woman. The women had his sympathy. His female patients were of different religions, nationalities and cultures. Violence has no racial discrimination, he thought. We can all kill another human being, if we are pushed too far. We all walk a tightrope in life, one false step either way and we fall off. Fortunately most of us keep our balance; we can usually control our lives and tell right from wrong.

An incident room had been set up at New Scotland Yard. The killer had left no clues. The police had found no fingerprints, no footprints, nothing; it was as if a phantom had struck. It seemed that the young men had been shot from a fairly short distance; someone had got very close to them or probably from a stationary car, usually in wet weather, therefore, leaving no tyre tracks. All they had to go on were the four eight-inch silver-plated bolts and so far they had drawn somewhat of a blank on those.

Very clever, he thought. He stopped pacing and walked into his smart kitchen and made a cup of strong filter coffee before returning to his desk.

"C'mon, c'mon," he shouted impatiently, as he spun the ball of the optic mouse to bring his computer out of sleep mode and waited, fingers poised over the keyboard. He had been struggling with several ideas about the murders and wanted to feed them into his computer while they were still fresh in his mind. He heard the familiar muffled sounds of the hard drive examining itself, then finally the soft crackle of the computer coming back to life. He pressed the function key that would call up the programme he wanted. The photos of the young men he had loaded earlier onto it came to life and he zoomed in on the pictures, examining them minutely as he looked for clues as he worked on into the small hours of the morning.

David Myers was a widower and self-made man at the top of his career and at forty-six one of the best in his field. He acknowledged to himself that he was a workaholic, a lonely man in many ways, though he would never admit it to anyone. He had always liked the company of women and found that sex came his way without looking for it and he found some solace in it, but mostly they were only brief encounters.

He was somewhat of an avoidant, not willing to give too much of himself. For the last eight years he had lived in this way, alone in his luxury penthouse apartment in the West End of London. There was no evidence of a female around; it was essentially a large bachelor's pad.

A lady in her fifties, Mrs Jackson, came in three times a week to clean, sort out his laundry, and helped when he entertained the odd guest. Usually he just ordered the food from Harrods or Selfridges, even though he was quite a good cook himself, but he never seemed to have the time or the inclination. The caterers just brought it in, cleared it away and he was quite content living that way. He had conditioned himself to living alone, but lately he seemed to have reached a crossroads in his life. He had all the things he needed, money and position, but no one to share them with and he didn't really want to die a lonely, miserable old man. He had once joined a dating agency, but that had been a disaster, being philosophical he knew that one of these days he would meet the right woman.

"Oh well..." he sighed out aloud and thought. "Maybe someone will come along soon."

He didn't know how soon!

Originally he had come from a humble working class family in the West Country and had won a scholarship to Cambridge. After graduating he had worked his way to the top of his profession, vowing that he would never be poor again. He had been married once to a very rich, beautiful and talented woman five years older than him, who developed Multiple Sclerosis, and whom he had loved very dearly.

David recalled how one wet and windy winter night almost nine years ago, a hit and run driver had mowed her down as the car mounted the pavement, whilst they were coming out of the Royal Opera House in London. She had been killed instantly, right before his eyes. He thought he would never recover from it.

Even now he still dreamed about her, he should have spent more time with her and not been so compulsive about his work. For the first time in his life, he had known real pain. She was everything he had always dreamed of, and in rare moments of seriousness even now, he still said she was the only woman he had ever loved, and he meant it.

David had been absolutely devastated and even to this day still remembered vividly the way the car had ploughed into her wheelchair crushing it and as she fell out of it, her body was dragged along the wet road, torn and bleeding. It was a stolen car and the police were never able to trace the driver. That was how he had first made Paul Forrest's acquaintance when he was a Detective Constable earlier in his career.

He vowed to himself then, that he would never marry again. He could not endure the hurt of someone he loved being lost forever. She had been funny, sexy and beautiful and he had adored her. To him, it had always seemed that the moments spent with her were tinged with magic. Until she died and left him with a resounding emptiness and an overwhelming sense of loss that he actually thought he might kill himself.

He had also gone into deep depression for over a year and found little solace in drink, but with the help of Paul Forrest, who pulled him out of his grief, they had become firm friends. There had been other women since, several of them, to fill the nights and days, but he had never loved another woman, nor did he want to. Loving was too painful and he did not want to go through any more pain and loss.

Fortunately over the years' time had slowly healed him and he felt that he must give of himself once more and find a companion. He was a very confidant man and very attractive to the opposite sex. He had a vast fortune invested and he was single. He was just six foot, with a pleasant voice, a kindly yet handsome face that quite often looked cheeky and amazing changeable blue eyes.

Sometimes he looked extremely good looking when he wasn't frowning and carrying the world on his shoulders as he was now. His body was in good shape; he spent two evenings a week at the gym beneath the modern building complex where he lived. He also swam in the pool and played squash once a week and he always took his holidays abroad when he had the time and kept up his expensive tan on the sun bed at the gym.

He worked on his computer into the early hours of the morning before taking another break. When looked at himself in the kitchen mirror, his twinkling blue eyes with their long black eyelashes, stared back at him with self-criticism. His greying wavy hair was badly in need of a trim. He would get it cut over the next few days, he thought as he made his way back to his study. As he sipped his coffee, he reviewed his present life-style, was he becoming boring, he wondered? Had he lost himself completely in his work?

Suddenly his thoughts were broken, as the nearby telephone rang out. He glanced at the decorative Ormolu clock on the large marble mantelpiece over the fireplace and noticed it was three am. At first he didn't answer it, but it rang out persistently. The answerphone cut in; it was his friend DCI Forrest. He reached over wearily and picked up the receiver.

"Hello, David here," he answered somewhat abruptly. He really hated being interrupted when he was working.

"Hello David, sorry to disturb you at this late hour," Paul said apologetically. "Just wondered if you were still awake and if you'd come up with anything yet?" he asked eagerly.

"Well... Paul, not really, though I'm pretty sure it is a woman, unless she has a male accomplice. It's not just the gut feeling I have, there are several pointers that could make it so, on the other hand, could be a man, but he would probably suffer from OCD syndrome. It seems to be so well manoeuvred."

David cleared his throat before continuing.

"I've been going through some of my own files on some of my female patients, but I don't think it is any of them. This is someone new, someone very clever, she or he knows exactly what they are doing and to whom. It has all been very carefully planned and it's almost as if he or she has some inside information on the victims."

"You're very sure that it is a woman, aren't you and what do you mean planned, inside information, are you saying there's a leak in the department?" Paul questioned David quickly.

"No, not necessarily your department, it could be any department anywhere. The timing is always right. The weather conditions; little things like that, whoever it is, is a stickler for detail. Maybe it is a woman who has planned the killings, but not actually done it herself, perhaps she does have an accomplice." David paused and took a sip of his now, lukewarm coffee.

"I thought at first it might have been a gay killing, but the victims were not gay, were they, the thing they all have in common is, they were all junkies and beat up their women and were small time dealers. So?" He paused again.

"I would say that we have definitely got a serial killer on the rampage. Assuming that it is a woman, I would think that she is somewhat older than her victims are. I wonder if she has ever done this before, in another town, or another country even, might be a good idea to get on to Interpol and check on any similar deaths over the last few months or even years." He suggested to his friend. "Who knows how many more are going to be murdered?"

They spoke for several more minutes before they said their goodbyes. David replaced the phone slowly, deep in thought. His adrenaline starting rushing again, he no longer felt tired and he fed more data into his computer again, it was around 4.30 am when he finally packed up.

He decided he was going to take some time off from his practice and pursue the matter more thoroughly, so he phoned and left a message on his office voicemail for his elegant, blonde secretary Samantha to cancel his appointments for the next few days.

Thank heavens for her, she was not only beautiful but intelligent with it, he often wondered why she had never married, but then she was dedicated to her job and if ever there was an important function for him to attend he could depend on her to be by his side.

He was going to dig up more information and pay a visit to his old school pal, Dr. Michael Akaro at his Drug Rehabilitation Centre in Palmers Green. He had not seen him for some time and they had plenty to catch up on. Two of the victims had been found in that area so perhaps Michael might come up with something, they had often helped each other out in the past and North London seemed the most likely place to start. He knew the person in question would not be satisfied until she or he, had wiped out every young drug abuser around, or until the police caught up with him or her.

"Mind you," he muttered to himself. "Whoever the killer is, he or she is certainly doing society a favour, at least there are four less bums living off my tax money."

"Oh my God!" He exclaimed aloud. "I shouldn't be thinking like this, it's not politically correct."

He shrugged his thoughts aside. He had his own ideas how people like the four victims should be

48

treated. They would've died young anyway; there were very few geriatric drug addicts around. He sighed deeply, turned off the computer, then the lights in his study and made his way to his large, opulent bedroom, recently redecorated and refurnished by one of the top interior designers in London.

***

David awoke around 8.30 am, even though he had not had many hours sleep, his mind was clear about what he was going to do over the next few days. He showered and changed into some casual, but smart clothes, gulped down a cup of coffee and a piece of hot buttered toast. Checked his answerphone was on, picked up his wallet, mobile phone and car key and took his private lift down to the underground garage, where his brand new pale blue metallic Mercedes sports car was parked.

He gazed at it lovingly. He'd only had it a week and was dying to try it out properly. Just going from his apartment to work had not given him much chance to appreciate its performance. He pointed the key at the car, opened the door and settling into the driver's seat, started the sleek car and drove slowly towards the security gate, pointing his remote control handset at the sensor and drove out into Park Lane, and then headed towards North London, hoping to find out more from his friend Michael Akaro.

As he drove along on that dreary April morning, he turned things over in his mind again. The Pathologist had extracted one lethal silver-plated bolt from each of the victims' genital areas.

There were no witnesses at the time of the killings. The police had spent hours door knocking, but to no avail. It seemed like a phantom had come out of nowhere, shot the men and then disappeared. The killer couldn't go on forever and not be caught. How many more young men would be killed?

Whilst he drove along, he punched out Dr. Akaro's number, on his hands-free car phone.

"Hello Michael, it's David, I just wondered how you are and would it be okay to drop in on you this morning? I am not far away in fact, I'll be with you in about ten minutes, traffic permitting. Oh, by the way, get the coffee on." He laughed heartily and nodded as the man at the other end of the line spoke.

"Why hello David, you just don't drop in without some ulterior motive. Yes, okay, see you soon, bye."

Michael was a man of few words, but he had always come up with some good ideas in the past. He knew what his friend's real reason was. He'd been expecting a visit earlier than this.

CHAPTER FIVE

NORTH LONDON - 2004

Dr Michael Akaro originally came from Jamaica and he ran a Rehabilitation Centre for drug addicts and alcoholics in North London, but he got very little help from the State, it was run mainly on a charitable basis. He also held rape-counselling sessions for women; he was a brilliant West Indian doctor who had given up a successful private practise in Richmond to help the unfortunates in society - *as he called them.* In David's view an impossible mission, but he kept his thoughts to himself when he was with his friend.

Michael and he had studied together many years ago in Cambridge and had always kept in touch over the years, helping each other out on various occasions.

The Rehab centre came into view, on the left hand side of the street, past a small pharmacy with iron bars covering its windows. The block was dingy, there were two small sex shops, several decaying small stores, a small dingy hotel that had been closed for many years and a minicab office that was still functional which needed a good coat of paint on the outside.

On the other side of the road most of the buildings were vacant and boarded up with corrugated iron sheets over the doors and windows. He saw an old woman in almost ragged clothes, pushing a supermarket trolley with all her worldly goods in it, then a middle-aged man sitting on a step in front of a closed shop vacant-eyed from drugs, mouthing words to no one in particular. A woman of uncertain age who looked like she was on the game, leaned against the door of one of the closed shops smoking a cigarette watched him driving by and David felt revulsion that there were such places in North London where one could buy a woman's body or anything at all, very cheaply.

David knew that Michael spent most of his days in the ugly old 1930's red brick building with the green mosaic trim missing most of its tiles. It had once, long ago, been a small private hospital. Other derelict buildings covered in graffiti lined the blocks either side of the Rehab Centre. It was too small really, with windowless corridors, paint peeling from the ceilings and the smell of dirty people and dirty deeds.

He drew up outside of the shabby building and parked his expensive car right outside of the front door on the pavement, hoping that no one would try to damage it. If he got a parking ticket it was just too bad he thought. He doubted whether Parking Wardens were very welcome in that area.

He picked up his mobile phone from the passenger seat and put it into one of the pockets of his Barbour jacket lying on the small back seat and then checked that nothing of value was left inside of his car on view, in case the odd opportunist might try to break in. Not that he was too worried; it had satellite tracking that was, if they could get the car started. Hopefully he would have all four wheels left on his return. Getting out of his vehicle he leaned over and then grabbed his Barbour jacket, shut the door and set the sophisticated alarm system and walked into the run-down building.

The exterior brickwork needed re-pointing and the front door was covered in old cracked paint of some unidentifiable colour. The pane of glass in the middle of the shabby door was badly cracked and had been mended with wide brown masking tape to stop it from falling out. The building was badly in need of a face-lift. He made a mental note to pop a generous cheque in the post to Michael to help towards some of the refurbishment that was so badly needed.

As he went through the equally scruffy inner doors, a good-looking black giant of a man, his head shaven and a gold earring in his right ear, came forward to meet him with his large right hand outstretched.

Doctor Akaro was around six foot six inches, weighing in at twenty-one stone and made of solid muscle. Usually people were a bit scared when they first encountered him, but he was a gentle giant, except when aroused.

"Hello David, so nice to see you after all this time." His deep cultured voice boomed out and he smiled widely, his bright even white teeth contrasting heavily with his coal black shiny skin.

"Sally looks who's here," he called over his shoulder to a young lady sitting at a rickety desk. "Two of your best coffees please!"

The pretty black girl smiled at him; she adored the big man and would have laid down her life for him. He had taken her in off the streets where she had been forced to earn money as a young prostitute, since she was fourteen, to feed her brother's drug habit, after they had arrived in London from Jamaica five years ago. Her brother had eventually overdosed and Michael had found her sleeping rough after a client had beaten her up. She now worked for him and shared a flat just around the corner from the Rehab centre, with two other Jamaican girls he had also saved from the streets in a similar situation.

He guided David through the door of his rather shabby office - cum - surgery and pulled an equally shabby chair over to his desk for his friend.

"Not quite so up-market as your place," he joked. "But it serves its purpose and maybe one day, who knows?" He grinned wryly.

David laughed; his friend always came out with the same comments, every time he visited him. He looked around the room and raised his eyebrows at the tatty posters on the walls.

"I'm afraid we can't have any of your antiques or priceless paintings around here, they wouldn't last five minutes with my clientele. Somebody would certainly steal them." Michael said amusingly and his laughter also boomed out resonant and loud, like his voice.

Sally entered the room without knocking, holding two large steaming mugs, her pert breasts bouncing against the soft fabric of her lime green blouse as she moved.

"Only got instant, I'm sorry David we can't run to one of those expensive coffee makers like you've probably got in your office!" She commented with a broad cheeky grin on her pretty dark-skinned face.

"Fraid we don'ave any of dat exotic coffee dat you most likely used to." She drawled in her Jamaican accent and made a cheeky face at him as she placed the two mugs on the doctor's desk.

Then she turned slowly and wiggled her hips provocatively at both of them in her short tight black Lycra skirt and left the room. David turned slightly in his chair and watched her depart. Michael followed his gaze as Sally left the room.

"Not bad eh, er...! So how can I help you, David?" He asked as he shuffled some papers around his large old oak desk to cover up his embarrassment at his remark about Sally.

The big desk had been a present from David some time ago, after he'd cleared out some of his late mother's furniture. David had been very close to his mother and after she'd died Michael had been there for him, as he had also been when David's wife had been killed. The two men were an unlikely pair; their friendship had been cemented, many years ago during their University days in Cambridge. The other scholars had nicknamed them, David and Goliath, because of the difference in their statures in those days.

Before reaching for his coffee, David handed his friend some notes from his jacket pocket that he had printed out the night before.

"Here, have a look at these while you're drinking your coffee, see what you can make of them, perhaps you might even know one of the victims."

Michael studied the papers for a few moments.

"Yes the fourth victim, Gary Medway, was definitely registered here, so is his girlfriend. She had only recently been *main-lining*, so it's not been too difficult to get her off heroin onto Methadone. In fact she is doing pretty well. That nasty boyfriend of hers has finally got what he deserved, I'm afraid to say!"

He took a long gulp of his coffee before continuing.

"Gary had been trying to get her back onto the streets to pay for his own habit ever since their child was born. Cindy refused so he continually beat her up. She's a nice young woman actually and tries to help the other unmarried mothers here. I really don't know how she got involved with him!"

He heaved a large sigh. "She comes here quite often to get away from him but she'll be okay now he's out of the way. God moves in mysterious ways. *Praise the Lord*!"

He quoted in an ecstatic tremolo as he turned the Big Man's name into something that sounded like *LO-OR-R-D* as he raised his eyes and his big hands towards the ceiling. He was a great churchgoer and fervent gospel singer at his local Gospel Church and very well liked.

"Someone's certainly done her a great favour!"

He looked across the big desk at David and knew the remark had hit home.

"Yes David, I've changed my mind somewhat since the last time I saw you." He gave an embarrassed smile, as he was very aware of David's thoughts on people such as Gary Medway.

Dr. Michael Akaro was a dedicated man, helping addicts of all kinds, who were really sincere about drying out. But he also had a low opinion of people such as the four victims of the Serial Killer.

"Funny enough Cindy told me only just last week that once she was completely cured, she was going to leave Gary and go back to Manchester. Her parents were so pleased that she was going to leave him and they were ready to help her financially, when the time came. I suppose she's under surveillance by the police? Well, I can tell you now, it wasn't her, that girl wouldn't hurt a fly. Just tell your friend Paul Forrest that from me please, David," he exclaimed loudly as he banged the desk with one large fist to emphasise his statement.

David nodded. "Yes, I certainly will when I speak to him later."

Michael continued. "She's only just seventeen and a half poor kid; she'd been with that bastard since she was fifteen and a half, when she first came to London. Well providence has stepped in and helped her, thank the Lord!" Once again he raised his eyes and hands to the ceiling again.

"Well my friend, want to tell me about it?" He questioned raising one eyebrow quizzically.

The two men spent the next two hours deep in conversation, exchanging ideas and going through Michael's records. The doctor made a few calls to other rehabs to find out if the victims had been registered with them. It seemed two had, one at Finchley and the other in Golders Green.

"My goodness, time has flown." Michael commented suddenly looking at his wristwatch.

"I've got two patients due soon and Mrs. Lawson, bless her, will be here in about five minutes, she's always on time. She's a lovely lady helps out with the young children as well as the unmarried mothers, absolutely wonderful woman I couldn't do without her now. I know she gives them money sometimes and food and clothing for their kids." He rambled on. "She's er..."

David interrupted him. "No, I don't think I've met her, have I?" He asked as he conjured up a mental picture of a dour Scots lady handing out gifts like Father Christmas to the poor and needy, in her late sixties with bobbed grey hair and a dark moustache on her upper lip. She probably dressed in tartan tweeds too he thought.

"Ah...well she's one of my benefactors, as well as doing voluntary work here at the centre three days a week. Very attractive, late thirties I think, looks younger, beautiful lady. She looks a little sad at times, very lonely, lives on her own."

He paused and looked meaningfully at his friend and then grinned.

"Not short of a bob or two, well educated, drives a nice car, has a house in Richmond, very respectable woman!"

"Don't try that again Michael, the last time you played cupid, it was an absolute disaster. Do you remember that evening at your house, and that dreadful woman you introduced me to! Did she find anyone eventually to take her on?" David laughed as he recalled her.

"Yes, I do remember her, you're right you wouldn't like Sarah, too independent. She lives alone in Richmond with her cat, in a lovely house. However, she has been very generous financially to everybody here, she and Sally get on so well, she comes over here three times a week and everyone loves her."

Michael looked away and fiddled with a ballpoint pen lying on the desk before continuing.

"I met her several months ago at a charity evening; she walks with a slight limp, an accident I believe. No. You wouldn't want to meet her."

He got up from his desk and made out he was going to show David to the door.

"I know what a busy man you are David. I don't want to keep you any longer."

"Oh… all right, I'm not that busy today and stop matchmaking." Teased David.

This was one of his friend's favourite pastimes. Michael was a very happily married man with five wonderful children and a beautiful Jamaican wife and for years he had been trying to find someone for David. Usually Michael's comments went over his head, but somehow today they hurt him, maybe it was time he found himself somebody, who knows she might be quite nice after all. I'll stay he thought just to please him and satisfy my curiosity.

"Okay you've sold her to me, I'll meet her, and maybe she will have some ideas about the killings. Being a woman." He added.

At that precise moment there was a light tap on the office door and a tall, slim, elegant and very attractive blonde lady entered.

She was dressed in a simple white round necked cotton blouse, a well-fitting just above knee-length black skirt, black stockings and black leather court shoes. She wore very little jewellery, just a thin gold chain around her neck with some sort of gold charm that shone through the fine fabric of her blouse. Around her left wrist was an elegant gold wristwatch.

Michael boomed out. "Sarah, my dear, absolutely marvellous to see you today, I should like to introduce you to an old friend of mine, Mr. David Myers. We were at Medical School together." He grinned and gestured towards David.

"David. Sarah Lawson one of my Guardian Angel ladies, as I call them."

David got to his feet and politely extended his right hand and he just stood and stared at her as he took in the details of the lovely blonde woman standing before him.

She came across the office with her hand outstretched and a smile on her beautiful face. Their eyes met and the room seemed filled with a wealth of silent messages and emotions. She was amazingly beautiful and he realised he was staring at her like a star-struck teenager.

Michael looked from one to the other. He felt the strong attraction that passed between them, and smiled to himself. He knew he had done the right thing in telephoning her earlier and asking her to come in that day whilst his friend was still there.

He always knew what he was doing. There was still a little of the witch doctor left in him from his ancestors!

David didn't know what had hit him.

"Er...hello..." He stuttered as he extended his right hand.

They shook hands. His grip was cool and firm as his fingers gently closed around her long pale hand. He noticed she wore no rings on her fingers.

"Nice to meet you." He cleared his throat nervously. "I've heard so much about you...er."

He realised he was stuttering and still holding her hand. He quickly released it as if it had burnt him.

She glanced at his face and smiled as she noticed it was tanned and faintly lined around his grey-blue eyes, he looked strong and determined and his curling greying hair badly needed a trim. He obviously didn't have a regular woman in his life at the moment she thought. His body seemed to be in very good shape and he wore a navy T-shirt and denim jeans with expensive trainers.

She was very impressed by this handsome man standing before her.

So this was the famous Mr. David Myers!

She too wasn't quite sure what had hit her either.

David noticed her nervousness, her quick smile, as she looked at him and he smiled back, his strong hard face softened and the lines around his eyes crinkled into their well-worn pattern. His cool blue eyes warmed to her. He liked her; in fact he was almost speechless. Trying to act nonchalantly, he immediately took his Barbour off the back of the chair he was occupying and put it on a small stool nearby and offered it to her and stood awkwardly to one side, not quite sure what to do next.

"I hope it was all good." She smiled at him.

Michael broke the silence.

"I was just telling my friend here of all the wonderful work you have been doing and the help you've given me over the past months. Would you like a cup of tea, my dear?"

Sarah nodded not trusting herself to speak again. A small pulse in her neck started to throb. She wasn't quite sure why. Was it excitement or fear?

Michael walked over to the office door and called through to Sally. There was a muffled reply.

"Um…I must leave you for a few minutes. I've someone to see to in the outer office." He left and shut the door quietly behind him.

Sarah and David started to talk at the same time.

"It's...er...I…" They both said together.

Then they smiled at each other and burst into laughter.

"Yes, well, I come here a few times a week, I help out with some of the unmarried mothers you know," she explained to David.

Her mind was in a whirl, she just didn't know exactly what to say to him.

"Yes, I know, Michael was telling me. I've known him for a long time we were both at Cambridge together. He's a very good doctor and counsellor."

Oh God, I'm rambling on he thought, I can't think straight. I can't think of anything intelligent to say to her, she must think I'm an absolute idiot.

"Yes, he has mentioned you might have a few ideas..."

Sally entered at that moment and placed a large ceramic mug, shaped like a frog on the desk in front of Sarah.

"Hi, how're you today Sarah? No sugar, right? Must get back to my desk."

She looked hastily at them and quickly left the room, but not without noticing the electrifying atmosphere between them.

"So tell me about yourself Mr. Myers." Sarah said quietly, her composure starting to restore itself.

"David, please. I'm here on the case..."

"The case?" Queried Sarah innocently.

"Yes, those terrible killings, surely you've read about them in the newspapers?"

David started to pace the room slowly.

"You know the four killings in the North London area. They were killed just recently." Oh, I'm making a mess of this he thought.

"Yesss...um. I have read something about them." She looked at him intently as she weighed him up.

So Mr. David Myers, she thought, you're the man I've read about, the man who says the killer needs help. If only he knew who I am she thought as she leaned forward and picked up her mug of tea and held it to her lips. It was very hot and she blew into the mug, using the few seconds to think about what she would say next.

"Yes, dreadful isn't it? What a terrible world we live in nowadays, and all this crime. Your job must be so very stressful." She took a small sip of her tea before continuing.

"Perhaps you would like me to show you around the centre, you could speak to some of our visitors here, maybe they could be of some help to you."

She knew she was floundering, but he didn't seem to notice. He seemed more interested in her at that moment in time. She smiled at him and inclined her head to one side.

"No, I'd rather not today thank you, I must be going, I don't want..."

What did he want? He asked himself silently.

He wanted to take her in his arms; he wanted to kiss her. He just wanted to be alone with her. Maybe he should invite her for dinner, or maybe it was too soon. Thank heavens she couldn't read his thoughts. He was so utterly and completely bowled over by her, he hadn't felt like this since he was a teenager.

"I wonder if you... umm..." he started.

At that point Michael re-entered the room and David was able to gather his composure.

"Well I'm so very pleased to have met you." Sarah said. "If I can help in any way, please let me know, you can always contact me here at the centre. Excuse me, but I must go now Michael, one of the girls wants to see me. Goodbye Mr. Myers."

Sarah left the room hurriedly and David turned and watched her in a trance-like state.

Michael looked amusingly at his friend and noticed how flushed he was and knew that Sarah made had a great impact on him.

"Well did you two...?"

"Well? Well what?" Queried David turning back to look at Michael. "Yes, we discussed the case briefly, and she offered her help if I needed it, she said that I could contact her here if I needed to." He replied quickly.

Michael raised his eyebrows. "Good, I knew you two would get on, she is really a lovely lady. Well, you must excuse me also David, I have some work to do, and no doubt you'll be in touch with both of us, very shortly!"

"Uh, yeah…yeah," mumbled David as he stood up.

Michael got up from his chair, reached over and shook hands with his friend.

"Oh, in case you need to get in touch with Sarah, this is her mobile phone number. I know she won't mind me giving it to you. You might want to get in touch with her about something else, sometime," he said as he handed David a small piece of paper with two telephone numbers on it.

David looked at it and then hastily stuffed it into the small pocket on his T-shirt and left hurriedly, he hardly heard Sally saying goodbye to him. As he stepped into the street outside he breathed deeply and made his way towards his car. It was still in one piece, he noticed thankfully. He bleeped the remote control key and the engine started up; he opened the driver's door and sat for a few moments deep in thought.

Suddenly there was a tapping on the front window and Sally stood, here arms outstretched holding his Barbour jacket.

"Yours I believe, you left it behind, and you were in **such** a hurry to leave!" She commented amusingly.

He pressed the switch on the window and she dropped his jacket onto his lap and with a secret smile turned and ran back through the Rehab door and then turned and waved.

He hardly noticed her and with the piece of clothing on his lap he shifted into drive and drove off slowly towards the West End of London.

As he drove along, he felt something inside of him that he hadn't felt for a long, long time. He was in love. It was as plain and simple as that and he grinned at himself in the rear view mirror as he drove straight through a red light and nearly hit a car side on.

David felt like a young man again. This is ridiculous he told himself, I have just met her, I have to get my life in order, no woman is going to upset my equilibrium, but he couldn't get the image of Sarah Lawson out of his mind. All he could think about was when they would meet again.

The case of the serial killer seemed strangely unimportant now, but he knew he must give it a lot of thought later when he got home. He wondered if he asked her out to dinner whether she would come or not, he patted the pocket on his T-shirt with her phone number inside, Michael had obviously realised the attraction between them. Good old Michael, perhaps his matchmaking this time would work. Though, if he dropped into the clinic tomorrow, as he was planning, he would probably bump into her again if she was there and ask her out to dinner. He knew of a lovely little intimate Italian restaurant along the River by Hay's Wharf. The thought excited him as he turned things over in his mind.

Suddenly he again had to brake violently as he saw another car in front of him. This has got to stop he told himself, I'm a fully-grown man, well balanced, in my mid-forties, I must control myself, but all he could see in his mind's eye was Sarah. He drove into the underground garage, locked his car and took the lift up to his penthouse.

The place was in darkness, he suddenly felt extremely lonely. He was fed up coming back to an empty apartment. He needed company, basically he needed a woman to come home to and he'd just met her. His mind was in turmoil, all he could think about again was Sarah. His analytic mind told him, he knew nothing about her, who was she? Yes he would definitely visit Michael tomorrow morning and perhaps over a long lunch he would find out more about her.

* * *

Sarah too was thinking along the same lines as David as she drove back towards Richmond that afternoon. No man since Julio had affected her like that. What a wonderful man David was, polite, educated, very presentable and very attractive. He also had the air of confidence that came with money. He seemed too good to be true. Could she, was there the remotest chance that she could again find happiness?

What about the present situation? It would have to stop, but she felt quite safe, no clues had

67

been left behind. No one had ever seen her; the killings would have to stop, maybe no one would ever know. She felt no fear or excitement just a strange feeling of apathy and it worried her slightly. Could she live with the knowledge of the revengeful murders? It was like a symptom of emotional disintegration.

Over the past few months, she'd often reflected on the humiliation she'd endured at Julio's hands. Revenge had not actually been sweet, as the old cliché went, it was almost frightening, especially now. However, it had been very necessary she told herself. Perhaps one more time, she wasn't quite finished yet. Women like her, with no one to speak to at the time, no one caring what was happening to them in their own homes. When she thought back to her time with Julio, it was as if it had all happened to a different person, not her. Thanks to his father she was at last free, why had she been such a fool to stay with his evil son for so long? She would make a phone call when she got back to her house.

She shook her head to clear it and turned her thoughts back to David, perhaps she could find an excuse to phone him. No, let him do the entire running. If her intuition were correct, he would be in touch with her very shortly; perhaps tomorrow if she went to the Rehab Centre there might be a message from him. She pulled up in her driveway; her cat, Picasso, was sitting on the doorstep waiting as always.

Getting out of her car, she bleeped the key and it locked and then she walked quickly towards the front door, glancing from side to side, as if expecting someone to jump out at her. That was another habit from the past that she must control.

Picasso got to his feet and stretched himself and then followed her through the door, rubbing himself against her stocking clad legs, purring loudly as she switched off the alarm. She turned and locked the door behind her, then scooped up the bundle of blue fur and gave him a big cuddle and a kiss on his nose.

"Well, Picasso, I have just met the most wonderful person today, you would really like him."

She carried on talking to the cat in her arms as they entered the kitchen and she switched on the lights and then put the cat down and set about opening a tin of food for him as she told him about David. Suddenly she had feelings of doubt. Julio had been all of those things in the beginning, and then it had turned sour. She had kept her emotions locked away for so long, could she ever trust another man? Where was Julio now? Would he come back again and terrify her? She questioned her judgement. I have become very bitter, she thought and almost recluse like in my lifestyle - just my cat and me!

Tears welled up into her lovely eyes, she suddenly felt very, very lonely. Who was David Myers anyway, besides being a friend of Michael?

She knew nothing about him. But she needed someone to love her and most of all to protect her. Unless she was wrong, she had the feeling he could be the one. But she must act reasonably. Certainly her behaviour with Julio from the first searing encounter, when she had indulged herself in sheer

69

lust, could not be classified as controlled or reasonable. But the feeling she had now for this man, whom she had just met, was not one of just lust, she felt she could trust him and they could have a realistic friendship. She also knew that she was about to play a very dangerous game.

He was a clever man, and he was the expert on the case of the serial killer. She made her way back to the hall and picked up her extension phone that was on a small antique table.

***

Sarah lay back on her bed after her shower and thought about the events of the day. She felt she had reached a crossroads in her life, which way should she go? As far as she could see she had two choices, stop the killings now and hope no one ever found out or continue to dice with her future.

As much as she would like to lead a normal quiet life, she knew she it would be very difficult until Julio was thoroughly exorcised from her system.

Picasso jumped up onto the large bed, purring loudly and gently kneaded her stomach with his paws and then lay across her purring softly and rhythmically. She stroked his head and slowly drifted off to sleep. Her arm fell to one side, back onto the bed. He could feel the tension slip from the body of his devoted mistress.

The great blue cat blinked several times and watched her through his slanted amber eyes for a few seconds, reassuring himself that she was sleeping soundly before he closed them and drifted off to sleep as well, tucked into her back.

BOOK FOUR

EXODUS XX1 Verse 24: eye for eye, tooth for a tooth, hand for hand and foot for foot.

CHAPTER SIX

MARBELLA – 2003

Sarah's nightmares had come back again. Summer had come and gone. The weather was getting chilly, especially at night. Even though they had agreed to a reconciliation Julio was up to his old tricks, he was out late yet again. Sarah knew that she was trapped in the relationship until she could find a way out. She decided that she would have to appease him even though she suspected that he was once again getting out of control. This was not the right time to stand up to him, but one day there would hopefully be a way out.

Julio had been away all day he hadn't even bothered to phone in to check on her. She wished he would never come back, perhaps he'd had an accident and crashed the Ferrari and was lying dead in a gutter somewhere in Marbella. Perhaps he was already dead in some mortuary. She really did not care about him anymore. All she wanted to do was to leave him.

Life was becoming intolerable, she'd had enough of him, the tension was building up between them again and she knew that shortly she would explode. They constantly quarrelled. He had taken to drinking heavily and smoking dope most of the time. She knew he was also snorting cocaine whenever he could get any decent stuff.

She had found several books on drug abuse hidden away in a wardrobe in the spare bedroom and wondered to whom they belonged. As she had so much time on her hands, she had taken to studying them in great detail and was now well aware how dangerous he could become.

Somehow she had to get away from him. On several occasions when he had left her all day and night in the apartment, he had locked her in and unplugged the main phone from its socket and taken it with him, leaving only the extension phone by their bedside that only received calls, she could not dial out from it to phone anyone.

On two other occasions he had even put her on a long chain with a padlock attached to the bed frame, just like an animal. It was only just long enough for her to wander around the bedroom and he had left a bucket for her to use as a toilet. Was there no end to the humiliation that he enjoyed subjecting her to she wondered?

He had become completely paranoid about her and had delusions that she was looking at other men and receiving phone calls from them. He had even accused her of being unfaithful to him a number of times.

She recalled one time when she had been let out to go shopping and taken his car and returned late because of the busy traffic, he had grabbed her and thrown her onto their bed, torn off all her clothes, smelt them and her body to see if she had been with anyone.

"You're mad, completely and utterly mad." She'd screamed at him incredulously. "You're not only mad, you're absolutely obsessed, leave me alone Julio, and let me go, let me go back to England. Please." She'd begged of him. "I won't tell anyone of your behaviour, but please, please let me go." She had burst into tears of helplessness.

She was so tired, she wasn't eating, and she had lost a lot of weight and felt mentally drained. He had only laughed at her, a strange weird laugh, then stalked out of the apartment leaving her lying naked and petrified on the big double bed. The bed they had once shared and loved each other on.

Her shopping was all over the hallway floor, milk spilt, eggs broken. She had no daily help anymore. Julio had sacked Maria, he didn't want anyone around her and he was scared she would use her as a means of escape. The apartment was filthy, but she just didn't have the energy to do anything. He sexually abused her regularly, raping her whenever his need for her was strong; he forced her into anal sex and used to call it lovemaking. She felt utterly filthy.

He was insanely jealous about her past and forced her to repeat things again and again about the former men in her life and her sexual activities with them. She wasn't allowed to go out alone anymore. Sometimes he would stick one of his long black hairs across the outside of the front door so he would know if she tried to get out, or anyone tried to get in.

If ever she managed to get out of this relationship, it would be a long time before she entered into another one, she was put off men for life and she would never trust another man again. At least today he had not tied her up before he left.

Once she'd asked him why he locked her in.

"For your own protection." He'd told her.

He was even paranoid about their cat and used to leave it locked out so she couldn't have it for company.

She lay on the bed, looking up at the ceiling, sick with despair and terror. It was 02.30 am by the little clock on the dressing table. There seemed to be a party going on downstairs from one of the rented apartments, laughter and loud music filtered through the floor. She wondered if she would ever lead a normal life again and laugh too and then she burst into tears of despair.

"Oh my God! Oh my God!" She screamed aloud to the empty bedroom. "Help me please, what shall I do?" She sobbed even louder, but no one would hear her over the loud music.

Suddenly, the phone by the bedside rang out shrilly and she jumped with fright.

"Hello, hello..."

There was no answer.

"Hello...hello..." She repeated nervously.

There was only heavy breathing at the end of the line. She instinctively knew it was him. What the hell was he playing at now, she wondered, checking up to make sure she was still alive or whether she might have jumped over the balcony?

No, she wouldn't give him that satisfaction; she'd push him over the rails before that happened.

She replaced the receiver, but the phone immediately rang again.

"I'll be back in about half an hour. Be ready for me, I'm strong and hard tonight," he hissed down the line and hung up before she could answer him.

Sarah pressed the light switch on the headboard and glanced over at the clock again, it read 02.35 am.

As she sat up in bed she caught sight of a strange woman in the mirrored wardrobe running the length of the right wall, from floor to ceiling. She realised that it was her; she looked dreadful, haggard, pale and thin.

Julio liked to watch himself in the mirrors when he had sex with her. He would also fondle himself and masturbate in front of her, then force her to lick him clean. She felt debased and he just used her thin body for his own satisfaction. Lately one of his favourite ways, was anal sex, which she hated, it was so painful. She was also afraid of catching Aids from him or some other sexually transmitted disease, as their sex was always unprotected and goodness knows whom he went with when he did not come back at night.

Thank God she was on the pill; she thought at least she couldn't get pregnant. But her supply was diminishing.

Sarah knew there would be trouble that night, when he returned, she could sense it. Her loathing for him was becoming as obsessional as his black love for her. He no longer even tried to hide his addiction from her; she had seen the disposable needles and other drug related paraphernalia lying around in the bathroom.

Her thoughts went back to one morning when she had caught him sitting naked on the edge of the bath having a fix.

Around the upper part of his left arm was a length of thin-knotted rubber tubing. By the side of him on a small glass shelf was a small bottle of still Spa water, his gold Dunhill lighter, a spoon and a small packet of crystallised powder.

Of course he only bought the best heroin or whatever took his fancy; he could afford it, he often bragged to her.

He boasted that he had never shared a needle, as he was terrified of catching Aids, like some of his friends, so he went for regular check-ups. She knew that one day he would catch it. The sooner the better, as far as she was concerned. She shuddered, was there a possibility he already had it, could she be infected, was that why she had got so thin?

She recalled that she had just stood staring in horror at him, whilst he injected himself.

"So now you know bitch, I'm a drug addict and I have been one for a long time! Want to try some? It might take that snooty English look off your miserable English face." He had yelled at her.

His face was ashen white and strained, the black circles around his eyes made him look evil as he stared at her swaying slightly.

"Quick, Sarah," he'd shouted. "Take the needle out, take the needle out for me God dammit...too much...I..." He whispered.

Then as the drug rushed into his system he calmed down slightly, but she instinctively knew he was in trouble. He had used too much. Suddenly his eyes started to roll back into his head and his breathing became laboured, large beads of sweat broke out on his face.

"Quickly," he ordered. "Now, now, take out the fucking needle, I can't, I…"

He's going to OD, she'd thought with terror, but at the same time with sadistic relief.

She watched him a little longer, then reached over very slowly and withdrew the hypodermic from his bulging vein, released the tubing completely and threw it to one side. It bounced onto the bathroom floor like a wounded snake; she also threw the syringe aside with distaste. He passed out and also fell to the floor. Sarah stared at him for several seconds mesmerised, her beautiful face contorted with hate and disgust for him.

"I hope you're dead." She'd shouted at his unconscious figure and with a swift movement of her left foot she lashed out and kicked his body with a great deal of satisfaction, again and again.

"Go on die, no one can accuse me then. Die!" She shouted again at the prone figure. "The police and doctors will verify that you have overdosed, it will prove that you are an addict, and I shall be in the clear." She kicked him even harder, and then burst into tears of rage and relief.

He still didn't move. She knelt down and peered at him, his eyes were closed and his breathing was very shallow. He could be out for the count she thought.

Getting to her feet quickly she fled into the bedroom and pulled one of her large suitcases out of the top of the wardrobe and hurriedly started to pack. As she looked around the bedroom, she noticed he had left a wad of money on the dressing table together with the keys of his car and the lounge safe. Now was the time, she could leave. Hastily she stuffed some of the money into one of her shoes and as she packed, her body trembled with fear; she scarcely knew what she was doing. She snapped the suitcase shut and pushed it under one side of the bed out of view and then started to get dressed.

Suddenly she became aware of a slight noise behind her; it was Julio, standing in the entrance of the bedroom in a pair of underpants. She turned and he came over to her, his old charming smile back on his face.

"Hey *querida*, what're you doing, where're you going?" He asked her menacingly, gazing at her through hooded eyes as he ran his hands over his naked chest and down over the large bulge in his underpants, his feet were bare.

"I'm leaving you. Now! I can't take any more Julio." She cried out in desperation. "I can't take any more of your nonsense, your drinking, your drugs, everything." Her voice was high pitched with a mixture of anger and fear.

He stared at her for several seconds. "I'm sorry you had to see me like that."

He spoke normally, quietly as if trying to soothe her nerves. "Please darling, don't leave me, I promise as from today I will kick the habit that was the last time, that's why I took so much." He smiled dreamily at her.

"I've kicked it before you know, in fact, many times, just give me one month." He started to plead with her, almost whining. "I'll get some tablets again from my doctor, they helped me last time. Do you remember how I was when we first met? I was cured."

He looked imploringly at her, his little boy expression on his face. He knew she couldn't resist it.

"Sarah, my love, my world, I love you, only you. Please don't leave me now. I cannot live without you, we shall get married, we'll have babies, please don't leave me."

He fell to his knees in front of her, his hands together as if praying. "Please don't leave me." He begged her again.

Sarah's mind momentarily flicked back, of course the little white oblong pills in the bottle all those months ago by the bedside. What a fool, how stupid she had been to believe him when he told her they were vitamin pills. She had been so ignorant and so much in love with him then. But hell, she was learning fast! Marry him, have babies, he was most certainly insane, did he honestly think that she would marry him? She looked at him contemptuously.

"You are a liar, you bastard, you'll never stop taking drugs, look at you," she sneered at him.

"I will, I promise you babe, I will. You don't understand I've been taking drugs ever since I was sixteen years old, just after my lovely mother died.

It was my father's fault. It was so traumatic you see, at first the doctors put me on tranquillisers, they took the hurt away."

He tried to explain. "Unfortunately I got hooked on them, and then I got in with a bad crowd. I popped all sorts of pills, I also smoked grass. Then one day I tried heroin and became well and truly hooked after the fourth fix. I was then only seventeen."

He hung his head in shame as he was obviously remembering something from the past.

"Over the last eight years my father has sent me to several private clinics for treatment. He even sent me to The Betty Ford Clinic, when we lived in the States. He has spent thousands and thousands of dollars on me. But, I can kick it this time, I know Sarah, with your help. I can because you love me, don't you?" He questioned her miserably.

"You know my father doesn't really love me, he hates me, he blames me for my mother's death, it was a heart attack, I swear to you I did not kill her. Okay he gives me money, but that is not love I never see him, he's always away with that young English bitch of a wife. I hate her. I have to deal with his accountant or stupid P.A."

He looked imploringly at her as tears were falling down his ashen face. His black eyes were bright with the heroin; he started to fiddle with the gold chain around his neck as he spoke.

She knelt down beside him and touched his right arm tentatively. She started to feel sorry for him he had never opened up to her before. Then the warning bells started ringing again in her head. The books, what did they say?

Drug users can be very plausible, especially when they've had their fix.

Could she really believe him?

***

Her mind sprung back to the present evening as she heard the front door bang noisily. Julio stalked into the bedroom, he smelt of beer and cigarettes and he was in a very ugly mood.

"So, bitch, you're still here then?" His speech was very slurred and he swayed around in front of her trying to focus on her.

"What the hell is that noise?" He shouted at her and a long stream of abuse issued from him.

"Shush Julio it's only the new tenants in the flat downstairs. The Agent must have rented it out again. They're probably just having a party by the sound of it."

She spoke quietly trying to calm him down. The last thing she needed at that time of night was an argument.

"I'm going down to tell them to shut up. These are my father's apartments and I have the right," he shouted at her drunkenly as he stamped on the floor. Turning he left the bedroom, and then slammed the front door loudly after him.

A few minutes later she could hear raised voices, then silence. A door banged and after a few minutes the door of their apartment slammed shut as well. Once again he entered the bedroom.

"I told them, I would call the police. That scared them. That stopped them, bloody foreigners, you're all alike." He belched loudly, and then farted. Turning from her he went to the bathroom to relieve himself.

He returned to the bedroom. "Come here whore, I want to fuck you, English whore."

He reached over and tried to grab her, instead he fell down by the side of the bed and suddenly started giggling then got up from the floor, His enormous penis was hanging out of his trousers. He'd forgotten to zip them up and he'd got a massive erection.

"Hey look at this, wouldn't you like it tonight, whore?"

He started to taunt her. "I've been upstairs all evening, having fun with those three Filipino girls and done it to all three of them, it was wonderful, you should have been there to watch. They are so young and beautiful, not like you, old and ugly. They could certainly teach you a thing or two." He laughed insanely and belched loudly again.

Sarah looked at him, hate and disgust written all over her tired face.

"I expect they can, after all they are all whores and I'm not. You make me sick you're so disgusting. Why don't you go back to them, if they are so good? I really don't think you could do anything anyway, in your present state. Look at you, you filthy stinking Spanish pig."

She spat the words out angrily. "Get out you stupid..."

Before she could finish her sentence, he leant over the bed and grabbed her by the neck, almost strangling her as he pulled her across and pushed her face into his genitals.

"Go on, smell it, smell someone else on me. You cow." He yelled in anger. "You snooty English whore, don't you call me a filthy Spanish pig!" His face was black with fury.

She tried to pull away from him, but he was too strong for her. He pushed her face further into his crotch.

"Smell bitch, smell."

She could smell the stale female body odours and cheap perfume all over him. It made her want to puke. Would there never be an end to this degradation?

"Go on put it in your mouth." He ordered as he thrust his offensive tool between her lips.

Right you asked for it she thought incensed with anger. Sarah opened her mouth widely and bit down hard on the offending member, so hard that she drew blood. She could taste the saltiness of him mixed with the girls' odours and it took all of her willpower not to vomit on the spot.

He screamed loudly, pulling himself away as she stood up quickly and moved back slightly, then she spat the blood into his face.

Julio snarled with pain and pushed her from him with great force against the mirrored wardrobe doors. She hit them so violently that one of the mirrors shattered and fell into a several large pieces around her body and legs, narrowly missing her bare feet.

"You Spanish idiot," she shouted back at him in his language. "You could have killed me then."

The noise of the mirror shattering and her shouting at him made him even angrier, he jumped across the bed and pulled her towards him again, slapped her hard around the face several times, then punched her in the stomach with all of his strength. She fell into a crumpled heap to the floor. Then he stood up and started to kick her doubled up body, as she lay completely stunned on the marble floor. With a satisfied grunt he fell back onto the large bed and fell immediately into a soporific sleep.

***

Sometime later Sarah came round; she was on the floor of the bedroom in a heap, naked and icy cold. Her whole body was a mass of pain and her face felt like an inflated balloon. She got to her feet unsteadily and walked over to the dressing table mirror. Her face was an absolute mess. Dried blood clung in blobs to her nose, she touched it gently, it didn't seem to be broken, but it hurt a great deal. Her bottom lip was badly split and her left eye was swelling fiercely, it was almost closed.

Turning she noticed the long glass slivers of the broken wardrobe mirror laying scattered around the floor. It all came back to her, as she caught sight of herself in the other mirrored door, she was covered in red blotches where he had punched and kicked her body. She knew she would be black and blue in a few hours' time.

I must pick up the broken glass, she told herself, trying to blot out the pain of her face and body. If only she had the courage to drive one of the pieces of mirror into him or slash his throat.

She knelt down and carefully piled the pieces of glass up, as one would build a house of cards. Then she reached for her flimsy robe that he had torn off her earlier and wrapped it around her cold body and crept through the hallway and into the kitchen to get some old newspapers to wrap the broken pieces of mirror in.

Returning she carefully wrapped up the pieces one by one for fear of cutting her hands. When completed she lifted up the heavy pile and took them back to the kitchen and dumped them into the large black plastic dustbin on the small balcony outside of the kitchen area. She entered the lounge and collapsed onto the big black leather settee with sheer exhaustion and pain. Julio hopefully, wouldn't wake for several hours; she should be quite safe for the time being and she needed to think.

Much later that day when she awoke, she found herself on the settee. She could hardly move with the excruciating pain in her body. Her face now felt like two inflated balloons, memories of the night before came flooding back to her. A whimper of pain escaped her bruised and cut lips as she tried to sit up. She felt dizzy from the effort and lay back against the big cushions, pulling the front of her dressing gown open that was twisted around her slight frame, she looked down at herself. Her breasts and stomach were covered in dark bruises. Bile rose in her throat, she thought she was going to throw up but somehow she got to her feet, and pulled herself together with a tremendous effort.

Once she had managed to stand up, she slowly and painfully walked into the bathroom and looked at her damaged face in the wall mirror. Suddenly her bare toes touched something soft and furry. She stepped back quickly and looked down with her good eye and let out a tortured scream. Her beautiful Persian cat lay dead at her feet. He looked as if he had been beaten to a pulp... by Julio? The cat had never harmed him, not even so much as a tiny scratch. Sario had always adored him, *oh why, why*? She kept asking herself. Was it because he hated her so much?

She knelt down trembling and caressed the once lovely cat, which was now a bloody, furry mess. Tears of sorrow mixed with incredible anger rolled down her cheeks. She raised her face to the ceiling and shouted with rage.

"You black hearted, evil devil, just you wait, one of these days I'll get you for this."

Sarah was lost for words. Through a blur of tears she reached over to the nearby bathroom chair for a towel hanging there and wrapped the mangled body in it. Then clutching it to her chest, she rocked backwards and forwards sobbing, trying to will life back into the pathetic cat. She stood up with the sad body pressed against her bruised breasts and looked once more into the mirror through her right eye. Her nose had swollen. The left side of her face black from the beating, her left eye completely closed and her bottom lip nearly twice its normal size with a deep cut covered in dried blood.

"Oh my God," she breathed. She sniffed hard trying to clear her nose, she wondered if it was indeed broken, the pain was excruciating and tears welled up again and ran down her beaten-up face.

She kissed the top of her dead cat's head, and then leaning over the bath, she reverently placed him in it. Later she would give him a decent burial, down in the garden under one of his favourite bushes.

She felt nauseated with rage and sat down on the small chair next to the bath and rested her head in her hands, trying to catch her breath as she hyperventilated. She thought she was going to pass out with the feeling of hatred inside of her. The waves of loathing, anger and hatred coursed through her battered body.

A few minutes passed and she slowly became calmer. She would pay him back somehow, when or where she didn't know, but she would somehow. She would pay back all men like him somehow, she vowed to herself. Slowly and painfully she pulled herself up to a standing position and wrapped her bloodstained robe around her tightly and walked into the master suite.

Julio was still asleep, snoring loudly with his mouth open. It was nearly three o'clock in the afternoon. She stood over him, glaring down at him with overwhelming loathing, willing him to die. She was appalled by his appearance. Once he had been so good-looking and fit, now he was bloated with all the alcohol and drugs he had consumed over the years, she thought his liver was probably affected and knew he would not live to a ripe old age.

He looked as if he hadn't shaved for a week, he also stank of stale body odour and the whole bedroom smelt of him. His bare arms, she noticed, were covered in needle tracks, even his groin and ankles where he had tried to find more veins. She decided she would move into the spare bedroom, she no longer wanted him near her.

She was resolute now, her cat being killed was the final straw, she had found her inner strength and she would leave him as soon as possible.

"I hate you, how I hate you," she mouthed venomously at the stinking inert figure stretched across the large bed.

Julio did not wake. He grunted, then farted in his sleep and turned over. She stepped back, she did not wish to waken him, let him sleep it off until tonight. She would bide her time, he could rot in hell for all she cared.

He started snoring loudly again and she noticed that he must have vomited in his sleep, it was caked all around his mouth, the rancid smell turned her stomach and it was also on the floor on his side of the bed.

She stepped over the dried vomit and reached for his wallet and keys and very carefully she picked them up and crept into the lounge. He wouldn't even know if she took some of the money out, he'd think it was the Philippino girls who had stolen the money from him when they were all together; let him go and beat them up instead of her.

She'd had enough. They were probably used to that sort of behaviour from their clients, filthy tarts. Hurriedly she tucked a wad of euro notes and dollars into her dirty dressing gown pocket, together with the keys. Then she quietly replaced the wallet by his bedside and returned back to the lounge. She would deal with him later.

Slowly she walked towards the hidden safe and opened it. Inside laid a small pearl-handled gun and several envelopes with various currencies in them.

***

Julio had trouble forcing his eyes open. With supreme effort he managed it and blinked several times. His eyes felt crusty and bloodshot. He knew he had a very serious hangover and he knew he'd overdone it again with the drugs and sensed that something was very wrong. For a moment he was completely disorientated and then he remembered where he was. The curtains were closed and he had no idea if it was day or night. All he could remember was that he had been in Puerto Banus at the Rio Coco nightclub in the VIP section with some of his friends and they'd been snorting coke. He'd told one of the heavies to bring over the attractive Philippino girl he'd seen on the dance-floor and she had introduced him to some of her friends. Later they had gone back to her apartment and he remembered the fantastic sex, the ammies, the pot, the drinks etc. Then everything had gone blank.

He got up unsteadily and put his hand down to his throbbing cock. It was extremely painful. Very slowly with his eyes closed and the top half of his body rigid, he sat up, and then swung his long legs over the side of the bed. Immediately he felt nauseated and a pain shot through his left foot. He looked down and saw that he had trodden on a splinter of the broken mirror from the night before and it had imbedded itself into the ball of his right foot. He cussed loudly in Spanish.

"*Cojones*, what the hell is that?"

As he reached down slowly he took a deep breath and quickly nipped out the piece of mirrored glass and blood flowed from the wound onto the luxurious white rug on his side of the bedroom floor.

"Sarah, where the fuck are you bitch?" He yelled out loudly. "Quickly, I'm bleeding to death, it hurts, help me." He sounded like an angry petulant child.

Sarah was in the spare bedroom lying on the single bed, her body still throbbing with intense pain from her severe beating. Let him bleed to death, her inner voice told her. You might get some peace then!

"Sarah," he bellowed again. "Where the hell are you woman?"

She sighed loudly. Better go and see what he wants, he'll only keep shouting until I do, she told herself.

Somehow she managed to lift herself painfully off the bed and slowly walked through to the other bedroom, still wrapped in her filthy crumpled robe pulled tightly around her slim body. Waves of pain seared through her and she gasped at every step.

"Yes, Julio, what is it?" She asked him wearily through her clenched teeth and bruised lips.

Looking at his outstretched legs, she saw several droplets of blood falling onto the white rug from his foot. He'd obviously stepped on a one of the glass splinter and she was pleased and she wanted him to suffer a bit for what he'd done to her.

"I'm sitting here, bleeding to death and you just don't care!" He moaned.

"Care? Care? No, I don't care at all, why should I? Last night you nearly killed me, so why should I care about you now? I hate you, I hope you do bleed to death!" She replied coldly, staring at him with enmity written all over her swollen face.

Her tone brought him to his senses. He looked away from his cut foot and stared back at her in complete horror. Had he done this to his lovely Sarah? Oh no, he thought, not again, he couldn't even remember doing it. He knew he'd been very stoned and very angry when he'd come back from the Philippino girls' apartment. They had all been chasing the dragon, then later one of them had handed him some tablets, they'd made him so horny and he'd had all three girls, one after the other, then he must have passed out for some time.

His head was thumping badly as he tried to think. Of course, Sarah had bitten his penis, he looked down at it, it was swollen and red and he wanted to pee badly. My god, he thought, I hope those bitches upstairs are clean. He had to get to grips with himself he didn't need dirty little foreign sluts when he had his lovely Sarah. Or did he still have her? He must try and ease up on the drugs.

The alcohol he knew he could handle, but the drugs were blowing his mind again. He must not repeat the things he'd done in the past, his father would be furious with him. He was due back in Spain shortly and this time he knew that his father would not forgive him, and he would certainly cut off his generous allowance and completely disown him if he saw him in this state again.

Looking at Sarah he realised that it was almost a repetition of what had happened some years ago in America when his father had managed to cover it up with the help of an associate. He knew Sarah would most certainly leave him now, she'd warned him, but he'd taken no notice of her.

"Oh, my darling, I'm so, so sorry. Come here." He forgot his own pain and straightened up and tried to gather her in his arms.

"Don't darling me, you disgusting bastard. Don't you dare touch me, you evil devil, don't come near me, don't even think about it." She snarled at him, her bruised face contorted with disgust, hate and rage. "Look what you've done to me. Just look at my face and body!"

She pulled open the soiled dressing gown and let it fall to the floor. "Also, what about my cat, my lovely Sario, you killed him. How could you? He never harmed you he loved you. You're...you're worse than any animal."

Sarah burst into tears of outrage and pain and slumped onto the end of the bed in a crumpled heap sobbing hysterically.

Despite what she'd said, Julio reached over and gathered her trembling body into his arms and held her against him, trying in some way to absolve himself.

He bit his bottom lip, closed his eyes and bowed his head. Yes. What had he done? What could he say now to comfort her? He wanted desperately to tell her the truth. He wanted to tell her how sorry he was, he had never meant to harm the cat, but she seemed to love Sario more than him. He knew he desperately needed her to help him. Instead he whined and lied. It seemed he no longer was able to distinguish fantasy from truth.

"I didn't mean to, I found him downstairs under a bush crying and in great pain, I think he was hit by a car or something. So I just put him out of his misery. You would have done the same, I didn't know what else to do, so I brought him upstairs and I was going to tell you about it."

He felt some of his confidence coming back. Perhaps she would believe him, she was always complaining about how fast the Spanish people drove their cars.

He's crazy, he is really crazy, she thought looking at him and I know he's lying.

She pulled away from him and looked him in the face.

"You're utterly and completely mad. Do you really expect me to believe you? You're so full of the shit you put into your body, you don't know what you're doing or saying. I swear if you thought dogs' pee would give you a kick, you'd inject it or drink it, or bathe in it. You disgust me, you filthy, evil smelling apology for a human being." She shouted at him in Spanish and then spat in his face.

Julio blinked several times as her saliva ran down his face. His befuddled mind was trying to take it all in and he couldn't accept what she was saying. He knew he was right and she was wrong, how dare she spit at him his brain told him.

"Anyway, I'm glad he's dead, you always loved him more than me. You were always holding him and kissing him." He shouted at her.

"And me! What about me? Just look at me Julio, look what you have done this time, look at my face and body." She shouted back as she pointed to herself and managed to break away from his strong grasp.

Julio looked at her through his bleary eyes and swayed slightly and was immediately overcome with fear. His mind told him that this had happened before, in fact not just once, several times, he had blacked out in the past in the States a few years ago when he had actually killed a young girl because he had been so stoned. His father had covered up for him, contacted an associate, who had got rid of the body and paid the family off.

The victim had been a young Mexican girl from a very poor family. They had taken the money and said nothing. Was the nightmare starting again? He had nearly killed Sarah. He really did love her. He'd never loved anyone so much, not since the death of his sister. She was the only normal person in his sordid life that he had ever loved, besides his mother and he was trying to destroy her mentally as well as physically.

What if he had killed her? His father was not around to clear up this mess. Damn the drugs, damn the alcohol and damn those two men who had sexually abused him when he was a young boy. Damn everybody, most of all him. Maybe the doctors at the clinic in California were right after all; he was a Psychopath. He suddenly remembered the terminology perfectly: -

One suffering from a behavioural disorder, resulting in indifference to his obligation to society. It is often shown in acts of violence and anti-social behaviour. The specialist had also told his father that he was a manic-depressive - a person suffering from a type of mental illness, characterised by periods of elation and periods of immense depression made even more severe by his drinking and drug abuse. He also suffered from psychosexual disorders i.e. a range of disorders that are related to sexual functions.

He had told himself at the time that was the reason he took drugs and drank so much. He must sort himself out before his father arrived. He also had to gain Sarah's confidence again. He knew that would be the most difficult thing to do!

"Please forgive me, just give me one more chance and I'll make everything up to you. I promise. I beg of you Sarah, just one more chance, if things don't work out, you can go back to England, I won't stop you and I won't even contact you ever again. Please help me." He wailed.

Sarah focused on him with her good eye, the saltiness of her tears as they ran down her cheeks, stung her cut lip badly. Could she believe him? Or was this another of his tricks?

Julio reached out and touched her face tenderly, what had he done? His body shook with grief and realisation. He needed a fix desperately, but he had to control himself. Methadone. He would ring his uncle, who was also his doctor, as soon as possible.

He knew he would help him again, so as not to shame the family. He pulled Sarah to him again and crooned softly in Spanish to her. Her body was very cold and he pulled the duvet off the bed and wrapped it around her. She looked so frail and tired.

Sarah sighed deeply, feeling the warmth of his body against her, all she wanted at that moment was to be held gently, all her mental energy was depleted, and she wanted to go back home, back to England. She sensed that Julio was genuinely sorry this time and very frightened. They needed each other for the time being and she would take advantage of it. Let him feel guilty about what he had done to her, maybe he would come to his senses at last, but it was too late.

She knew her body would heal in time, but the mental scars would take a long, long time to leave her. She could not deny that there was a burning compulsion to get even with him.

"Okay Julio," she said pulling herself away from him.

"If you are really sorry you'd better do something about it. First of all run me a deep hot bath that should ease some of the pain and bruising. Also I need a drink, a brandy perhaps, something to perk me up a bit. There should be enough left in the drinks cabinet!"

He re-arranged the duvet around her before he left the bedroom and walked into the bathroom and turned on the light. There lying in the bath was the mutilated body of their cat, wrapped in a bloodstained towel.

Julio gasped with horror, he felt dizzy and sick. The cat's body was stiff in death, his eyes bulged open and his little pink tongue looked pathetic as it hung sideways out of his mouth. Had he really done that to the poor thing? He'd loved it too in his own way, what was happening to him?

He turned away and retched, vomiting into the toilet. He wiped the puke from his mouth with the back of his right hand and then he started to sweat and tremble profusely he needed something to calm him down, perhaps just a little something, until he could see his uncle. No, he told himself, I must fight it. *I've done it before and this time I will really stop all this nonsense.*

He flushed the toilet, rinsed his face in the hand-basin, and then took a deep breath and reached over into the bath and lifted the pathetic little body into his big hands, carried it onto the kitchen balcony and put it in a black bin-liner. Later he would bury the cat under some bushes downstairs in the large garden area.

Returning to the bathroom he washed out the bath thoroughly, then rinsed it, poured some disinfectant around and rinsed it again. Then he ran a deep, hot bath with some of Sarah's favourite *Femme* bath gel in it and turned on the Jacuzzi switch. The water bubbled softly. He knew in his befuddled mind that Sarah had made him do this on purpose. It had certainly shocked him back to reality.

He walked back slowly to the bedroom; she was lying still wrapped in the duvet, fast asleep. He awoke her gently and helped her to her feet, the duvet fell back from her naked body and once more he was overcome with shock at the sight of what he had done to her. He fell to his knees and kissed her ankles and legs, he was getting an erection and it hurt through the thin material of his briefs. She always had this effect on him.

Sarah was fully aware of what he was trying to do to her. Did he honestly think that he would arouse her in the condition she was in? But against her will he was turning her on, he was like a drug to her, if only she wasn't so sexually addicted to him. A bit like him she thought, she was hooked on sex and he on drink and drugs. She pulled herself hastily from him.

"No Julio, leave me alone," she begged in a weak voice and wearily she sat back on the bed.

"Please leave me alone, leave me in peace. I'm going to have my bath now. I assume you've cleaned it out for me?"

She threw the duvet aside and limped into the big bathroom. Her limp would last a long time she knew. Her right hip and pelvis felt as if it was fractured from the kicking that he had given her. She put her good leg over the bath first and slowly lowered herself into the steaming scented water. She lay back in the large Jacuzzi and closed her eyes, feeling the warmth of the bubbling water soothing her battered body and she started to drift off into oblivion.

Julio came into the bathroom and watched her and then grabbed his white towelling dressing gown from behind the bathroom door and left, closing it quietly behind him. He knew better than to annoy her again and would have to tread very, very carefully from now on. This could be the end of their relationship. He was not dealing with a stupid young peasant girl, but with an intelligent woman. He walked into the lounge and poured her a large Remy Martin and took it back to her.

***

Sarah spent the next three days in bed in the darkened spare room. She ached all over. Julio waited on her hand and foot, trying very hard to show her how he had changed.

She enjoyed it immensely and had no intention of getting out of bed unless she needed to attend to her bodily functions. Julio in the meantime had managed to see his uncle and obtain some medication to help him with his drug problem. He had also cut down on the cigarettes and alcohol, and cleaned himself up again, had his hair cut and given the cat a decent burial.

Sarah knew he was trying hard. He slept in the master bedroom and left her alone.

Slowly she was healing physically and somehow her brain was functioning again. She was thinking of a plan of escape.

Julio still disappeared for several hours a day, but at least he was sober when he returned. He had phoned his father in London and was told by his secretary that he would be arriving in less than a week and left a message for his father to call him so that he could meet him at the airport and take him straight to his favourite hotel. Julio didn't want him to see the state that Sarah was in.

His uncle had given him a supply of Methadone and some other tablets together with a strict warning that he would tell Julio's father if he did not clean up his life-style. His uncle also told him that if he carried on this way he would kill himself, his liver was in a very poor state and he doubted whether he would survive another five years without having a transplant it was so badly damaged.

***

Julio knew he had not really been born evil as his father had often told him. Many years ago it seemed, as a little boy, his Spanish grandmother had taught him right from wrong and to believe in God's way. Then his beliefs were shattered at the age of twelve when two drunken men in his grandmother's village up in the hills sexually abused him. That was when he had his first major breakdown. That was also the start of his schizophrenia and wild tantrums. Yet at times a little part of him that he barely acknowledged these days, escaped. It told him God was still about somewhere trying to help him. But, most of all he could only acknowledge the devil and forces of evil, abnormal sex, alcohol, drugs, gambling anything that was bad for him. Sex to him, was a way of punishing himself as well as others, for what he had gone through, especially violent sex. Under the influence of drugs and alcohol, he seemed to lose control and his mind would blank out.

He had been sent to Public school in England at ten years old and only went back to South Africa, where his parents were residing at the time, for his holidays. At twelve he was sexually abused when

100

he was on holiday with his grandparents in Spain. At around sixteen on one of his summer holiday visits to South Africa he was first introduced to marijuana and locally brewed beer by some of the local lads in the town.

When he returned to school two gay pupils, who constantly admired his good looks pestered him and eventually invited him into their study, they had frightened him at first, but at the same time, he was curious as he watched them performing in front of him and then they took turns with him.

He'd never quite got over the sensation of a male penis up his anal passage. Often he wanted to try it again with them after that, but he knew it was forbidden. He wondered sometimes if he was actually a latent homosexual.

BOOK FIVE

PETER 1 Verse 2: Grace and peace be multiplied unto you through the knowledge of God.

CHAPTER SEVEN

LONDON - 2004

Upon returning to his apartment, David worked all through the night and eventually he fell asleep at his desk. He awoke with a start; the phone on his desk was ringing out loudly.

"Hello... David Myers here."

"Helloooooo!" Boomed a loud voice. "I'm sorry to ring you so early, but I've got some information for you, could be a lead!" Exclaimed Michael Akaro excitedly.

"Oh, sorry, you just caught me...er, what's the time?" David stuttered, still half asleep.

"About 7.30. What, still asleep or do you have company?" Asked his friend jokingly.

David shook himself, 7.30 am, where was he? His neck felt terrible and he ached all over as he rubbed his eyes hard and tried to put his mind into gear.

"Uh no, I got up early to do some paperwork," David lied to his friend. "Tell you what; I'll ring you back a bit later, someone's on the other line. Okay!" He replaced the receiver hastily.

Was he going out of his mind? Thoughts of Sarah came flooding back to him. He must phone her, to see her, today. He would ask her out to dinner tonight. He tried unsuccessfully to blot her out of his mind. He really must concentrate on the Serial Killer case. Leaving his study he made for the bathroom, he needed a cold shower to wake himself up.

About three quarters of an hour later and a cup of strong coffee, David rang his friend back.

"Yes Michael, sorry about that, wasn't quite awake! What have you got for me?" He asked, now that he was fully awake. "Okay, yes, I can come and see you. About what time? Around eleven thirty that's good."

David slowly put the handset back. Interesting he thought, at last I might be onto something.

**

The phone rang out by Sarah's bedside and wakened her from a deep sleep. So soon, was it David, had he somehow got her phone number? She lifted the receiver carefully and took a deep breath.

"Hello, Sarah Lawson here. Oh yes, Michael, lovely to hear your voice, yes, yes, of course I'll come in tomorrow instead of today, usual time? Bye now, thanks for letting me know."

She was shaking like a nervous schoolgirl. Perhaps David would be there again. That's why he'd not rung. Maybe she should give him a ring, no, she couldn't do that she didn't have his number, but Michael would probably give it to her, if she asked. No, she told herself. He was too much of his own man. He was the type that would have to make

103

the first move, he could get her mobile number from Michael and she knew she mustn't chase him.

Well at least she had the day to herself, she could relax, perhaps go shopping something she hadn't done for a long time. She needed a few new clothes, something smart, but more up to date than most of the things in her wardrobe. She leaned back against her pillows and sighed deeply. Picasso started to snuggle down against her warm body and yawned.

"Oh no, you don't, my lovely," she laughed. "I am getting up now. You can stay here if you want to, but I'm going downstairs to make myself a cup of tea."

He looked at her through his bright copper colour eyes, then yawned and snuggled down into the soft duvet with a long cat sigh and curled himself into a ball.

She swung her long legs over the side of the bed, padded across the bedroom, picked up her turquoise silk dressing gown from a chair nearby and wrapped it around her slender body. Then quickly she ran down the stairs barefooted into the kitchen, filled her electric kettle and made her way through to the hall.

Her early morning paper and mail lay on the doormat. She picked them both up and returned to her kitchen dropping them onto one of the worktops whilst she made her tea. Having poured her tea she looked through her mail. Most of it was junk and she binned it before looking at her newspaper.

The assassinator of the drug addicts had made front-page news again. In many ways it made her feel ill, but in other ways she could feel the burden of carrying her pent-up hatred and anger for Julio lifting, almost floating from her mind and body. She could also feel the numbness that she constantly had in her right leg from one of his vicious beatings, tingling with a new kind of sensation. He had cracked her pelvis and badly bruised her from the beating and kicking when she had lain helpless on the floor of her house after he had tracked her down in England some months previously.

The words sprang out at her: -

DAVID MYERS, THE WELL KNOWN FORENSIC SCIENTIST AND PSYCHOPATHOLOGIST ON THE CASE, PROCLAIMED YESTERDAY AT A MEDIA INTERVIEW: - THE KILLER IS ALMOST CERTAINLY FEMALE. WE ARE LOOKING FOR A VERY CLEVER WOMAN, SOMEONE WHO IS NOT NECESSARILY NEUROTIC OR PSYCOPATHIC OR EVEN A SOCIOPATHIC NUTCASE, BUT SOMEONE WHO HAS PLANNED EVERYTHING VERY CAREFULLY. SHE IS OUT FOR REVENGE - RETALIATION. SHE HAS OBVIOUSLY BEEN HURT BADLY, MENTALLY AS WELL AS PHYSICALLY BY A MAN OR MEN AT SOME TIME IN THE PAST, PERHAPS EVEN AT THIS PRESENT TIME. SHE HAS NOW GOT THE APPETITE FOR KILLING AND SHE WILL STRIKE AGAIN, BUT WHEN AND WHERE NO ONE KNOWS, BUT ON THE OTHER HAND SHE MAY NOT, NOW THAT SHE HAS BECOME ALMOST A CELEBRITY.

It was a feature article and also quoted several theories by the police as well as Mr. Myers comments.

"I'm not neurotic or a psychopath. And I am certainly not a sociopathic nutcase!" She shouted aloud to the empty kitchen. "What's the matter with all of them? I'm only trying to exorcise the evil memory of Julio in order to live a normal life again. Why should women be treated in this way, used and abused? Surely Mr. Myers of all people should know that!"

She carried on reading the rest of the article.

Mr. Myers went on to say that: - *Inside a murderer was something that was inside of everyone. People should know this so they could know more about themselves. He concluded the article with - if she needs help, would she please ring New Scotland Yard, say who she is and ask for DCI Paul Forrest. A special phone line has been set up that will be put directly through to his office. Please call 0800 - 798 - 7988. Her call will be treated confidentially. We want to help her. An incident room has also been set up and anyone with any information, please also contact DCI Forrest no matter how insignificant it might seem.*

More like catch her. Sarah thought. Besides she had other things on her mind at present, her blanket of gloom was being lifted. Perhaps a little spiritual help might be a good thing. She would go to church and pray, it was a long time since she had entered a church, in fact not since her Aunt's funeral, let alone pray. She knew where she would go, she would go to Oxford, visit the grave of her cousin and aunt, do a little therapeutic shopping there and then visit St. Mary the Virgin's Church.

CHAPTER EIGHT

OXFORD - 2004

Sarah stepped from the bright afternoon sunlight into the cool gloom of St. Mary the Virgin's church. For a moment she could see only shadows and the vague outlines of pews as her eyes became accustomed to the dim interior and she could see more clearly. Suddenly she noticed the lone woman parishioner seated at the back of the church, her head bowed low and wondered if she too had a dreadful secret to confess and was seeking forgiveness.

She looked around her and noticed the ornamental wrought iron frame with its many candles burning brightly and she walked towards it and selected an unlit candle and placed five one pound coins into the box on the side and lit it from one of the others. She also bowed her head and said a small prayer and crossed herself.

Though Methodist parents had raised her originally before they had died in a road accident, later on in life, her Aunt Meg who had been a devout Catholic had looked after her and taken her to attend her local Catholic church and shortly after that she had been baptised into the faith. Then she had been brought up as a Catholic, but she was not fanatically religious, she did believe in God though and she let the silence envelope her as she prayed and asked him for strength and peace in her life once more.

She felt at home in the beautiful church with its big stained glass windows. The richly decorated stained glass windows above her glowed with sombre hues where the sun was trying to filter through.

Staring up and around her, she felt a sense of disquiet and her gaze moved to another window.

Sarah rose to her feet and turning she walked into the Chancel of St. Mary the Virgin and quietly sat down on one of the pews and made the sign of the cross. She reflected and meditated on her past life and now the new future that she was going to face. She had not prayed in a long time and hoped it would work.

Looking up at the seven stone-carved figures of Saints above the altar, she asked each in turn for their help.

The Madonna stood in the middle with the boy Jesus in the crook of her left arm. Sarah's lips moved in silent prayer once again as she asked forgiveness from the Mother of Jesus.

On either side of the Madonna, stood St. Mary Magdalene and St. John. On either side of them were St. Frideswide - Patron Saint of Oxford and St. Hugh of Lincoln. St. Catherine stood next to St. Frideswide and St. Edmund of Abingdon to the right of St. Hugh. It seemed that the seven statues looked down at her coldly and accusingly, but at the same time pity for her.

Surely during their time on earth their lives were not completely flawless, they had after all been flesh and blood, surely they had been tempted and they had sinned and been forgiven by God. What did the future hold for her, she wondered? She needed love now, pure unadulterated love. She had so much love to give; she needed also understanding and comforting. Tears prickled her eyes and ran down her cheeks. Suddenly she felt so alone, so unhappy.

"Please God, please forgive me. I only did what I had to do. I hope in some way that I have also avenged the people that Julio hurt in the past. Please help me now and forgive me for my sins."

She whispered in prayer.

Her thoughts turned to David. She knew that he would be the man she wanted to share her life with, but how? She was the instigator of the killings, but he must never know, she knew he would contact her through his friend Michael and she knew that he would protect her.

Michael knew a little about her past, but not all the details. He had helped her get her strength back after Julio had beaten her up again, in London. She must get back to London, David might have called and left a message on her answerphone, she knew that Michael would have given him her home number and probably her mobile number as well.

Had she turned her mobile on, she searched her handbag and started to panic. Had she left it at home or was it in her car she wondered? She had to get her brain under control; she was acting like a stupid teen-ager with her first love. She had to find out if he had called her.

Hurriedly she picked up her big shoulder bag and rushed out of the Church into the bright afternoon sunlight, she all but ran back to where her car was parked and trembling with excitement she pressed the button of her remote control transmitter and entered her BMW. She could not see her mobile anywhere and panicked, and then she fished around under her driving seat. It had fallen down onto the floor. She grabbed it and there was a message from an unknown number, she pressed one of the buttons and listened to the message.

Hellooo Sarah, if you pick up this message in time, would you care to join me for dinner this evening at around eight thirty. Are you free? If not, I fully understand.

Thank heavens she thought feeling very exhilarated and saved his number.

Already she felt better. She looked at her watch, it was three thirty. Her fingers were shaking again as she quickly called up his number. It rang out several times and then went onto his voicemail. He was not in, but she left a message for him. For several moments she sat in the driver's seat collecting her thoughts before driving back towards London. With trembling fingers she turned the key in the ignition as she saw a Traffic Warden approaching her car.

CHAPTER NINE

LONDON - 2004

David looked across the table at Sarah. He knew he had done the right thing calling Sarah that morning and inviting her for their dinner date albeit was rather short notice.

He watched the rise and fall of Sarah's breasts as she breathed. The movement sent erotic messages to his brain and then passed them through his body. He could feel himself hardening and grinned, he felt like a young man again. It was wildly erotic and a little mad, one of those crazy moments that one has in ones' teens. As he sat opposite her at the table for two in the intimate little Italian restaurant he'd carefully chosen, he knew she would bring new meaning to his dull life.

A light pink glow from the wine spread over Sarah's smooth cheeks and she seemed to lose some of her reserve. He had almost forgotten what it was like to be with a real woman again, instead of one of the bimbos in the past that he had wined, dined and bedded, over the years mainly for company.

This lovely woman sitting across the table from him was very different. As he looked at her in the subdued lighting of the restaurant, he noticed how youthful her skin looked. She wore very little make-up, but then, he thought, she didn't really need any with her almost perfect fair skin.

He sat there feeling relaxed, eating, listening and enjoying her warm eagerness, taking pleasure in just being with her.

Her shoulder-length pale blonde hair swung with the movement of her head as she started to indulge in animated conversation. Her well-shaped breasts rose and fell against the fine silk fabric of her cream blouse.

He noticed briefly that she did not wear her gold chain beneath it tonight; just a simple string of exquisite pearls replaced it. On her right hand she wore a beautiful diamond and ruby ring. He wondered jealously who'd given it to her. On her left hand nothing. Looking across at her he realised how much he wanted her. In the past, he had always been scared to commit himself, he had conditioned himself never to marry again or to enter into a lasting relationship, but now he felt that he had reached that time in his life when he wanted to fill his loneliness, he wanted her beside him, to share his life.

Better be careful though he thought, it was a little too soon, he hardly knew her. His mind wandered and he really didn't hear what she was saying.

Suddenly she stared up at him, her full lips parted.

"But enough about me how was your day?" She asked, bringing him back down to earth as she leaned across the table and touched his left hand shyly. She smiled her lovely smile at him and his heart melted.

She seemed to shimmer with energy, yet he knew she was very strong willed but he wanted her badly. He wanted to lean across the table and take her in his arms and kiss her passionately.

"So, tell me David, what exactly is your role in this investigation?"

She needed to find out more about him, how his mind worked, how much he knew. As she spoke he noticed her small aristocratic nose, fine cheekbones and huge astonishing blue eyes with their long lashes. He wished he could decipher exactly the colour of her eyes. She was a striking looking woman, not a weak looking beauty the kind he despised and he liked her presence so close to him.

"Oh, Michael and I had another meeting this morning as you probably know. He came up with some good ideas. It's a very difficult case you know. Er...then I just did some wandering around and thinking and here we are tonight enjoying a lovely dinner." He smiled back warmly at her before continuing.

"As you know I am first and foremost a Psychiatrist. Psychiatry is the study of disorders of the mind. I normally deal with conditions such as depression, anxiety, and schizophrenia in my everyday practise in Grosvenor Square. However, over the years the police have called me in on many occasions for my other profiling skills, and then I deal with the criminally insane and mentally abnormal people. I look into the mind of the murderer and have specialised over the years in Serial Killers."

He took a sip of his wine before continuing.

"I expect you've read the present articles in the newspapers," he said seriously. "Avenging Angel, that's what the media are calling the killer. She is becoming quite the heroine and the police don't quite know how to handle it. Literally thousands of women have been ringing and writing into the newspapers, the TV stations and even the police are praising her. Of course it is a woman you know!" He stated.

"In fact I myself would like to meet her and thank her for what she is doing, but keep that to yourself!" He laughed embarrassingly and took another sip of his wine before continuing once more.

"She is making the public very aware out there, of what goes on in the real world. There are many monsters around beating up women and children and causing havoc."

He reached across the table and took her hand. "If anyone ever did that to you, I would kill them too!" He proclaimed vehemently.

Sarah smiled back weakly. My God, if only you knew she thought, biting her bottom lip. She realised she had almost said it aloud. The blood drained from her face. Certain feelings never healed; if one was lucky they stopped bleeding and became a little fainter in ones' mind. The brain always stores things like a computer, touch the right key and everything comes flashing back onto the screen.

She felt sick as the waves of nausea swept over her. Did he know, could he know how much she was involved, was he saying these things to test her, was this his way of telling her he knew she had something to do with the events?

She took her hand away abruptly and reached for her glass of red wine. He didn't seem to notice the movement.

"Yes, but how can you be so sure that it is a woman?"

David continued.

"Because these are desperate murders. It is also my gut feeling, I am very rarely wrong, they are so clear-cut. Of course, on the other hand, what kind of woman is she really? Her mind must be in terrible turmoil, and she needs help desperately or she could just be a plain cold-blooded killer, doing it for kicks. I don't think it's the latter, though. I wish I could meet her and get into her mind and find out more, she has been so deeply hurt. I feel for her. I know I could help her."

Sarah managed another weak smile and tucked a strand of hair that had fallen across her face, behind one ear. She could feel the blood slowly coming back into her cheeks. Fortunately, it was dim in the restaurant and he had not noticed the colour drain from her face.

"She is probably a very nice person deep down inside," she proclaimed. "She obviously has been very deeply hurt at some time or other, you're right, I wish she would seek help from you, but how would she know that you really intend to help her and not just report her to the police and they would lock her up forever."

She looked across at his gentle face. Please help me, she prayed silently to him. Her lovely blue eyes welled up with tears.

David looked into her big sad eyes. "Hey, what's all this then?" he chided. "We're supposed to be having a relaxing, pleasant meal and all I can talk about is work and upset you. Have you finished,

116

would you like anything else, a cup of coffee perhaps?"

Sarah shook her head and reached for her small black DKNY handbag hanging on the back of her chair.

"No thank you that was a lovely meal. I just…" She broke off. What could she say? She knew that she was falling in love with him.

David looked across into her eyes, both realised that they both wanted and needed each other very much that evening.

He glanced around the restaurant and beckoned to a young woman selling roses from a shallow wicker basket, she came over and he selected several long stemmed red roses and handed them to Sarah.

He signalled to the waiter for the bill and also asked him to call a taxi. "Shall we go back to my place?" He asked quietly.

She looked at him and just nodded.

***

He had no idea what had awakened him, until he heard her cry out again. Her cold shaking body was covered in beads of moisture. He held her tightly against him until she came out of it.

"Bad dream?" He asked in a whisper.

"Umm…" she mumbled as she snuggled against him and dropped back into a deep peaceful slumber. Her shaking had stopped and she was safe again. In the morning she apologised for waking him with her bad dreams.

"That's why people sleep together, so there is someone around to rescue them from their nightmares," he told her gently as he turned to her and kissed her lovingly.

She kissed him back with feeling as well as great passion; her hands began to slowly explore his muscular body. Her right hand lazily stroked his stomach, pulling the fine hairs around his belly button between her fingers, working her way down deeper to a thicker bush. She pulled away slightly and smiled at him.

"I want you to make love to me now, David, proper love, not like last night!" She said softly.

***

She had made no attempt to stop David from having sex with her the night before, but now she wanted him so much and she was ready to give herself completely to him, he made her feel relaxed and wanted. He had been there to see her through her nightmare.

He answered her by pulling her forward to kiss her, tasting the inside of her lips and her tongue; kissing her until her long body was pressing urgently against his. Her lips trembled against his. He softened the kiss, sliding the edge of his tongue along her lower lip, urging her to open her mouth again. He wanted to taste her more than anything in a long time. He knew that he had found someone whom he could love and possibly marry.

She made an achingly sweet, soft sound against his mouth. David swallowed up the tremulous cry as if he were a starving man being offered food after a great fast. He immediately craved passion; he felt her clutching at him, his own body was throbbing with an urgent need to possess her.

118

He had never met a woman like her and he knew he would not be content until she was his. His hands began to move over her beautiful body. Their skins and beings became one. Their blood raced and pulsated through their bodies, they were as one as he filled her with his pulsating manhood so gently and so powerfully that it was as though her entire existence had never been about anything more, or anything less, than being with him. They held each other tightly not daring to let go, for fear of losing each other.

She felt his breath in her hair as he held her. His fingers lingered on the nape of her neck, the touch made her shiver with longing for him. They were generating a heat that threatened to incinerate both of them. His hands explored the length and breadth of her back, the nape of her neck and her arms, as he drew air into his starving lungs before again seeking the eager welcome of her mouth.

In those moments after he felt an extraordinary tenderness for her, she had rekindled feelings in him that he didn't think he would ever have again. They had made love, proper love and not just lust.

They both lay back and recalled the night before as they nestled in each other's arms.

***

After the taxi had dropped them off at his penthouse, they had rushed into his bedroom. His hunger for her matched her own need for him. They had torn off their clothes in their haste to be rid of them and their desperate longing to feel the flesh of each other. He remembered kneeling in front of her admiring her naked body and then, with deliberate

119

slowness, pulled off her black silk lacy topped hold-up stockings, looking up at her all the time, devouring her with his eyes. Then his hands caressed her hips and his eager mouth found her and his tongue was finding every secret place on her body.

He had felt Sarah's body stiffen, and then relax as her legs gave way from the ecstasy he was giving her. She had screamed with joy as she felt herself climaxing and fell back onto his big bed, but still he held her hips, still continued to pleasure her and she lost count of the times her body arched with passion. Then he was upon her and thrusting into her and she felt his flesh, his sweat and their animal passion for each other.

She also had never experienced such pleasure and feeling for any man in her life. Not even Julio whom she thought she had loved in the beginning. She knew that she had found real love now, not just animal lust this time. Could she dare to think that once again she had found the right man in her life? She breathed deeply and sent up a little prayer.

***

David was now at peace with himself as he lay back on the big bed reflecting. He knew now that he was truly in love with her. He lifted his head and looked over at her, her face was flushed, yet beautiful, and almost serene, she smiled happily.

"When you smile at me like that, I could eat your lips David murmured as he shifted onto his side.

120

With one finger, he smoothed the hair off her forehead and back behind one ear as he gazed into her lovely blue eyes.

"I love you Sarah. Will it last?"

"It will last my darling. Forever," she whispered.

Maybe now I'll be able to find peace and no longer be afraid of my ghosts she thought vaguely remembering that she had cried out in the night. She didn't regret sleeping with David. It was not common practise for her to jump into bed with a man on their first date, but somehow this was different, they had not disguised their need for each other. She knew that her prayers had been answered at last.

BOOK SIX

EXODUS XX1 Verse 25: Burning for burning, wound for wound and stripe for stripe.

CHAPTER TEN

MARBELLA - 2003

Sarah knew that she was screaming out, but she could not wake up as she relived her nightmares again.

After spending three whole days in bed, Sarah decided that it was time to get up and sort out her life; she had a lot of thinking to do as she had to formulate a plan of escape.

She took a good long look at herself in the tall cheval glass by the spare bedroom window that overlooked the blue Mediterranean Sea. The stark whiteness of her bra and panties stood out against the purple and yellow bruising on her body. She pulled a pair of jeans from the wardrobe and a cotton T-shirt and pushed her feet into an old pair of flat sandals. Then she took a careful look at the state of her face in the dressing table mirror.

First she applied some Vaseline to her cracked lip to seal it, then some light foundation to the area around her bruised eyes. She brushed her hair and pulled some short wisps over her forehead and around her face to disguise the rest of the bruises. At least she looked a little more human and not so much like a punch-bag!

Julio knocked timidly on her bedroom door and she called out to him to enter. He pushed the door open tentatively and stood and stared hard at her as he bit his bottom lip and held his breath wondering what she was going to say to him. He was afraid as he looked at her.

Sarah turned and just stared back at him. "What do you want now?" She asked wearily.

"Oh, well, Sarah, you look better, you do know I'm truly sorry." He said with a meek voice.

He said it with such sincerity that she found herself actually believing him.

His face was grey and drawn and a thin line of sweat covered his top lip. She knew he was suffering, but true to his word he seemed to be making an effort to stay clean. She felt a small rush of sympathy for him, but quickly checked it. She was also pleased that his nearness was not affecting her anymore, she felt almost cured of him too. Now she felt stronger and able to cope with her life again.

"I know you are sorry, Julio, but being sorry will not bring back my cat and will certainly not bring back the feelings I once had for you. I will never, ever, forget or forgive you for what you have done to me. We are finished. Do you understand? I am leaving you when I am fully recovered. I am going back to England. I need money from you for the flight and some other things."

Her voice was icy cold as she spoke to him, her blue eyes dark and unforgiving.

"You can't leave me, I'll kill myself. You can't leave me, I love you, I love you," he shouted at her. "I love you."

He started to shake uncontrollably. "I'll never let you go, never. I'll kill myself."

"Oh, don't be so damned dramatic." Sarah sneered at him.

He took a step towards her and then raised his right hand as if to strike her, but thought better of it and lowered it and curled his hand into a fist by his side.

She ducked instinctively covering her face knowing that she had made the right decision to leave him.

Julio stepped back as he realised that he was threatening her again. Jesus, he needed a drink or something else to steady his frayed nerves. He ran from the bedroom through to the kitchen, clawed one of the kitchen cupboards open and found a half bottle of Bacardi tucked away at the back of it.

A few days before he had poured away all the hard alcohol that was in the cocktail cabinet in the lounge in an attempt to give up drink. The Bacardi was all he could find. He poured himself a stiff drink then searched in the refrigerator for some Coca-Cola. Unsteadily he poured it into the white rum, raised the glass to his lips and downed it in one big gulp. He banged the glass down on the marble topped kitchen table and it shattered into pieces and he stalked to the front door slamming it behind him, not even bothering to lock it, he needed a proper fix badly.

Sarah sat down at her dressing table, trembling with fear; he had almost struck her again. She must get herself ready. She had to get away very soon. She still had the money she had taken from him, hidden away in a shoe. He had never even noticed it was missing from his wallet.

The noise of the front door slamming brought her back to her senses. She heard the keys jangling on the inside. She was not locked in. Swiftly she ran down the hallway to the door and turned the key in the lock. Now he was locked out. She burst into hysterical laughter; for the time being she was safe.

About an hour passed, still Julio had not returned, she felt more relaxed now, it was around eight p.m. and she doubted whether he would return that night. She felt sure he had gone somewhere to satisfy his cravings.

She waited for several moments in case he might come back for the keys and then phoned her Aunt Meg. Carefully punching out the numbers with trembling fingers and spoke to her for about half an hour, trying to explain things to her. Aunt Meg, bless her, never asked any questions, just listened. She only said at the end of the conversation.

"My darling, if you need money and a place to come back to, you can rely on me. I'll ask my Bank to make an electronic transfer of a thousand pounds to you; will that be enough? Where do you want it sent?"

Sarah was so choked with emotion it was hard for her to give all the details to her aunt.

"Tell me all your troubles when you come back to England my darling, I'm waiting for you. The Bank of Bilboa, Marbella, you said? Okay and the account number."

She repeated the number back to Sarah.

"Don't forget to give me a ring regarding your flight details and I'll meet you at the airport if you like."

"Thank you auntie, yes of course I will." Sarah whispered. "I will ring you as soon as I know my final details. No you don't have to meet me that will be all right. I'll get a taxi or go on the train to Richmond and then take a taxi. I don't have much luggage. I love you Aunt Meg and thank you again." Sarah's throat constricted, she couldn't say anymore.

"I love you too, my darling. I'll be waiting; don't forget to phone though as soon as you arrive at Heathrow."

"No auntie, I will ring as soon as I arrive. Bye."

Sarah put down the phone, she felt very comforted and strong after talking to her aunt, she knew now she had the courage to leave Julio, Spain, and all her troubles behind.

But what she didn't know was that she would never speak to her Aunt again.

She sat down on the chair by the phone in the lounge and burst into floods of tears, a mixture of self-pity and relief, and wondered how on earth she had managed to get herself into such a mess, how she had put up with Julio all these months. What had she done to deserve him? She plucked a tissue from the Kleenex box by the phone and blew her nose hard; there were so many things to do. Then she got up, removed the keys from the front door and put them into one of the pockets of her jeans.

It was getting dark now and she welcomed the darkness, it hid her feelings. She walked over to the huge black leather settee and flopped onto it and closed her eyes.

A few minutes went by and there was a slight noise at the front door. It opened slowly and a form appeared in the doorway, lit only by the dim landing light outside. A tall man stepped into the apartment; he flicked the light switch by the front door, and then gasped in complete surprise when he saw her in the room.

She had jumped up terrified from the settee when she'd heard the door opening, thinking that Julio had returned and somehow managed to unlock the apartment door.

"Oh, excuse me. Am I in the right flat?" He questioned in perfect English.

"Well I don't know, are you? Who are you anyway?" She asked in a wavering voice as she reached for the lounge light switch by the door.

The room was flooded in light. She forgot about her bruised face for a moment, then realised he was staring at her. She put her hand up to her face and turned to the right slightly, her long blonde hair falling over it, trying to hide her bruising.

"My name if Juan Carlos Gonzales, and who may I ask are you and what are you doing in my apartment?"

"I'm Sarah Lawson."

She stared back at him and suddenly it dawned on her; she could see the family likeness. "Are you by any chance, Julio's father?"

"Yes my dear," he replied softly as he closed the front door behind him and walked over to her.

He dropped his black leather briefcase onto the floor and reached over pushing her hair from her face.

"Oh, my God! So, I see my evil son has been up to his old tricks again," he stated coldly. "I'm so very sorry, I can only apologise for what he has done to you."

She jumped back sharply.

"*Apologise, apologise*. That's all you two ever do is to apologise, look at my face! Would you like to see my body as well?"

She made as if to raise her top to show him.

"How dare you stand there and say sorry so casually, you bloody Spaniards, you're all the same!" She screamed at him and the little spots of saliva that flew from her mouth landed on the front of his pale grey Armani suit.

"My dear, lady," he put up both hands resignedly. "I did not mean it like that. I just know what my son is capable of doing. Please try and calm yourself."

Juan Carlos was extremely angry, not with her, but with his son and himself; he knew that this lady standing in front of him had been terribly beaten-up by his son. His own flesh and blood! Was history repeating itself again?

"Can we sit down and talk this through perhaps?" He smiled warmly at her, trying to win her confidence.

"I mean no harm to you, we Spanish are not all the same, as you put it. At least, not this Spaniard!"

He gave a slightly nervous laugh, studying Sarah, she reminded him so much of his first wife, slim, blonde and beautiful.

Sarah also laughed a little tremulously at his reply.

"I'm sorry too, do come in, can I offer you something, a coffee perhaps, I don't have anything stronger I'm afraid."

Her left hand pulled nervously at her hair trying to cover her bruises. Julio's father made her extremely twitchy; whatever must he think of her? She looked around; the place was so untidy.

"I'm sorry the place, it's..." she looked around her. "I haven't been well. Now she was apologising again and she let out a small hysterical laugh as she nearly burst into tears.

"My dear Sarah, calm down, I can see you have been through a lot recently. A coffee would be fine. I'll sit down while you make it. I am rather tired from my journey."

He lowered himself wearily into a nearby black leather armchair. Sarah went into the kitchen and made a pot of coffee for both of them and returned with the tray, placed it on the low coffee table in front of the settee and sat down to pour.

"What exactly did you mean by your apartment, when you first came in? I thought this was Julio's place. He said that you had given it to him for his twenty fifth birthday." she said feeling embarrassed at being caught in the flat.

"My son says many things. He is a habitual liar, another of his vices, I'm afraid. I said he could live here whilst I was out of the country. Actually I very rarely stay here. I either go back to my house in Puerto Banus, or stay in one of the local hotels. You see my second wife and I live at present in an apartment next to the Spanish Embassy in London since I've been given the position in England. She is also English like you." He explained.

" I suppose in many ways the apartment is his, or will be one day when I die, in fact the whole block will be his. But what are you doing here? Excuse me, but you are not like his usual type of girlfriend. Not that I have met many of his girlfriends, we don't see each other very often." He raised his left eyebrow quizzingly.

"Well, Julio and I have lived together for several months, I feel awful, and I feel like an intruder into your life, you obviously didn't know about me." She paused, waiting for his reaction.

"Well, I wouldn't exactly say that I didn't know about you. I knew from my solicitor, who incidentally is my first cousin, and also from my brother the doctor. He said that Julio had an English woman living with him, but he wasn't sure exactly who and also he didn't know that you are such a nice lady." He smiled engagingly at her.

Sarah felt even more embarrassed by what he had said and the way in which he was staring at her.

Julio had told her that his father was a womaniser, were they both alike in their choice of females? Or had Julio lied about his father too. She was very confused and did not know what to believe.

She liked the look of the man sitting opposite her and felt drawn to him; he seemed so kind and sympathetic. Julio had claimed that his father was a brutal, handsome gallivanting man and his mother had been deeply unhappy and died of a broken heart. He'd also said that he had suffered a very traumatic childhood and his grandparents had played a big part in his younger years when his parents had not been around for him. He also claimed that his father had been the catalyst of his mother's death.

"How do you like your coffee?"

"I'll have it strong and black, no sugar thank you."

He looked questioningly at her. "Have I offended you in some way?" He asked as he reached over for his coffee.

"Not exactly, I am a bit bruised, but otherwise ok I suppose now."

She thought, I'm becoming paranoid and she tried to smile back at him. "You're not exactly as I pictured you either." She exclaimed getting some of her confidence back.

"I just wondered what a lady like you is doing with my perverted son. Don't be shocked at my words. I know exactly what he is like. It is not the first time that he's beaten up a woman, but I expect you already realise that by now."

Juan Carlos sipped his coffee and looked over the rim of the cup before continuing.

"I suppose Julio has told you some dreadful stories about me. How much I hate him, I've never been there when he needs me, and I killed his mother with my womanising ways, so on and so on."

Sarah stared back at him.

"Well, sort of...um, something like that." She replied hesitantly realising how much Julio had indeed lied to her.

"Julio, I would say is full of delusions, irrational beliefs. Call them what you like. His drug filled mind is full of torment. I feel sorry for him. I do not hate him. I'm afraid for him. He is a very sick young man. I no longer know what to do about it. I don't know how to help him anymore. He is shockingly clever, he is also sadistic and has always managed to get what he wants, to do what he wants all of his blighted, predatory life and no one has ever been able to stop him."

He paused again and took another sip of his coffee.

"I don't expect that he will ever give up his drugs and alcohol. It all started a long time ago you know. When he was twelve years old, two villagers sexually abused him when he was staying with my mother and father up in the hills during one of his school holidays. The two men who did it hated him. He brutally tortured one of their hunting dogs. He killed it you know in a very gruesome way. I will not upset you with the details at present."

Juan leaned forward in his chair as he talked to her. "There is little to be done for him now. It is affecting my work and most of all my marriage. My young wife, Diana, I know is scared of him, she will not come to Spain with me, but she doesn't say too much to me about it. I try to keep them apart as much as possible, I too am afraid for her. At the moment she is away looking after her sick mother.

She usually goes there when I am away, Julio doesn't know that. I do not trust him either. At the moment he is occupied with you, but I am afraid that one of these days he will turn up in London. I suppose he beat you up in one of his uncontrollable drug filled rages."

He looked at Sarah with great sorrow on his face. "Oh my God, how many times does this have to happen?" He shouted, as he looked up at the ceiling, clenching his fists, his eyes closed in horror and desperation.

Sarah looked at him sympathetically. "I do not know much about him being sexually abused, he told me a few details but not the whole story, but of course he blames it on you entirely. He said it was two of your labourers in the village. Tell me what exactly happened then?"

"No, it was nothing to do with me. They were acquaintances of my father. The dog used to bark a lot, especially at night, so one night when Julio was staying with his grandfather he half strangled the poor beast with its own lead, then cut it up into pieces while it was still alive and left the bits in a cardboard box on their doorstep. The two men came to my father's house, they knew it was him and they took Julio away, bound and gagged him, beat him up and then sexually assaulted him." He paused for a moment.

"I of course felt very guilty about the whole matter, but there was nothing I could do at the time, I was not even in Spain when it happened, I just had a phone call from my father, he glossed over things of course, it was only later when I returned to Spain that I learnt the truth." He paused again and sighed deeply.

"The police of course believed Julio, as he was so young and the two men were jailed for five years. I was horrified about the whole affair, when I eventually found out the truth. I managed to pay for them to be released from jail and another large payment to them to keep their mouths shut. That was when I realised what my son was capable of doing. The matter was hushed up and kept from my first wife. She was not a strong woman as she'd already had a heart attack that left her very weak. So believe me, I know him and what he is really like. I've seen some of the women that he's beaten up over the years. It disgusts and infuriates me. I have paid people off many times to cover up for him, so I would not lose my position and protect my good name, I don't think I can handle it anymore."

He sighed deeply again and leaned back into the large chair. He seemed to physically age ten years in front of her.

"You're so completely different from anyone else he's ever been with. What are you doing with him, please forgive me for asking, but you are somewhat older than him?" He asked tentatively.

"Yes I am several years older than him. I'm a fool, but honestly, I didn't know what he was like. He was so charming in the beginning. Now I am caught up in a situation that I am not sure quite how to handle. I have to get away from him." She explained, and then told his father a little about herself and how they had met.

"Oh yes, I know my son is very charming, especially when he wants something or somebody. That's all part of his character pattern. He is schizophrenic as well as being bi-polar. I had hoped he had changed after the last lot of medication. Er... would you mind if I smoke?"

Sarah shook her head. "No of course not, I'm used to it, Julio smokes like a chimney and it has never worried me."

Juan pulled his gold Dunhill lighter and gold cigarette case from the inside pocket of his jacket and clicked it open.

"Do you?" He asked as he held out the case and offered her a cigarette.

Again she shook her head. "No thank you, I don't smoke."

He lit up slowly and inhaled deeply, then blew out a long stream of smoke across the room before continuing and then placed his lighter and case neatly together on the olive wood coffee table in front of him.

Sarah studied him. He was certainly a very good-looking man, lightly tanned, with a full head of hair greying at the temples, dark brown eyes not unlike his son's and the same well-shaped nose and sensual lips. She reckoned he was in his early fifties. The word Diplomat was written all over him, he held himself well and was full of bearing, even though he looked very tired. He wore an expensive light grey Armani suit, cream silk shirt and plain light grey tie and Gucci shoes in charcoal grey suede.

He leaned forward a little, resting his elbows on his knees and looked at her intently.

"When he is charming he is wonderful, but when he's not, he is evil. I think he was born evil. His mother had a very difficult birth with him. I thought she was going to die. But she pulled through and it left her very weak. I don't know what went wrong. I have in fact always tried to be there when he needed me, even though he denies it all the time."

He tapped some ash into the large onyx ashtray she'd provided.

Little did he know it was the one she had hit Julio with!

"I received a message a few days ago that he wanted to see me, so I jumped on a plane at the first opportunity. You know I can't always just take time out when I want to. He doesn't know yet that I have arrived. No one except you and my wife Diana knows that." He sighed deeply before continuing.

"May I stay tonight? I can sleep in the spare room or even on the settee, as I am very tired. But if you prefer I will book into a hotel. Do you know if he will be back tonight?"

"I really don't know, I don't think so, he just left, slammed the door and went, leaving the keys behind in the lock. Usually he locks me in these days." Sarah explained, not bothering any more to hide the truth from his father. He might as well hear some more horror stories about his son.

"If he needs a fix as badly as I think he does, I doubt whether he will return tonight, or even tomorrow, he will find somewhere to go, I hope that he never returns again anyway."

"In that case, I shall certainly stay; at least you will be safe if I am here. He would not dare to cross me? He needs me." Juan Carlos stated emphatically.

"Yes, I would like you to stay and I would feel safer if you are here. I'll change the bed in the master bedroom, he's been sleeping in there, and I've been in the spare room."

She got up and left, pleased to do something to occupy her thoughts. She'd really had enough of this family, though she had to admit to herself that his father seemed to be a very decent person as well as a very worried man.

Julio's father appeared a few minutes later in the doorway of the master bedroom.

"Thank you very much, I do appreciate all that you have done for me, perhaps in some small way I can help you also. Can you call me about 7.30 am? We will talk further on the subject in the morning. I will try and help you as much as I can. You must leave and go back to your country. Goodnight Sarah."

He reached over and kissed her hand.

Sarah left the room, returned to the lounge and put out the lights. She too had many things to talk about tomorrow and she needed a good night's sleep as well.

CHAPTER ELEVEN

MARBELLA - 2003

The next morning Juan Carlos and Sarah talked earnestly over a light breakfast. He noticed she looked better and had applied heavier makeup over her facial bruising that looked as if it was fading a little. He also felt better himself and didn't look so grey with tiredness and worry.

Sarah stared at him across the big plate smoked glass and stainless steel dining table as he started to relate some of the terrible things his son had done over the past years.

He reached across the table and covered her left hand with a comforting gesture.

"I want to help you," he said earnestly. "It is the least I can do, but I must continue my story about him. Please do not condemn him too much, after all he is still my son, heaven forbid, my own flesh and blood, I never knew that I would sire such an evil child, also it is not entirely his fault that he is the way he is."

He stopped for breath and sighed deeply.

"Unfortunately there is a streak of insanity in him. It comes from his mother's side. I found out that her father was schizophrenic as well as being bi-polar and at times he was very violent toward his wife and children, which in latter years was controlled by medication. I never knew anything about it until several years after I married Angela. That was when she told me about it and swore me to secrecy. She said it had bypassed her being a female child. She'd had many tests and it seemed to come out in male children only. "

Juan paused for several seconds.

"I have always tried to hide it from my side of the family because my mother would have been very upset, though my present wife Diana knows about Julio's drug and drink independence, but she does not know the complete story. It would frighten her too much. She absolutely hates him anyway and will not have him in our home. You would like her. You would both get on so well together."

He smiled fondly at the thought of his young wife.

Sarah stared hard at him unsmilingly. She wondered if Juan was as big a liar as his son, but what else could she think? She was so desperate to get away from the evil Julio.

"Please continue. I will listen, but I will make my own judgement, I cannot promise not to condemn him, especially after what he has done to me. He should be punished!" She stated flatly as she pulled her hand away from his.

Juan stared thoughtfully at her across the large table, before continuing, as he hunched over his coffee cup, with a cigarette burning steadily between his long, thin, well-manicured fingers.

Sarah noticed that he was almost a chain-smoker, not that she was surprised with all the pressure he must be under.

"Fair enough, I do understand, I'll tell you about him. My first wife, Julio's mother, Angela, was from South Africa. White of course, of Anglo Dutch decent, a beautiful blonde. In fact you look very much like her. I expect that is why he was so attracted to you in the first instance. He has a thing about blonde women. When I met her she was working at the Spanish Embassy in Capetown. Her mother had recently died and her father was in a nursing home, she was in effect all alone really." He said wistfully, feeling completely drained of spiritual and moral force as he tried to recall an image of her, but was unable to.

He stubbed out his cigarette and immediately lit another with trembling hands.

"Excuse me, I know, I smoke too much, but I get so nervous not knowing what my son is up to next. I have had this bottled up inside of me for too long. I couldn't really tell anyone about my first wife and her misgivings, though Diana has probed and I know she is not stupid."

"Julio of course was a beautiful looking baby and completely spoilt by Angela, and also by my side of the family, especially my mother. My present wife Diana, whom I married nearly five years ago, knows very little about the past. She has never liked Julio and certainly doesn't trust him. He loathes her. He is eaten up with immense jealousy because of my love for her. She is only seven years older than him, blonde and beautiful like you. Perhaps one of these days we'll have a child together, I pray every day for it to happen, Diana has already had two miscarriages."

He smiled sadly at Sarah and shrugged his shoulders.

"I have a weakness too for blondes. Julio never forgave me for marrying again, especially to such a young woman. He said it was disrespectful to his mother, but a man has his needs you know. I was lonely after Angela's death for so many years and I also needed a presentable wife in my position."

He paused again and inhaled deeply on his cigarette before stubbing it out in the big black onyx ashtray.

Sarah reached over and poured him another coffee and she noticed his eyes were brimming with tears.

"I left the army when I was twenty one and entered the Diplomatic Corps. My family always had plenty of money and I like the good things in life. My father had good connections, so it was easy for me. I also knew I would make a good Ambassador for my country."

He took a sip of his coffee before carrying on.

"I was sent to England for the first two years of my term and then to Capetown. There I met and fell in love with Angela - *Angel or messenger* - is the translation you know. She was so beautiful, only just twenty-one. I was twenty-five then. Six months later we were married and after a year she gave birth to Julio. I was ecstatic. I had everything I wanted. A beautiful wife, a lovely son and an exceedingly good career ahead of me. Life was good then!"

He paused, smiling at the memory and then drained his coffee cup before he continued.

"My term was extended for another five years. We had another child in that time. A delightful daughter, we named her Eva after my mother. She was the clone of her mother, blonde and blue-eyed. The complete opposite to Julio, he has inherited his

141

dark looks from my side of the family. They were such a contrast. Everyone stared at the two children wherever they went. I had no idea he would turn out to be quite so evil."

Sarah was enthralled. This was the first time she had heard about him having a sister.

Juan lit yet another cigarette and blew a long stream of smoke into the air and smiled at Sarah.

"I hope I am not boring you too much Sarah?"

"No, not at all!"

"Well, things started to happen when Julio was about six years old. Eva was about three years old then. The Dutch nanny, whom we employed, told me one day that Eva was covered in bites, scratches and pinch marks. It was of course Julio. The nanny caught him one day and brought him straight to me. When confronted, he told me quite flatly, that he hated his sister. He was jealous of her, he had been number one before she came along and he did not wish to be around her."

Juan shook his head from side to side with exasperation before continuing.

"Imagine a six-year-old child talking like that! The nanny advised me not to make too much of an issue about it, as it would only make matters worse. I had intended to spank him, but instead I spoke harshly to him and sent him to his room. He just stared back at me with his coal black eyes and informed me, he didn't care! *'Mummy will let me out, you see!'* He shouted at me and stamped his foot. Of course I had to be careful because my wife had become very sickly after having a second child. It was such a difficult birth, she had to have a

Caesarean section; she had never ever been strong and she took a long time to recover."

He paused again and sighed.

"I kept an eye on Julio and he kept his word and left Eva alone, for a while. He would just look at her with his dark eyes and laugh menacingly and make gestures at her. He was always so jealous of her up until the day she so tragically died. Yet deep down inside I know that he really did love his sister in his own very strange way. It would seem that he destroys everybody that he loves!"

Juan stopped talking and took a handkerchief from his slacks pocket and wiped his eyes.

"When he was ten I sent him to boarding school in England. He had become unbearable and I thought it was the best thing for him. I regularly received reports of his bullying, but the large sums of money I gave to the school's restoration fund etc., squashed the many stories from getting out. I was in due course transferred back to Madrid for a period of one year. Angela stayed on in England and I used to fly over every weekend and she was completely unaware of what was going on at his school." Juan stopped to take breath once again.

"Eva loved Spain when she came over for her summer holidays and her new Spanish family. During Julio's school holidays he spent half with his mother in the UK and the other half always stayed with his grandfather in the hills, so that was one problem solved. He and his sister rarely met up with each other. It was during this time that the village men attacked Julio on one of his holidays there. My father put him in a hospital in Malaga and I returned to see him. I just told his mother I was going on a business trip to Spain. When I returned to England I asked for a transfer and was sent to South Africa again, my wife of course was thrilled as she had never been very keen on living in Spain. I just could not tell Angela what had happened to her beloved son, she never saw the bad side of him. Her weak heart anyway would not have stood up to such a trauma."

He stopped yet again to light another cigarette before continuing and then started coughing.

Sarah noticed how heavy his breathing was and was not sure if it was the cigarettes or emotion from telling the story. If anything he seemed to smoke more than his son.

"That was Julio's first mental breakdown, he would get better, then something else would trigger it and he would be on medication again. The doctors said many things, it could be in the genes and probably something to do with his age and he would grow out of it. None of them seemed to be able to give me any real answers! I knew better, it was inherited from his Dutch grandfather and I knew the lunacy would get worse. As Angela got older she too started to show signs at times. The dreadful mood swings, the violent tempers, the headaches and so on, but it was so much stronger on the male side. I also think that the medication that she was on at that time for her heart, might have caused some of the trouble. I hope I'm not boring you?"

He exclaimed again as he looked across the table at her and then heaved a big sigh as he cupped his head in his hands before continuing and ran his fingers through his thick hair.

Sarah stared wide-eyed at Juan wondering how he could have carried the burden so long without cracking up.

"No, not all, I find it all so interesting; it gives me such an insight into Julio's behaviour. Would you like some more coffee or perhaps something to eat?"

No, she was not bored. Everything was starting to fall into place and she was full of sympathy for him.

He shook his head. "No thank you, only coffee please."

She once more went into the kitchen and made another pot of filter coffee and brought it back to the dining room and poured him another cup.

"Please carry on Juan."

Juan sipped some of the coffee before he resumed his story.

"I flew back to England with Julio, because of course he had to return to boarding school. I stayed on for a week and he seemed to be coping really well. The Matron was monitoring his medication and he seemed to love the school, so I returned to Cape Town. Things were quiet for a long time and then one day I received a phone call from the Headmaster telling me that Julio was in trouble again. He had been drinking and using drugs. He was coming up to his fifteenth birthday by then. I once again flew back to England to do another cover-up job, warning him that it would be the last time and that I would cut off his allowance.

145

Everything was quiet again and he spent the next two school holidays with his grandparents in Spain that year."

Juan stood up and paced the room as he continued his story.

"The next year he came out to Cape Town for his summer holidays and sixteenth birthday and behaved himself impeccably at first. About two weeks later I caught him out. We of course had several servants in those days. One manservant, a maid for my wife, two young black girls of fourteen that helped out, a gardener and a youth of sixteen who used to do odd jobs around the settlement. One morning I was passing Julio's bedroom, the door was slightly ajar so I pushed it open to have a chat with him. He was sitting naked on the bed and masturbating in front of the mirror. I caught a quick movement in the glass and I saw the reflection of the young man, naked sitting next to him. I instantly dismissed him. He wasn't really to blame though as I found out later, because Julio had already threatened him with dismissal if he did not obey him. When confronted, he said - *so what! Young men do those sorts of things all the time, I was just experimenting!* I couldn't believe it. We never spoke of it again. I could not mention it to my wife, she was almost bedridden by then and the shock would probably have killed her."

He stopped pacing and walked over to Sarah and looked her straight in the eyes as if looking for an answer.

She stared back at him, wondering what words of sympathy she could say, but nothing came to mind. She just wanted him to continue his story about Julio.

Juan started to pace the room again.

"Angela and I had not had a proper married life since the birth of Eva. I sometimes sought solace in the arms of another woman in another town. Julio found out, he had followed me one day, confronted me with it and started to blackmail me, morally and financially. Imagine! His own father! I went along with it, because I loved my wife and I didn't want to upset her. So I gave him copious amounts of money to keep him quiet. He bought as much marijuana and hashish or whatever he wanted, he had also started drinking the local brew."

Juan drew on his cigarette once more and sighed deeply as he continued the story.

"The servants all indulged of course whilst off duty and he would sit with them rolling up his joints and drinking and he picked up the local language quickly, he's very intelligent and speaks several languages fluently, you know. He left at the end of the summer holidays and returned to school. Eighteen months later there was more trouble and this time he was expelled. He was approaching eighteen years old then. He came back to South Africa and started visiting the brothels and there he hit the hard drugs."

Juan stubbed his cigarette out and stood near Sarah before continuing.

"Meanwhile his grandparents in Spain both died in hospital within a week of each other when there was an influenza epidemic and they left all their money and property to Julio. The property though was in trust until he was thirty, so he could not sell the land until then. Even so he had become a very rich young man overnight. At least he stopped blackmailing me. He didn't need my money anymore thank God. I don't think though there's very much left now because of his habit. I know he's been dealing again, and it's not long before he is thirty, if he lives that long, the way he's going on. His uncle has warned him, but he takes no notice of anyone."

Juan paused and ran his right hand through his thick head of greying hair.

"What could I do? One day I asked him what he intended to do with his life and that it was about time he stopped all these things. Do you know what he did? He spat in my face and told me to go to hell, as I was in no position to preach to him. He accused me of being a womaniser and beating his mother and so on and so on. His drug filled mind was full of delusions. I shouted at him and struck him across the face. That was the one and only time in his life that I had ever hit him. I should have done it a long time ago, but I am not a violent man. He told his mother of course. He used to spend a lot of time with her, amusing her with his jokes but, she never noticed how stoned he was as she was usually under some sort of sedation herself. "

Juan stopped and rubbed the back of his neck with both hands as if to relief the tension in his shoulders before continuing.

"One day he told her about my affair. He spared her nothing. He told her I had been unfaithful to her, cruel to him, etc. She of course believed her beloved son, she got out of bed and came screaming to me in my study. She was like some demented creature. I admitted to her about my one affair, she didn't believe me, she chose to believe Julio. He just stood in the doorway with an evil grin on his handsome face. Her heart couldn't take it and she had a massive stroke. One week later she was dead. He had in effect killed his own mother. He broke down and had to be sent back to Spain to a private clinic owned by my brother. Once more he was put on medication. I stayed on in Cape Town for a while, my wife was buried there alongside her parents in their family plot and my daughter was coming up for fifteen, a lovely young lady and the image of her mother. Eva never knew what Julio had done as she never saw any evil in him like I did. *To her he was her big brother.*"

Juan stopped talking, as the effort of the story seemed to be draining his energy. They moved from the dining room into the lounge area where it was more comfortable and sat down on the large settee.

Sarah looked at him. "He told me he was sixteen when his mother died."

Juan leaned back into the comfortable settee and sighed.

"No, he was eighteen then, another one of his lies, I'm afraid, he no longer knows the truth. Do you want me to continue?" He asked his eyes full of tears again. "The rest is not very pleasant!" He said as he brushed his tears aside

Sarah looked at him in sympathy and noticed how old he seemed to appear. He'd had certainly aged considerably over the last few hours of his being in Spain. Julio had a lot to answer for. He really needed punishing. She knew for sure that when the time was right she would be the instigator of his punishment.

She smiled at Juan trying to put him at ease.

"Yes, I would like to hear more, you need to tell someone don't you after all these years. It is not good to keep things bottled up forever. Maybe I can help you. What is in the past is past, but sometimes it is possible to mend the past and carry on to a better future."

She felt her physical beating was nothing to the mental one that Juan had suffered for so long.

"Well, I left South Africa and was transferred to America, Washington, to be exact. That's when things really came to a head. Eva attended college there and by then she was nearly eighteen and a half. Julio came out to the States a year later. For a while he was very quiet and very well behaved. I thought perhaps that he had been cured with all the treatments that he had undergone for such a long time. But no, within six months he had fallen in with a bad crowd, using crack and goodness knows what else. He was very quickly getting through a lot of his inheritance. He'd used the land as collateral and borrowed from a bank on one of his trips to Spain and then he started demanding money from me again, saying he would tell the Embassy about me. What could I do? I gave him the rest of the money that his mother had left him that had been in trust and invested and told him to get out of our lives. He went and once more my life was peaceful, even though every day, I wondered when I would get a phone call from him or about him. He dropped the name Gonzales and changed it to his mother's maiden name. He called himself - *Jacko von Jonge* - and he also adopted a South African accent. He had plenty of money again, so he could keep up his life of flashy cars and women, no trouble in finding dope and dealing in it. I didn't want to know, sometimes I prayed that he would die, but it wasn't to be. Thank God I had my wonderful daughter Eva. She was the only thing that kept me from going insane."

He reached into his jacket pocket and took out his handkerchief and dabbed his eyes, then drained his cup of lukewarm coffee, before taking a cigarette out of his case, but he did not light it he just played with it between his fingers.

"One day I had the fateful call from an associate of mine, someone who knew Julio, and told me he was in a lot of trouble, would I fly to New Orleans? I knew something terrible was brewing and I needed to protect my daughter. I had to shield her from her evil brother. I told her I had to go on a business trip so she stayed with some friends whilst I flew to New Orleans. He had beaten up and killed a fifteen-year-old black prostitute, her family was demanding money for their silence and so was her pimp, who incidentally, was her brother. He threatened to find Julio and kill him. So he had no money again, or very little. I also found out he was dope peddling again and owed a lot of money to his supplier and he'd also threatened a man in a bar with a gun, and then shot him in the leg. It just seemed to get worse and worse. Of course, I paid up. I had to. I contacted my *associate* who had in the past rendered a lot of special services for me, at a price of course. He found out where my son was living and just bundled him into a car and drove to Mexico and he was thrown into a clinic to dry out, yet again!"

Juan stood up and started pacing the room and with shaking hands lit his cigarette before continuing.

Sarah stood up and emptied the nearly full ashtray noticing how many ends were in it. Juan was obviously addicted to nicotine she thought. She couldn't believe Julio could be so cruel to his family and get away with it. She returned to the lounge to listen to the rest of the story.

"He was in the clinic for about eight months. Don't ask me how I managed to keep it quiet, let alone work, but I did. Fortunately he was booked in under the name of Von Jonge. When he returned to our house in Washington he was like a zombie, full of drugs again, but this time proper medication to quieten him down. In fact the doctors had even spoken of corrective brain surgery, but I drew a line at the time, I wish I hadn't now, that might have been the answer to his addictions and mental disorders, but at the time I felt it was too drastic, now I know better."

He looked at Sarah and shrugged his shoulders as he drew deeply on his cigarette and sat down again.

"Eva was a wonderful comfort to me. She was nineteen and a half and an extremely lovely and good hostess whenever I entertained, thank God that

I had her. Believe it not, she was actually pleased to have her brother back. She of course knew nothing of what had been going on. One evening I returned late, Eva thankfully was away at one of her friends for the weekend. I found Julio sitting in the kitchen, his clothes covered in blood. I thought he had hurt himself. But no, he had been up to his old tricks again. He had not been taking his medication and he had gone out that night in search of some drugs and got caught up with a young Hispanic prostitute and her pimp who had accidentally stabbed her instead of him and he had tried to help her. Or so he said! Of course I didn't believe him, how could I?"

He stopped talking and looked at Sarah to see her reaction and shook his head in an exasperated movement.

"I desperately needed help yet again. I phoned my *associate* once again who sent a man around to the girl's apartment and he disposed of her body in a dumpster somewhere. She was also a drug user and when the police found her body, her death was just written off as another junkie. My *associate* kept Julio under cover for about three weeks. Then he came back into my life and killed his sister, albeit it was a tragic accident. ***His own sister!*** He took her for a car ride stoned out of his brains and drove up the freeway the wrong way, straight into the path of an oncoming truck. She died instantly in the crash. He was quite badly injured and spent a long time in hospital. How I wished it had been the other way around. Would there never be an end to his wickedness. I don't know how I didn't kill him myself."

He stood up and looked at the ceiling and shouted. "Oh Lord! Will I never be rid of this monster? "

Juan took a deep breath and sat down again before carrying on the story.

"Julio off course dried out again during the time he was hospitalised, and then we returned to Spain. Now you know how I feel about my son. God help me, I have tried and tried again and again, I only hope I can keep this killer away from my second wife. I know he will kill her if he gets the chance, he is so insanely jealous of her. If only..."

Juan finally broke down in front of her.

Sarah said nothing as he sobbed deeply releasing his pent-up frustration of many years. Several moments passed before he managed to pull himself together.

"I am so sorry. Oh my dear, I am apologising again!" He tried a watery smile. "I must help you before he gets back here, perhaps we can help each other in the future. Come with me."

He stood up and grabbed her hand and almost dragged her across the room to the wall safe in the corner of the large lounge, opened it up and shuffled some of the contents around. He turned and handed her a small pearl handled nickel-plated Beretta 9mm gun.

"Here take this, it is small enough to put in your handbag, but lethal enough to do a lot of harm. You might need it one day!"

He also handed her some bullets. "I have a larger calibre gun at the Embassy in London, for my own safety, you understand! Now take this sterling money also you might need it. I want you to take this too. I could never give you enough for all the pain you have endured at my son's hands. It might come in handy one day in case you need to sell it."

He also handed her a small red velvet box. Inside was a magnificent ring with a big ruby surrounded by large South African diamonds.

"This was Angela's engagement ring, I want you to have it, and she would have wanted you to! Diana knows nothing about this ring though. I would appreciate it if you said nothing about it to her when you meet her. She has a lot of beautiful jewellery that I have bought her over the years and would probably not accept it anyway as it would remind her of my past. It is worth quite a lot of money and if you ever need money, you could always sell it. I am surprised that Julio has never taken it and sold it!" He pressed it into her hand.

"Hide everything away, though, just in case Julio comes back."

Sarah left the room and hid the items in her suitcase in one of her shoes and pushed it under the bed. She returned to the lounge. Juan was standing up and reaching for his jacket that he'd left on a chair.

"I must go now and find Julio and make sure that he will not upset our plans. Thank you for listening to me, I feel so much better now, it's all been bottled up too long."

He took out his wallet.

"Here is my card at the Marbella office in case you need me. My mobile number is on it too. Get yourself ready to leave and I will ring you later. I'll arrange for you to fly back with me to England, I will also make sure that Julio is safely out of the way. Don't worry he won't come back here! I promise you!"

He picked up his briefcase, gave her a quick peck on the cheek and left quietly.

***

During the evening Juan phoned Sarah, everything was arranged. He would pick her up at seven o'clock the next morning and his chauffeur would drive them to Malaga airport. His private jet would be waiting for them. Meanwhile Julio was out of the way for the time being.

Sarah phoned her aunt, but there was no reply, so she left a message on the answerphone. At last she was leaving Spain. She was going back to England, to her freedom. Julio would only be a bitter memory.

Or so she thought!

BOOK SEVEN

2 PETER Ch. 1 Verse 4: Whereby are given
unto us exceeding great and precious promises…

CHAPTER TWELVE

LONDON - 2003/4

As Sarah drove back from the rehab centre, she
recalled the events that followed her departure from
Spain and how Julio had tracked her down shortly
after her arrival in England.

***

There was a soft thud as the Lear's wheels hit
the tarmac followed by a shrill scream of brakes as
the powerful jet decelerated down the runway at
Heathrow Airport. The flight from Malaga had been
smooth and very uneventful; she had slept most of
the way after Juan told her how he'd safely installed
Julio into his brother's clinic once again to dry out
and that should take him three or four months and
give Juan time to deal with his son. He would be
out of her life at last. Sarah wondered if that was
really true, she had a gut feeling that he would try
and contact her when he dried out. He would
somehow find out where she was, he wouldn't rest
until he'd destroyed her, but for the time being she
was back in England and felt fairly safe, especially
as she had Juan Carlos for a friend. She must try and
forget Julio and somehow relive her life again,
peacefully.

She felt an ache begin behind her eyes and her throat constricted, she blinked in an effort to dispel the tears of relief as she gazed sightlessly out of the small window. They had finally arrived back in England.

Juan nudged her gently. She turned and smiled weakly.

"We've arrived, my dear," he said softly.

The engine wound down to a muted whine as the jet wheeled off the main runway then cruised and slowly turned towards its allotted bay. Juan's Spanish chauffeur as well as being his bodyguard was in a black Mercedes limousine with diplomatic plates and heavily tinted windows waiting nearby for his passengers to disembark.

Sarah made a call on Juan's car phone to her aunt. Once again there was no reply and the answerphone clicked in. She had a feeling that all was not as it should be and she was very worried.

Juan insisted that he accompany her to Richmond. The car pulled up at her aunt's house and she rang the bell of her aunt's door several times, but to no avail. The house looked deserted. Sarah looked questioningly at Juan.

A neighbour across the road suddenly appeared in her doorway and called them over. She invited them in and broke the sad news to Sarah. She explained that her aunt had gone out shopping at the local supermarket two days before and had suffered a severe heart attack. She had been taken to Richmond Hospital where she was in intensive care on a life support machine but the doctors did not hold out much hope for her.

"Will anything ever go right for me?" Sarah asked Juan as they drove to the hospital and she burst into tears.

"You've had a bad time lately, my dear," he said sadly trying to find some comforting words. "But I'm sure she'll be alright. I'll make arrangements for her to have a private room as soon as we know what is happening."

When they arrived at the hospital, the doctor in charge escorted her to the relatives' room and informed her that her aunt had died about two and a half hours before their arrival and they had been trying to get in touch with her in Spain, he had left two messages on her phone asking her to call him. He handed her a letter with her aunt's handbag.

"We found this in your aunt's handbag when we were looking for identification. I think you should have it. If you need any help with counselling or help with the funeral arrangements, please let me know and I will notify someone to help you in this matter. Would you like to see her now?" He said kindly before he left the relatives' room. "I will send someone to escort you."

Sarah stuffed the letter into her handbag after reading it hurriedly and turned to Juan and burst into convulsive sobbing. He held her tightly trying to comfort her.

"Please help me," she whispered before passing out.

***

Juan and Diana looked after Sarah over the next three weeks insisting that she stay with them in their London apartment. Once the funeral was over and the Will read she said she wanted to move into the house in Richmond that her aunt had left her. She had also left her the rest of her Estate which amounted to a very large sum of money along with a lot of stocks and shares.

Juan took her next day to her aunt's house .As she stepped out of his car she turned to him and said.

"I want to thank you for everything you have both done for me over the past three weeks. If ever I can do anything for you, please call me."

He put a finger to her lips.

"Of course, but I am the one who is in your debt. I feel as if I am to blame for everything. Julio and his brutality, your aunt having a heart attack, it is my entire fault. I should have got you out of Spain before. If only I had known about what you were going through. There has to be some solution to this situation."

She looked at him and shook her head. "No. No. I should never have got involved with your son. I am the one to blame. I was so stupid, I was flattered by his attention and I was so desperately lonely at the time." Her lovely blue eyes glazed over with tears as she looked up at him.

He leaned over and kissed her on the cheek. "You know where to contact us if you need us, little one. Don't leave it for too long. I shall be in touch with you in the very near future anyway to see if we can resolve matters." He said as he got out of the car to escort her to her front door and then as he walked back down the garden path he turned and waved to her before stepping into his black Mercedes.

Juan settled back into the comfortable rear seat and sighed deeply, a plan was already forming in his mind, he had a contact that might be able to help or at least keep an eye on Sarah, but it had to be done very, very carefully.

Sarah waved back as the large car sped away out of sight and then stepped inside the house feeling very lonely. She knew that she had to be very brave and try and pick-up her life again and put the pieces together.

***

After a quiet Christmas in her new home, the next month was uneventful, she looked upon it as her healing time, or so she thought.

Early February she bought herself a good second-hand black BMW 3 series so that she was mobile. She also had started to feel lonely at times so she decided to adopt an abandoned cat from the local Cat Rescue Society.

She fell in love with a beautiful two year old English Blue and she named him Picasso. She also kept in touch with Juan and his wife Diana and visited them several times and they soon became firm friends. They came to know everything about Julio and how he had abused her.

Walking down Richmond High Street one day, she saw a card in the local newsagent's window.

CHARITY WORKER NEEDED FOR DRUG REHABILITATION CENTRE IN NORTH LONDON. SMALL REMUNERATION OFFERED.

PATIENCE AND GOOD SENSE OF HUMOUR VITAL!
Please contact. Dr Michael Akaro during office hours on 0208 256 76453.

Sarah vaguely remembered him from a charity evening that she had attended just before Christmas at the local Guildhall. She felt it might just suit her, as she was rather bored.

She had arranged everything in the large detached house to her liking. A new fitted kitchen and bathroom and the house completely redecorated from top to bottom, new carpets and curtains. A lovely paved patio, with her many flowering tubs outside of the lounge with French windows leading to her newly re-styled garden. She felt that it was time to work again. She did not need the money, however, as her aunt had left her very well cared for.

She needed to get out of the house though and it would give her something else in life to think about. Quite often memories of Julio would flash into her mind and she knew that she needed something to keep herself from continually thinking about her past. She phoned the centre as soon as she got home and made an appointment for an interview the next day and was accepted immediately. She felt that the position would suit her having experienced similar traumas to the patients that Dr Michael Akaro was helping. Perhaps working at the Rehab Centre would at last exorcise some of Julio's memories and help with the nightmares that she was experiencing of late.

***

Her life remained fairly uneventful for a couple of months, and working part-time had helped her considerably. She had also been able to confide in Michael about some of the events in her life. She told him about her two failed marriages and her time with Julio, but she left out several very poignant points. With Michael's help, Julio was gradually becoming a faded memory, until one fateful afternoon in April when she returned from shopping.

***

It had been a long day and she was tired. She put the key in the front door. As she entered a sixth sense warned her that something was wrong. There was an uncanny stillness about the house. Picasso had not come to greet her as usual. As she closed the front door gently, she wondered why. She looked around cautiously, the alarm was off and her kitchen door was ajar. She caught a whiff of male cologne, *Paco Rabanne*, that she instantly recognised and she gasped aloud. Julio was standing in the doorway of her lounge with Picasso in his arms stroking him. The cat seemed quite at ease.

"Hello *querida*," he said very softly, yet menacingly as he smiled at her.

Sarah had forgotten how good-looking he was, his gleaming black hair was combed straight back, rather than a few locks hanging casually over his forehead that he used to favour sometimes and somehow the effect made his eye sockets look far more hollow than usual in his sallow face. She also noticed that his face was thinner than before, and she could tell that he was still using drugs. She had learnt how to recognise the symptoms signs now that she was helping out at the Rehab Centre, yet his soft sexy voice made her stomach churn with fear as well as a certain amount of desire for him. He still had the same effect on her and he knew it.

She swallowed hard and moistened her lips, trying to compose herself as she closed the door behind her slowly, then suddenly the anger she had kept under control for so long welled up.

"What the hell are you doing here in my house? How dare you," she hissed through clenched teeth.

"I am visiting you, I missed you. It's been such a long time *querida*!" He grinned back cheekily his dark eyes sweeping over her body. "Did you really think I had gone out of your life forever?"

"But… how did you get in, the alarm…?"

"That was easy. I knew the code would either be my birth date or yours! Big mistake!" He smiled cockily. "I watched the cat, he was outside, and then he entered by the back door. Through his cat-flap and then later he came out again. I went around to the back and looked through the patio doors. I could see you have an LED flashing, but obviously not in the back utility room, because the cat didn't set the alarm off." He replied very nonchalantly as he grinned at her before continuing.

"So I broke in, it was so easy, I used a plastic credit card and slipped the latch on the back door and entered the kitchen. You really ought to change the lock *querida*! It is not good quality! Your insurance company will never pass it."

As he explained his movements to her, he continued to caress Picasso who was purring loudly. She noticed he still retained his strange control over animals. They always seemed to adore him.

"So, then I looked in the hallway and carefully crawled along the hall floor so I wouldn't break the beams of the sensor. By the way, they are set much too high you know. You really ought to update your system as well!"

He grinned at her again. "Then I just stood up and tapped in your birth date, hey presto, here I am." He blew her a kiss.

Once more the pent-up hate and anger flared up through her, how dare he come back into her life, how dare he invade her space after all this time! And this overruled all of her other feelings about him.

"You bastard, get out, get out of my house. I'll call the police." She leapt at him screaming, trying to hit him with her large handbag.

He laughed maniacally at her and threw the cat onto the floor and Picasso shot through into the utility room.

How many times have I heard that laugh she thought as her blood curdled at the sound? When would she ever be rid of him?

Julio smiled menacingly at her and then raised his right hand and slapped her face hard. She fell to the floor in a heap with the force of the impact. It happened so suddenly and so quickly that her senses were sent into confusion, not again an inner voice screamed - *not again*!

She thought this couldn't be true, this is not happening; it's a dream, a nightmare. She huddled against the hallway wall, trying to collect her thoughts as she held her head in her hands. The silence was broken by the sound of Picasso scratching violently with fright in his litter tray and she could feel the hate for Julio oozing out of her body like sweat, her heart pounded madly against her chest.

Julio stepped past her towards the front door and opened it.

"That is only the beginning. I'll be back, bitch," he shouted over his shoulder and he slammed the front door hard.

For several minutes she sat paralysed on the hall carpet, knowing that he was up to his old tricks, his evil mind games. Then she started to shake with anger and fear. Picasso came over to her and rubbed himself against her purring loudly as if to comfort her.

Gradually she took control of herself and rose to her feet, then all she felt was icy, controlled anger.

She ran to the front door and put the chain on and then ran into the lounge and picked up the extension phone and rang Michael.

"Julio is back, you remember the person I told you about, and he's just been in my house. Michael, I'm really scared, what shall I do?" Her voice trembled with rage.

"Okay, okay, slowly, slowly, now I want you to check every door and window and make sure they are secured, I'll be around as quickly as I can," he said matter-of-factly trying not to panic her anymore.

***

She ran upstairs and took the Beretta that Juan had given her in Spain, out of her underwear drawer, loaded it, and then phoned him to warn him of Julio's appearance in London.

Juan's private phone rang and rang and then the answer service eventually cut in.

'I am sorry but we are unavailable at the moment to take your call, please leave your name,

number and message after the beep, or you can get us on our mobile number 07790 210 3164.'

She tried his mobile number and the answering service also cut in with a similar message.

"Damn," she shouted, as she suddenly recalled that he and his wife were in Somerset visiting her sick mother and then he was due back in Washington for a conference.

"Juan, if you pick up this message, I must warn you that Julio is in London and be careful he is in a very black mood, God knows what he will do. I am so afraid. He was here, he broke into my house." She sobbed. What else could she do? She started pacing the house in fear and absolute terror.

The doorbell rang out shrill and long and she jumped with fright. She cautiously approached the door, the gun behind her back.

"Who is it?" She called her voice trembling for fear that Julio might have returned.

"It's me, Michael," his voice boomed out through the letterbox.

167

She quickly undid the door chain with trembling fingers and fell into his arms as he stepped over the doorstep.

"Thank God, I thought Julio had returned already." She said tremulously and then burst into tears.

Michael led her through into the lounge and sat her down on the settee. Unseen by him, she carefully hid the little gun behind a large cushion.

"Okay, I need to know what's happened, tell me about it," he said gently, but firmly.

"Oh, Michael, someone from my past, the one I told you about, Julio, I thought he was gone forever… I thought… I thought he was…" She stuttered.

"Okay, okay, calm down now, I'm here. Do you want me to call the police?"

"No, no, I don't want the police involved yet."

He sat down beside her and took her hands in his large ones. "Come on, I don't think you should stay here alone tonight. But how did he enter? You said you had a good alarm system fitted just a short while ago."

"It was…it is…I …I don't know he entered through the back door, he'd slipped the latch that's on the utility room door where the cat has his basket with a plastic credit card, he is very clever that way he even sussed out the code."

"What do you mean, he knew the code, how did he know the code and how did he know your address?"

"He guessed it; it was my birth date. You can never underestimate him. I must have been out of my senses when I armed it originally. Then I suddenly realised that I had left my address book behind in Spain when I left in such a rush, I suppose he found it and put two and two together."

"Okay, well first of all we must change the code, secondly get on to the security engineers that fitted the alarm system to reset the sensors and then have it linked up to the Police station. I'll stay here with you tonight if that's okay, I'll ring my wife and then I'll ring for a locksmith, we'll have new locks fitted in the morning as well. You'll be all right; somehow I don't think he'll return for the time being! Then I want to know more about him." said Michael.

He walked over to the phone and made the necessary calls. When he had finished he suggested that they have a take-away meal brought in.

Three quarters of an hour later over their Indian meal Michael carefully questioned her more thoroughly about Julio. She filled him in telling him some of the things that she had left out in their previous conversations.

He felt a tightening in the back of his throat and an overpowering tenderness for her, he just wanted to take her in his arms and comfort her. Instead he reached across the kitchen table and placed one of his large hands over hers and said,

"My dear Sarah, why didn't you tell me these things before? I could have helped you more, instead of you carrying around this burden on your shoulders, I know a good psychiatrist, and he would have helped you over this period."

"I don't need a psychiatrist. I couldn't tell you, I couldn't tell anyone, I felt so ashamed, and you know what it's like. Firstly I felt like one of your patients, secondly I felt sorry for him. Maybe it was because of his past, maybe I thought I was at fault. Oh, I don't know, maybe the time wasn't right. I've been such a fool Michael. I thought I could handle it all on my own. I thought I was strong enough, I never thought that he would find me." She blurted out and then smiled weakly realising what a complete fool she had made of herself.

"Sarah, he is one of millions in the world, who was abused as a child, and he's been using it as an excuse for getting high and getting by for years, saying life's not fair. Don't ever feel sorry for him. He is evil, one of these days he will get his comeuppance. Your secret is safe with me. Let's look at it in another light tomorrow. Now you need to relax and get some sleep."

***

Meanwhile outside Julio watched Sarah's house through some bushes from a neighbouring garden and had seen Michael arrive, but not leave the house. He decided that after waiting for two hours he would return the next day. He walked to the end of the road and flagged down a taxi to take him back to Soho. He sat sulkily in the back, his mind playing tricks. He wanted to know who her black boyfriend was, but he needed a fix badly. How could she have done that? How could she have betrayed him and taken a lover? Sarah could wait for the time being, he didn't think she would be going anywhere that evening. His mind was churning with all sorts of evil thoughts.

BOOK EIGHT

REVELATION Ch. 2 Verse 16:
Repent, or else I shall come unto thee quickly, and I
will fight against them
with the sword of my mouth…

CHAPTER THIRTEEN

LONDON- 2004

Michael spent the night at Sarah's house and slept in one of the spare bedrooms. He left early promising to ring her during the day and said he would try to return before lunchtime and told her to keep the house locked. Then he would take her to his home just outside of Kingston-upon-Thames where she would be safe until Julio could be persuaded to leave her alone. He still had a few friends who owed him a few favours and he would get in touch with them about the evil man.

After breakfast Sarah tried to collect her thoughts together and made plans to leave her house for a while. Michael had said she could take Picasso with her; there was plenty of room for both of them in his big rambling house and his wife and the kids loved cats.

She fetched Picasso's travel box out of the kitchen, gave it a good clean and popped in one of his blankets and put it in the kitchen with its door open so that he could crawl in and be ready for his journey. Then she went upstairs and started to pack a small suitcase for herself.

The doorbell rang out loud and clear. Sarah ran down the stairs thinking that Michael was back early and pulling the door open she came face to face with Julio.

Before she could even say a word, he quickly pushed her inside the hallway and slammed the door behind him.

"You were quick! So! You thought it was your boyfriend, your black lover?" He questioned her sarcastically and reached out and twisted her left arm behind her back. "Well is he then?"

"Is he what?" She replied with a tremulous voice.

"Your lover, boyfriend or whatever?"

"No, don't be ridiculous, I'm waiting for the …" she broke off.

"You liar," he shouted and raised his arm and slapped her face hard. The impact threw her against the wall and nearly knocked her out as she fell to the floor.

Not again, her mind told her, she had to collect her wits about her, and Michael had said he would either ring or try to come over during the morning, what was the time now she wondered as she lay back not moving, just staring up at Julio and all her hate for him pouring through her slight body.

The doorbell rang out again; she forced herself to sit up and waited for some of the dizziness to pass.

She started to mumble. "I must, answer it …I must…it's probably the security engineer." She instinctively knew it was Michael this time.

"Oh, no you don't," Julio snarled as he reached for her, pulled her to her feet and dragged her into the kitchen. "I'll answer it. Don't you dare make a sound," he threatened as he closed the kitchen door quietly behind him and pulled himself together to be polite to whoever was at the door.

Taking a deep breath and forcing a smile on his cruel face he walked to the front door and pulled it ajar.

"Oh hello." Boomed Michael. "Just passing, come to pick up some papers, is Sarah in?"

Julio looked at the huge black man. He decided he'd better be polite to this one. He was very much bigger than him.

"Yes, yes, my aunt's in, but she's not too well at the moment, she doesn't want to see anybody, she's waiting for the doctor, and it's some sort virus I believe." He put on one of his charming smiles. He didn't want the man to suspect anything.

Michael peered over the young man's shoulder, trying to look into the hallway, he wasn't fooled, and he knew he was lying. Something was wrong. He knew the young man in front of him was Julio, by the description that Sarah had given him.

"Oh dear, she works for me actually. I'm so sorry she does not feel well, er… tell her not to worry too much about work, she can call me when she is better. Bye."

Michael turned and walked slowly back to his car and drove off around the corner.

Julio stood at the door watching him drive away. Then turned and picked up Sarah's car key from the hall table and marched back into the kitchen where she sat trembling at her kitchen table.

Meantime Michael had slowed down and parked his car around the corner. Then he walked back to where he could keep an eye on Sarah's house.

Several moments passed and her front door opened. Julio looked from side to side and dragged Sarah through the door, by her left arm. He slammed the door behind them and pushed her forward towards her car. He unlocked the passenger door and thrust her inside roughly, then walked around to the driver's side, got into the vehicle and drove the car away with a screech of tyres.

It had started to rain heavily.

Michael swiftly ran back around the corner and jumped into his car.

***

Sarah fastened her seat belt and tried to remain calm, she didn't want to antagonise Julio.

"Where are we going?" She asked nervously.

"Shut up," he growled back.

Julio drove off at a high speed. The rain was coming down thick and fast and the roads were becoming very wet and slippery as there had been very little rain about. Sarah was terrified that they would have an accident. He drove in silence for several miles, not really noticing the oncoming traffic as he weaved in and out of it, his mouth set in a grim line.

"Julio, I really think you ought to fasten your seat belt. If we get stopped by the police they will pull us over."

"I said shut up, you bitch!" He lashed out at her with his left elbow.

She was slammed against the seat, winded by his blow. Suddenly he braked outside an off-licence.

Turning to her he said. "I'm going inside of that shop, don't even think of leaving the car or shouting for help, because I will kill you. Understand!" He snarled at her.

She nodded dumbly. She was terrified and knew he meant it, her stomach fluttered with fear. The past once more came flooding back to her of how he had treated her in Spain.

"I won't, I promise." She mumbled.

He switched off the engine and pocketed the key before leaving the car.

Julio pointed a finger at Sarah. "Remember, what I said, don't try anything!"

He slammed the car door shut in temper.

Several moments later he returned clutching a yellow plastic carrier bag and walked around to her side of the car and opened the door.

"Move over slut, you drive," he ordered.

Sarah unbuckled her seat belt and slid over to the driving seat. Julio got in and slammed the door.

The silence was suddenly broken. Her mobile telephone rang out. Thank God, thought Sarah it must be Michael, as she tried to reach for it in its cradle on top of the dashboard.

Julio pushed her hand aside roughly, tore the phone from the connector and pressed the cancel button.

"Here...key...drive." He shouted at her.

She took the key with trembling fingers and tried to put them into the ignition, it fell to the floor.

"Stupid woman, drive!" He reached for her as if to hit her again.

"I'm trying," she started to sob. "Don't keep shouting at me," she cried as she picked up the key and inserted it once again. This time the engine sprang into life.

"Drive, damn you woman, drive," he shouted.

"But where?"

She now shouted back at him as some of her confidence came back. She must let him see that she was no longer scared of him or else he would play on it and demoralise her completely.

"Just drive, we're going to Reading, in Berkshire, I have to meet someone. It's very important, damn you!"

She drove off slowly her heart pounding against her ribs with fright. She felt sick.

He pushed the electric window button his side and threw out her telephone and settled back into his seat, then he opened the carrier bag and took out a bottle of Bells whisky, broke the seal and raised the bottle to his lips, taking a long swallow.

***

Meantime, Michael who had tried to follow them had lost them due to the bad weather conditions and traffic and abandoned his chase. He stopped by the roadside and punched out her number on his mobile, there was no reply.

Reluctantly Michael knew that he would not be able to find them and decided his best course of action would be to go home and hope that Sarah would contact him. He hoped that his fears for Sarah would be unfounded, but in his heart he knew that something was radically wrong, but he was powerless to do anything.

***

Sarah drove on in silence, her heart had now slowed down a little and she was trying to think. If only he would drink himself into oblivion she thought and pass out, then she would stop and dump him somewhere. What on earth was he doing in London? She thought he was still in Spain or America? It had been a month nearly, since she had spoken to Juan. He probably wouldn't know that his son was back in London. She hoped he had picked up the messages she had left.

Julio continued to drink steadily as she made her way towards the M4, driving at a steady pace.

"Can't you drive this thing any faster?" He shouted.

"No, Julio, whether you know it or not, there is a speed limit in this country, we might attract attention from the motorway police, there are cameras everywhere. This isn't Spain you know! You wouldn't want us pulled over and stopped. Would you?" She commented, trying to keep her temper and humour him at the same time.

"Where did you say we're going?" She asked tentatively.

"Reading, you know **R-E-A-D-I-N-G,** as in Berkshire! Are you stupid or something, don't you understand English?" He yelled at her then he belched loudly. "I'm meeting someone. He's got some really good stuff for me. Understand?"

She nodded, her face hurt like hell, and she wondered whether or not that her cheek must be swollen from the hard slap he'd given her earlier on.

"So, uh, we're going to get some stuff, what is it this time? Heroin, coke, crack?" She asked quietly even though she felt the anger rising within her, as she knew that she must try and remain calm and not alienate him.

"You know I don't buy crack, I don't buy shit, I only take and deal in good stuff." He said disgustedly. "I met this guy see…in London. He gave me a name and address to go to. Okay! Just drive and stop asking me questions! Anyway it's none of your business, bitch."

He took another swig of his whisky and then fished around in the pocket of his jacket.

"Here, this is the address," he shoved a piece of paper at her. "It's near the station, New Washington Road, number 46."

Sarah hadn't a clue where the station was in Reading. She didn't even know the area of Reading, but she would find it. Hopefully she would be able to drop him off and drive away. She just had to keep her temper and treat him nicely. He was in one of his terrible black moods and very dangerous.

She turned to him; he was unusually quiet. He had fallen asleep at last.

"Thank God," she said aloud.

"Uh…what…what…?" He shook himself awake. "Are we there yet?"

He took a last swig from the bottle and threw the empty bottle onto the back seat. "Don't try

"Look I'm not driving round and round Reading. Besides, we need petrol."

She pointed to a garage. "I can ask at that petrol station over there, look!" anything," he slurred.

"We're nearly there, I think," she replied in a flat voice. "I'll just stop and ask the way."

"No stopping, no asking understand!"

If only she could get out and ask the cashier in the kiosk to help her.

"No you won't, I'll fill the car and I'll do all the asking you bitch, I don't trust you!" He no longer slurred, he seemed to be suddenly in control of himself again as he pointed towards the garage.

"Okay, stop over there then."

Sarah pulled into the petrol station and turned off the engine.

"Okay, you ask, you fill it up!" She snapped as she pressed the button on the main consul between the front seats and released the fuel cap cover and then handed him the key.

"Here is the key. I'm not going to run away, I just need the ladies' Julio I'm bursting!"

"I don't want it, but you just stay here, understand!" He ordered as he got out and walked around the car and fiddled with the fuel cap and started cussing in Spanish.

He came back to her.

"I don't know how to do it. You fill it, but don't you dare try to escape, I have a gun on me…

180

I'll ask the man over there the way and pay for the petrol."

He walked carefully over to the heavy glass door and entered inside.

The young man behind the cashier's desk looked at him warily. Julio ran his fingers through his long black hair and grinned at the man. He seemed completely sober now.

"Hi! Pump 5, I think!" He joked as he pulled out a platinum Visa card from the pocket of his expensive jeans and handed it to the young man.

The cashier glanced out of the window of his kiosk and moved back a little as he caught a whiff of Julio's alcoholic breath across the counter.

He took the card from him and swiped it on the small machine on the desk.

"Thank you sir, just put in your PIN number please."

Julio tapped in the number and the cashier handed him back the card when he had finished the transaction with the receipt.

"Oh…um… can you tell me where the station is please. It's okay, I'm not driving. My wife is." He grinned sheepishly. "I know I am over the limit, been to a farewell party, friend of mine."

The young cashier did not like the look of the dark handsome man standing in front of him, he seemed to have an evil aura about him, but he smiled back politely and gave him directions.

"Thanks."

Julio turned and strolled back to the car and got back in.

"Julio, I need the ladies urgently!" Sarah begged him between clenched teeth.

"Tough! You will have to wait until we're at our destination"

She didn't wish to argue with him. She knew it was going to be difficult for her to contact anyone, no matter how hard she made excuses.

"Well, where are we going then, did you find out?"

"Just turn left out of here, go to the roundabout, and then second right."

He slumped back in the seat, the alcohol in his system had not relieved his need, he was starting to shake, he needed a proper fix badly, and he was starting to sweat profusely, now the alcohol just made him feel sick. He belched loudly again.

"I feel sick Sarah, slow down a bit."

"Julio, if you are going to be sick, please do it out of the window, not in my car," she said evenly and flicked the window switch on her side. "I don't want to have to clear up your puke, you filthy stinking beast."

She slowed down as he vomited out of the window, and then fell back heavily against the seat.

"Here," she handed a crushed packet of tissues to him from the side pocket of the driver's door. "Clean yourself up, you reek of puke!"

She now felt more in command of the situation, soon she would be rid of him and she could drive away. She would find a phone and call the police and tell them where he was and what he was doing. Or so she thought.

He suddenly perked up. "There it is, there!" He pointed. "Stop, stop."

She turned into a run-down street and drew up in front of a squalid looking terraced house with its gate hanging on one hinge. Outside on the pavement stood a battered black, overflowing wheelie-bin, covered in graffiti and stuffed with several evil smelling black plastic bin bags that were perilously perched on top of each other, ready at any moment to fall to the ground whilst waiting for collection.

The small garden was a mass of weeds. Filthy torn lace curtains were hung up at one of the dirty windows upstairs, the downstairs bay window was boarded up with a piece of old rotting chipboard.

A black stretch Mercedes limousine, with heavily tinted windows was parked on the other side of the road. A young black man with his thick hair carefully braided in many tight plaits in an intricate design, who was attired in black jeans, a tight black T-shirt with several gold chains around his neck and black Nike trainers, was leaning against the bonnet smoking a cigarette with one hand and holding a mobile phone to his left ear with the other. He was oblivious to anyone walking by.

"Come on then, get out bitch!" Julio shouted at her, "and make sure you lock the car, looks a terrible area around here!"

Julio walked up to the shabby door and knocked twice, then once again and a small child of around five or six in a grubby pink dress and bare-footed, clutching a dirty teddy bear with only one paw, slowly opened the door.

She took her thumb from her mouth.

"Whaddayer want?" She asked in a sullen voice as she eyed them up and down.

"We need to see your dad!" Explained Julio quietly, not wishing to scare the child.

"Okay, come on in. Da..." she shouted. "Someone to see yer."

She put her thumb back in her mouth and led them through the dark rancid smelling hallway into the dingy living room.

Sarah looked around, there was certainly no way that she was going to use a toilet in the disgusting house, she would rather go in the bushes outside.

The little girl sat down on a shabby moquette armchair of some indistinguishable looking colour. She looked at them wide eyed, pulled her one armed teddy from behind her and hugged it and then put her thumb back into her mouth as she watched her father's visitors.

Nearby a very young baby in a dirty old blue plastic laundry basket, lay fast asleep. On a triangular shaped, melamine topped three - legged coffee table, lay four empty lager cans, a bundle of used syringes and an assortment of other paraphernalia used for taking drugs.

There were three other people in the filthy, smelly room. A young, thin mousey-haired woman wearing an old dressing gown over a pair of dirty jeans, with a black eye and cut lip, sitting in a shabby armchair and two men. One of them stoned out of his mind and kneeling on the floor swaying from side to side.

The other looked as if he was of Jamaican origin.

He was well dressed in a black shiny suit and black shirt open at the neck. His big head was clean shaven and shiny and he had an old knife scar that ran from the top of his forehead down to the bridge of his nose and then down to the corner of his lip on the right side that lifted his top lip up slightly and he looked as if he was smiling, but for that he would have been described as quite a handsome man. His eyes were a light amber colour. Around his bull-like neck he wore two heavy linked gold chains and he was sober. A smart black crocodile briefcase that matched his designer shoes lay on the dirty old vinyl covered settee he was sitting on.

"Hey, bro' I got some good stuff here, got da money?" He asked Julio in a deep voice.

Julio withdrew his wallet and waved it at him.

"Yeah, but I need to try the stuff first," he said in a low menacing voice.

The big black man flicked open the briefcase to reveal several plastic packages and full disposable syringes also in sealed plastic bags. He handed one of the bags of powder to him.

"It's da best, I tell ya." He said menacingly.

Sarah noticed that the black dealer had a heavy gold Rolex watch on his left wrist and two large diamond rings flashed on the third and fourth fingers of his right hand.

Julio pierced open the package with the long nail on his left little finger, then tentatively tasted it and rubbed some around his gums.

"Yeah, it'll do. Same price as you quoted to my friend last week?" He questioned.

The black man nodded his head slowly.

Julio opened his wallet and extracted a thick wad of fifty-pound notes.

The man handed over the briefcase with one hand and with the other took the notes. He took a small gadget also from one of the pockets of his jacket and ran it over the bank notes, he murmured under his breath, satisfied they were genuine.

Sarah watched in horror, but fascinated at the same time, she had never been with Julio when he was dealing. A strange ripple of excitement ran through her body before she reprimanded herself mentally, then disgust overcame her for what the men were doing in front of the small child. She wondered if the Social Services knew that her parents were taking and dealing in drugs, perhaps an anonymous call to them might be in order.

"Come on Ju…"

"Shut up woman," bellowed Julio as he stood up.

"Okay, if this is as good as you say, I'll need more, don't contact me, I'll let you know when I need to see you again," he said to the huge black guy, as he kicked out at the young stoned man who keeled over onto the floor.

"Come woman."

Sarah followed him outside to her car. He opened one of the rear doors and carefully wedged the briefcase down on the floor of the car between the passenger seat and the back seat and threw the tartan rug that was laying on the back seat over it.

"I'm driving this time, you're useless. But first I must have a proper fix," he said as he extracted from his jacket pocket, a ready prepared syringe that he had taken from the briefcase beforehand.

He pulled off the protective cap with his teeth, pushed his sleeve up with his right hand, tapped the main artery in the middle of his left arm and jabbed it into the first available vein near his wrist and then threw the used syringe out of the car window.

Sarah saw several track marks as she watched in horror and she recalled a similar situation in Spain. Surely he wasn't going to drive full of drugs.

"Julio," she begged. "Let me drive, please'"

"Shut-up, just give me the key."

She handed it over to him reluctantly. "At least put your seatbelt on, you could get stopped by the police." She warned him before going around to the other side of her car.

The heroin was seeping into his brain.

"Shut-up, I said. I'm perfectly alright, bitch."

He fiddled with the ignition and finally sorted it out. At first he drove reasonably slowly as he had now calmed down, until they reached the motorway.

It had started to rain again very heavily. The windscreens wipers of the BMW could hardly cope with the downpour. Cars flashed past going the other way, swerving to avoid the black car.

Oh my God, she thought we're going down the wrong side of the motorway and she remembered what his father had told him about the occasion in America with his sister. How on earth had he managed that?

"Julio, watch out, we're on the wrong side of the motorway. What's the matter with you?" She shouted and grabbed the handgrip on the passenger door.

"What? What? You stupid cow, they are going the wrong way, not me," he yelled back. "Shut up!"

Suddenly the headlights of an oncoming car driving straight at him blinded him momentarily. He swerved to avoid it. The car hooted madly and flashed his lights. Julio cursed out loudly in Spanish. At this point Sarah wrenched the wheel of her car to the left and they just missed a head-on collision. The side of her car grazed the central barrier and bright sparks lit up the night before the car spun around facing the other way. In fact it was the right way.

Fortunately for them there were no other cars at that point on the M4.

"Pull in you idiot," Sarah screamed. "There, over there, on the hard shoulder. But, for God's sake be careful I don't want to be killed or my car completely wrecked."

The shock of the car spinning round and her screaming at him seemed somehow to penetrate his befuddled, drug-filled mind and he eased his foot off the accelerator and pulled on to the hard shoulder.

Sarah was by now so shaken that she had wet herself with fright. "Get out you filthy bastard, get out of my car, what do you think you're trying to do? Kill us both?"

If only he would get out of the car, then she could drive off and leave him in the pouring rain. But she knew it was only wishful thinking.

His head lolled onto his chest and he started mumbling incoherently. Suddenly his head shot up.

"No, you get out, you cow. I'll move over. Bloody stupid country, everyone's driving on the wrong side of the road. It's not me!" He turned and slapped her face hard and she fell against the passenger door.

"Get out, you drive, I'm tired."

Sarah opened the door shakily. The night was black save for her headlights and the odd car flashing by. The rain was now even more torrential and the wind was cold and she was getting soaked to the skin. She sobbed with desperation as she walked around to the other side, opened the door and got in quickly. By the time she was in the car, Julio was fast asleep in one of his drugged comas.

She reached behind her and pulled the tartan rug away that was covering the briefcase and lifting her bottom she tucked the rug under her to protect the driver's seat from her wet skirt and wet knickers. Then she buckled up her safety belt. If only she had the courage to push him out and leave him. Why weren't there any motorway police about? Surely Julio's performance on the motorway had been picked up by one of the many cameras. That is if they are working she thought.

She looked around her; there was no one about. The engine had stalled as Julio had pulled onto the hard shoulder and the wipers were still going *clunk, clunk*, backwards and forwards. The noise was unbearable. She turned them off and she also turned off the headlights and sat in the darkened car trying to collect her thoughts, her head back against the headrest, breathing heavily. She felt completely drained, tears prickled her lovely eyes, and her face was sore and it felt even more swollen from the slap earlier.

Julio broke the stillness. He grunted and came too and said in a wheedling voice.

"*Querida,* drive on, I'm sorry. Come on we must get back to Richmond. I expect you're tired too." He leaned towards her and tried to kiss her on the lips.

"Don't you dare," she snarled through her clenched teeth as she started her car up and then shifted into drive and drove off with a start, throwing him sharply backwards onto the headrest and then forward onto the dashboard causing him to hit his forehead.

He started to shout at her again as he reached for his seatbelt. "You maniac, what are you doing?"

"You are the maniac, I suggest you belt up, you pig! And shut up."

She turned the wipers and lights on again. "I've had just about enough of you. The first police car I see I shall flash down. **Understand**?" She threatened.

He fell silent. That was the last thing he wanted to happen. He sat back and dozed off again. He would sort her out when they got back to her house.

Sarah drove back slowly the rest of the way to Richmond in silence, trying to think of a plan to rid herself of him, but her brain just seemed to be completely exhausted and she needed all of her resources to drive her car back to her house through the dark night. Fortunately the rain had started to subside.

***

She parked her car carefully in her driveway, in the cul-de-sac, the damaged side hidden by the sidewall. She had the detached house with fields beyond and fortunately her neighbour on the opposite side was away on holiday in France for several months. It was also late and she knew that her other four neighbours further down the road would be fast asleep by now.

Julio suddenly awoke out of his drugged sleep. "Get out Sarah and open the front door quickly," he ordered as he reached behind his seat for the briefcase.

She was wet through, and exhausted from the drive back. She opened the door and he pushed her into the house slamming the front door behind them.

He pulled her into the lounge, threw the briefcase onto one of the settees and pushed her onto the other low settee. "Don't move, bitch, I need a little something."

He fished in the pocket of his black leather jacket and pulled out a small bag of coke and a gold safety razor blade from a small thin gold box. He carefully pulverised the *snow spill* on the top of the glass coffee table into three fine lines. His diamond ring twinkled on his left hand. He rolled up a new twenty-pound note and carefully snorted the white powder lines off the glass top one by one. Then he wiped his nose and put the razor back in its little box. There was a slight residue left on the table and he wet the little finger on his right hand and rubbed it over his gums.

Within minutes he was fully awake and he quickly had a hard-on, he grabbed her and forced her into the hallway and pressed her against the hallway wall. She struggled and tried with difficulty to get away from him. He started to rip her clothes off. Still struggling and swearing at her, he clipped her across the face with his left hand and his ring made a small gash on her cheek. She stifled a scream.

"Julio, let me go, please let me go," she pleaded.

Her mind was whirling with a kind of mist and her body was unable to respond as she tried to pull away from him.

"Repent bitch, you are mine. You have sinned with another man. Get the fuck outta here, and get the fuck upstairs," he snarled.

"Keep still and do what I say. Get down on your knees and suck my dick, then maybe I'll let you go." He laughed insanely.

How many times have I heard that laugh in the past Sarah thought as her blood curdled at the sound? Would she never be rid of him?

Suddenly he changed his tactics and smiled at her.

"I'm sorry, I want you *querida*."

His eager hands moved over her breasts and down to her scanty knickers and he tore them from her and threw them on the floor. With ease he lifted her up, and carried her without any effort upstairs and dropped her on her bed. The cat went flying and darted down the stairs towards the kitchen and ran into his travel holder.

Then Julio pulled off his clothes and straddled her on the bed, one knee either side of her slight body, pinning her to the duvet. He started to run his hands over her body again. He felt just the faintest sensation in the middle of his palm as her nipples rose and stiffened. He didn't realise that it was merely a simple reflex on her part. A light breeze from an open window touching her would have caused her nipples to become erect in such a way.

She simply lay there inert. She felt disgusted by his filthy touch. Abandoning her breasts Julio sought his excitement elsewhere, further down. He had a fine sensitive touch. He knew just where to caress her. But she laid still and cold even her juices were not flowing from her, because of her fear for him. As there was no response from her at all, his desire quickly turned to anger.

She watched him as he looked down on her. He was so close she could smell the male scent of him and almost feel him, though he wasn't actually touching her. For one agonising moment as he leaned towards her, she thought he was going to kiss her.

She clenched her lips together and then unwillingly parted them as she struggled for air. Turning her head swiftly to one side, she wondered if he'd known that she had wanted to kiss him at that moment, before her common sense took over. She lay completely still knowing that it would only enrage him or perhaps deter him and he might go away. Instead he grabbed her by her blonde hair and lifted her head towards him and stared into her cold, expressionless eyes. They were flat, dead.

He slapped her across the face, twice and threw her back onto the bed, but she slid to the floor almost unconscious. Blood seeped from the left side of her mouth.

"Cold bitch, whore," he shouted at her in Spanish.

Then he reached for her once more, wanting to hurt her. He was unable to stop hitting her and kicking her. He clutched his psychosis closely to him, like an embrace. It turned him on; he often got his kicks this way and he released his erect penis from his jeans and fondled it. It was hard and throbbing, he knelt down beside her, his hand closed around the thick shaft and slowly, rhythmically he tossed himself off over her naked inert body. He screamed with ecstasy as he reached his pinnacle of pleasure. His semen formed a jetting arc over her, landing on her firm bruised breasts.

When he had finished he ran his fingers over her slim body and gradually made his way up to her slender neck. He gripped her around the neck with both hands and gently squeezed her windpipe, at first with a little pressure, then his anger took over and he pressed a little harder and then he released the pressure again, he did not want to kill her yet.

To Julio in his drugged fever, this harassment was a deadly serious business, with an importance and a meaning that could never be understood by anyone clean and sober. She had to be taught a lesson once and for all. She was his and no one else would ever have her, he was going to kill her. He was convinced that one day they would meet in heaven together and be united.

She nearly blacked out from the lack of air and as she gradually came round, she choked, fighting for breath. He leaned backwards slightly with his eyes closed as if in some sort of sexual trance as he once again applied even pressure. She once more choked and gasped. Suddenly he let go and keeled over, falling back onto the floor, he'd finally passed out with all the drugs and alcohol in his system and no food.

Sarah lay on her side for a few moments gulping in air trying to recover her breath and also waiting to ascertain that he had passed out. He started to snore loudly.

She carefully dragged herself up and sat on the bed, trying to stop herself shaking, then she got off the bed and reached for her baggy T-shirt on a nearby chair and quickly ran down the stairs and along the hallway, her feet silenced by the thick pile carpet. Reaching the front door, she frantically, but quietly turned the handle. To her horror nothing happened.

"Oh! Dear God, he's locked it and put the keys somewhere," she whispered to herself.

Having no choice, she ran back up the stairs to her bedroom to find the keys. They must be in the pocket of his jacket or jeans, she thought, she had to find them.

Julio was still in a stupefied sleep, snoring heavily. Taking a breath to steady herself, she forced herself to look through his jacket pockets, then his jeans. They were not there. She stepped over to the bed. Perhaps they were under her pillow.

Her bare feet suddenly touched something cold. She looked down and there they were on the floor shining in the moonlight from the window. Her heart was pounding erratically and her hands trembling as she bent to grab them. Taking another deep breath to steady herself, she started back to the front door. She was halfway down the hallway, when she heard a heavy tread on the stairs. In a panic she ran for the front door. Suddenly the footsteps were nearer. She swung around. It was Julio in his briefs.

Grabbing her he flung her against the wall. She barely even saw him move, she just felt the blinding pain that shot through her head as he slammed it back against the wall. The keys fell to the floor. She scrambled to her feet and fled to the kitchen, with Julio following her. Suddenly he was towering over her and grabbed her by the neck again.

She reached for the pair of large scissors in a wooden block on her new worktop by the sink behind her, grasping the scissors, and with superhuman strength, she plunged them deeply into the upper part of his left arm. He screamed out in agony and he slammed his right fist into her face as he released his hold on her.

She fell back onto the floor like a rag doll. Then he kicked out at her, her head, her body, over and over again.

For an agonised and blurred few seconds she was aware of being dragged by her hair and lifted before her senses were swallowed into a swirling, smothered ocean of black. The blood was streaming down his left arm onto the kitchen floor. He grabbed a nearby tea towel and wrapped it around his injured arm. Running upstairs he picked up his clothes from the bedroom, dressed as quickly as he could, took her car key from the bedside table and left the house, leaving the front door unlocked.

***

In the early hours of the morning Sarah regained consciousness, she was freezing cold and she was nearly naked.

Her face and body ached from the abuse it had received. The pain in the lower half of her body was excruciating. A thick tuft of her hair was on the hallway floor that had been viciously pulled out by him. She knew instinctively that he had done a lot of damage to her this time, more than ever before. She managed to crawl to the hallway phone and ring Michael's home, she knew he always worked late on his computer and she told him what had happened swearing him to secrecy.

"Don't call the police. Just come quickly please the front door is unlocked." She managed to tell him before she passed out again.

CHAPTER FOURTEEN

LONDON - 2004

Sarah felt as if she was in a long black tunnel. At one end was a pinpoint of light and it seemed to her that she was trying to make her way towards it, but it would have been so much easier to just drift off into oblivion.

When she next became semi-conscious, she drifted into the twilight between sleep and waking, dream and thought. The images that came to her were from her deepest past. Her mother, father and her aunt. Then the good memories of Julio, when they had been an item, which suddenly turned into bad. Someone was talking to her from a great distance, it was a deep voice. She slowly recognised it as Michael's voice. Then quite suddenly, she was awake.

"Hang on in there Sarah, you are alright now. I'm here now."

Then she wanted to drift away again. It was so difficult, she preferred the dark tunnel, and she felt safe there.

"Sarah. Sarah can you hear me? It's me, Michael. Sarah, come on, try to speak to me," he prompted her.

She sighed and began to fight her way back to consciousness. When she came to, she was in The Royal Richmond Hospital, in a private room organised by Michael and he was sitting by her bedside.

"How are you feeling Sarah?" He asked tentatively as he looked down at her.

She lay back onto the large pillows. She looked very small and wan. Her blonde hair was limp and dirty, with some dried blood clinging to the sides from the beatings she had taken around the head. Her cheeks were sallow. There were dark shadows under her eyes. Michael felt so guilty that he had not guarded her better and he felt so sorry for her, she'd been through so much, yet again.

She blinked several times, trying to focus on his face.

"How do I feel? I feel like shit! What happened, how long have I been here? What am I going to do Michael? Will he never leave me alone?"

She sighed deeply, and then winced with the pain that shot through her body as she struggled to sit up, only to fall back on the pillows.

Michael observed the bruising around her neck and on her face. Her left eye was nearly closed.

"You have been unconsciousness for nearly three days under sedation and you came round finally a few minutes ago whilst the doctor and I were here. We must tell the police, we have got to Sarah." He proclaimed earnestly.

"No, you cannot involve them, you can't do that, he'll kill me, you don't know him and he will find me. You don't understand," she cried.

"He'll even take it out on his father, somehow. I know him so well, he will seek revenge. Will you contact Juan please as soon as possible? His phone numbers are in my little blue phonebook by the phone in the hall, under Gonzales, Juan Gonzales.

You've still got the spare set of keys to my house, haven't you?"

"Yes, of course I will," he re-assured her.

"But for the moment Sarah you must think about yourself. You have been badly beaten up, your pelvis is cracked and you will be in here for at least another week. There might even be some serious damage to your liver or your kidneys from the amount of bruising on your body. My God, your lovely face is a mess. I don't understand what is going on, what haven't you told me everything? I understand one thing though; the person who did this to you is a maniac. Something has got to be done. I have to inform the police, when they find him, you must press charges."

"No, Michael I can't and I won't," she mumbled through cracked lips.

"I can't tell you now what it's all about. I can hardly talk at the moment, but I promise you, I will tell you the whole story when I am better. Juan will sort him out I know that and for his sake we need to keep the police out of it. Anyway what could we tell them?"

Michael thought for a few moments.

"I could tell them that you had phoned me and that an intruder had entered your house and you'd caught him in the act of robbery and he had beaten you up and then stolen your car. Well it would be half true, wouldn't it? It is what I told the doctors here. I know they won't, say anything. He has also taken your car, probably dumped it somewhere. I know that there has been a spate of break-ins in the area recently. By the way I cleaned up the blood in the kitchen and placed that small rug over the spot. I also sorted out your bedroom as well. I presume it wasn't all your blood!" He stated.

"I also stuffed your torn clothes into the bottom of your bedroom wardrobe and I wrapped you in your dressing gown, as you were..." he hesitated for a few moments, "er...almost naked in the hall when I found you."

He cleared his throat with slight embarrassment before continuing. "Alright, I won't tell the police then. But if it even happens again, God help me, I will, or if he starts harassing you, I will. You look all in, I'll go and leave you to sleep, it is the best medicine there is and I'll be back this evening. Just rest and try not to think about your attacker. As difficult as it may seem, you must try and start again when you are better and we must sort out what you're going to do. I'll phone Juan Gonzales as soon as I get back to my office, I promise. Now get some rest. Is there anything that you need? Oh, by the way, Picasso is at home with me, my family just adore him!"

Sarah nodded and tried to smile through her wounded lips.

"Thank you, thank you so much. I know you'll all look after him well."

He could see she was near to tears again and looked exhausted after their chat.

"You've come through a great darkness in your life and you will never again be so alone, so unhappy again." he explained. "I will help you all I can Sarah."

She looked at him with hope. "Can you promise me that?"

He nodded his head. "Yes. Not because I am a magician, but because you've got guts, you've faced your ghosts now and it's unlikely that you will ever have to face anything worse. You will have a good man come into your life soon. I promise,' he smiled.

"You know I feel as if I've been crying forever!" She sighed.

"There's nothing wrong with crying my dear, you have to let it out at times."

She was silent for a moment. "Michael, will I really ever stop crying, will I ever be really happy?" She asked sadly.

"If your life from now on gives you cause to feel happy, yes. If you have a sad and troublesome daily life, you'll always feel sad and troubled. You need to decide whether your life needs to change or not? Are you sure that working at the centre is not too emotional for you?" He asked gently.

"No, not at all, I love working at the Rehab centre, it helps me, and I feel needed and I have come to think of you as a trusted and dear friend. It's a gift you have, you know." She smiled gently at the big man. "That's why you're so good at what you do. You could be so much more successful, Michael."

"Yeah, I know, a close friend of mine keeps telling me that, perhaps one of these days I'll go private again, but at the moment I want to be sure that you are all right. Okay, how about only two days a week, until you're back on your feet properly?"

"Okay, but only for the time being, I like doing three days. I will be all right. I assure you. I will exorcise Julio in my own time. I've got you now as a good friend. I don't feel alone anymore."

She reached over and took hold of his left hand and squeezed it as tightly as she could, trying to draw strength from him. She felt she was in a dreamlike state where she couldn't comprehend what had happened; nothing seemed real anymore. In the morning she thought I will wake up and think that I've imagined the whole thing.

"Thank you for being you, for being there when I needed someone."

He smiled as he bent over her and planted a light kiss on her forehead before leaving the room.

Sarah slept for about three hours; during that time the doctor had been in to check her and at six o'clock in the evening a nurse woke her with her dinner. About an hour later when she was dozing again, she was aware someone else was in the room. She opened her eyes slowly and blinked them. A lazy smile appeared on her lips.

Juan had tiptoed into her room carrying a dozen red roses in one hand and an enormous box of chocolates under his arm and in the other hand a large basket of assorted exotic fruit. As he looked down at her he knew she was almost out of immediate danger now.

"Hello Sarah."

His soft voice from the end of her bed broke into her thoughts. He placed his goodies for her on a nearby table and came over to her and bent forward and gave her a kiss on each cheek. He could see her face was a startling white against the yellow and purple bruising and her eyes were filling with tears. He stroked her hair and moved nearer and sat on the bed beside her, pressing her slight body closer to his.

"Your friend Michael phoned me. I am so sorry Sarah. I shall never forgive myself for all the suffering you have endured because of my son. Have you told the police yet who it was?"

"No Juan, I haven't, I don't want them to know. I told Michael this. I don't want them ferreting about in my house looking for clues I don't want anyone excepting you, Michael and I to know what happened. I need time to think, to think about what I shall do. But be careful, Julio won't stop at this; he will probably come after you or worst still, your wife as he is bent on destruction."

She paused for a few moments before continuing.

"It's not only me, but also you and Diana are all in danger from him. I think he's gone completely mad, he's plagued by insecurities, and he's obsessional and completely neurotic as well as erratic. He is a drug addict who has problems with anger and a long history of abuse. He's a complete psychopath. Why do you still protect him so much? You must surely know that he will never be normal. We need to sit down and talk seriously when I am better."

Her eyes filled with ready tears of exhaustion and pain at the effort of trying to make Julio's father understand.

Juan released her and pulled up a nearby armchair.

"I know, I know, Diana has told me exactly the same after I told her the true history of Julio. I understand something has to be done about him. I'm just as scared as you are. Fortunately she is away at the moment, her mother has been taken into hospital, so she's pretty safe for the next few days and he doesn't know where her mother lives anyway. But unfortunately I have to go back to the States for a week. I'm going to try and postpone the visit if possible, but it is so difficult in my job. Then when I return I shall take her away for a while, somewhere where he won't find us." Juan explained.

"The main thing now, is that you get better, if you need anything, please let me know, do you have money to pay the hospital? Also when I come back we shall have our talk."

"Yes thank you, that's been sorted, Michael has done that for me."

They spent some time talking and making arrangements, before the nurse came back and ushered Juan out of the room.

She hardly noticed when the nurses came or went away. Over the next few days during the idle hours of recuperation in the private room that she had been moved to, everything came flooding back.

Not only in her sedated dreams, but also while she was awake and various other thin. Sarah had a lot of time to think about Julio and other happenings in her life. It was like watching a video of her past. Now she was alone she could admit to herself what she wanted. She wanted *revenge* as soon as possible.

She recognised it and she wanted justice as well as revenge. Not only for herself, but for all the women out there who had been abused and were being abused right now. For the women who were afraid of their partners and afraid for their children. She knew that fear was a powerful emotion and she had for a long time been afraid of Julio too. He had also been unimaginably cruel to her.

Sarah would punish Julio, for all the bad memories she had of him, she must exorcize him from her mind, and she must rid herself of his ghost that had haunted her for so long. She was ready now. Retaliation and Revenge, the words lay on her lips like a sweet kiss and she ran her tongue over them tasting their sweetness.

She knew must rid society of the drug addicts that preyed on people.

Revenge and Justice!

***

The doctor had taken her off her medication and now Sarah was just about ready to leave the hospital after nearly two weeks and was waiting for Michael to pick her up the next day.

She sat on the edge of the bed and gazed out of the large window across the well-manicured gardens. She'd just finished reading a novel about a very clever actress who used her talents to lie, seduce, blackmail and kill her way to the top of her career. It was a book for people who liked to imagine themselves in the role of a criminal, but knew it could not happen to them. To her it was not imaginary, she knew she could do it; she would find a way and get away with it.

She wondered how she could have been so gullible when she had lived with Julio. She had tried to ignore her past, forget the pain and live her own life, but she could see that she had been wrong, bitterly wrong. She had to destroy the ghost of her nightmares, to finally lay the ghost of Julio to rest. It had to be done before she destroyed herself and before he too destroyed more people.

She had the perfect weapon at home, hidden away. The little handcrafted crossbow that she had found in an old trunk in the attic of her aunt's house. Now that it was so carefully cleaned and restored, it would be the ideal weapon; she knew it was waiting to be used.

CHAPTER FIFTEEN

LONDON - 2004

Late the next afternoon Michael came complete with her cat in its travelling carrier and picked her up and took her back to her own house. She had already rejected the offer of staying with him and his family, she needed peace and quietness, time to think and hatch her plan and she needed to be in her own comfort zone.

Neither she nor Michael had noticed the tall man standing in the shadows from across the road.

Once Michael had left and she had closed the front door behind her she was suddenly afraid that she wouldn't be able to act normally, that she was too tired or too ill to keep up the pretence. She lifted Picasso out of his travelling box and cuddled his warm soft body against her chest. He was a wonderful source of comfort to her as he purred loudly whilst she smoothed his fur.

"Come on my lovely, let's go and have a rest upstairs."

She hardly seemed to have slept when the sound of the phone by her bed seemed to be ringing in the distance and awoke her. She groped for the phone, feeling resentful that it had woken her up. She fumbled the receiver onto the pillow.

"Hello," she croaked tentatively.

The line was quiet.

"Hello," she said more distinctly. "Hello Michael?"

After a pause she heard heavy breathing and her skin began to tingle with *goose pimples*. She knew immediately that it was Julio. It was a knowledge that was primal and instinctive that is built into most human beings.

"No bitch, this is not your black lover."

She sent the receiver crashing to the floor, then scrambled out of bed desperately and fell onto the carpet, her head buzzing and grabbed the phone again. She drew in a deep breath.

"Where are you? You bastard. Leave me alone. Just leave me alone, do you understand? Damn you, you bastard. Damn you Julio, damn you," she shouted. "Leave me alone, or I'll call the police. I mean it this time."

He laughed insanely. There was no mistaking the cruel and mocking tone before the line went dead.

She banged the receiver back onto its cradle, shivering with fright and then crossed her arms over her chest trying to steady her nerves, she felt chilled despite the warm evening. She had thoughts of locking herself in her bedroom, but what good would that do? It was not a fortress, only a house with windows that were easily shattered, if he decided to enter it.

The alarm system she had installed was only of use to her when she was absent from the house. She had not had a chance to have it updated and she knew that she must do it as soon as possible so that she could set it when she was at home as well out of the house, so that if anyone triggered the alarm sensor outside, it would then automatically notify the security company and they would call the house and the police if necessary and also have it set so that she could pick it up on her mobile phone.

I've had enough of being afraid of him she thought. I won't let him drive me away from my lovely house. I shall do it first thing tomorrow she told herself.

Sarah unfolded her arms and with trembling fingers she dialled 1471. An instant later a computerised voice informed her that the caller had phoned from a public phone booth and the number was withheld, and if she would like to make another call, please press hash.

She quickly put on her dressing gown, and hobbled over to her bedroom window checking that it was closed and then let the Venetian blind down and pulled the curtains together, and then she made her way painfully around the house checking that all the outside doors and other windows were locked.

She winced with pain as she hobbled up the stairs back to her bedroom. The doctor at the hospital had confirmed that her pelvis was cracked and the area around it was badly bruised and would take some time to heal. There were also several other contusions on her body, but these too would fade. He told her she would probably limp for quite a long time too and she wasn't to drive for at least another three weeks and then he wanted her to come back and he would check her over. He gave her a prescription for some anti-inflammatory drugs.

CHAPTER SIXTEEN

LONDON - 2004

Three weeks later when she arrived back home in a taxi in the afternoon, after her first day back at work at the Rehab centre she decided to have an early night.

She was feeling quite drained and she changed into an old T-Shirt and cut-off jeans and then made her way into the kitchen. First she was going to cook herself some penne pasta with pesto sauce that she had made the day before, preferring to make it with blanched lightly roasted almonds instead of pine nuts, and then topped with a little grated fresh Pecorino cheese. She had picked up a fresh Cos lettuce, a bulb of Finocchi (*fennel*), a cucumber and some tomatoes on the way home. A nice mixed salad would go well with it and to top it off she had bought herself a half bottle of Pinot di Pinot sparkling wine.

***

It is not going to be a hot shower tonight she thought, later she would take a long hot bath with lots and lots of bath foam in it. She caught a reflection in her kitchen window and a chill swept through her, as the face in the glass that stared back at her seemed not to be hers for a brief moment, it was Julio's instead. The hairs on the back of her neck stood up. Was he stalking her now? She shook her head to clear it and then looked at the window again. It had only been her imagination. She wouldn't put it past him though to stalk her. He certainly knew that she was back in the house when he had made that call two weeks ago. She must get a grip on herself. She turned on the flat screen TV in the kitchen and then concentrated on getting her dinner ready and her fear gradually passed.

Sometime later after her supper she stacked her dishwasher and then wandered through the house and turned off the lights, closed the curtains, checked the back and front door twice to make sure they were locked and then she went upstairs and pulled down her bedroom blind and closed the heavy curtains of her bedroom windows. When she had finished she once more did her security round, just to be sure.

I need a long, hot soak in the bath she thought. There isn't a physical or mental part of me that isn't irritated or worried. Then once more she repeated the same routine and checked the doors and windows again. Ever since she had returned to her house she was worried that she was becoming paranoid about security. She had still not contacted the security company and she made a note on a pad on the kitchen table to call them regarding her alarm system the next morning.

About an hour or so later after a delightfully long relaxing bath she peeped through her curtains and let her Venetian blind up a quarter of the way and then opened her bedroom window a little in order to get some air circulating. When she glanced down into the street, she noticed that it was deserted, except for a solitary stroller, whose silhouette she couldn't quite make out. Was **he** out there, was **he** watching her? No she told herself, I am becoming paranoid about him being outside too. Perhaps it was someone walking their dog.

Julio hadn't rung again in the last three weeks, he won't she told herself, not after I threatened him with the police. Maybe he has even left the country again, she thought as she shut the heavy curtains tightly and settled into her bed with Picasso.

Despite her physical and mental exhaustion after her first day back at work, Sarah was unable to sleep well. She woke three times in the night and found herself listening intently for any sound that might suggest someone was in the house. The first time she awoke, it was one thirty am. The phone ringing broke the silence. Her instincts told her to ignore it, but she knew that Michael often worked late at home; it could be him checking to see if she was all right.

She reached for the telephone. "Hello, hello."

All she could hear was deep breathing and some crackling down the line, then silence. Instinctively once again she knew it was Julio and from the static noises on the phone he was obviously using his mobile. Was he outside she wondered? Her stomach turned over with fright as well as anger. Would he never give up?

"Okay, that is it, I am calling the police, now," she shouted down the phone before slamming it back into its cradle.

Sarah knew the threat might scare him again. She was not going to let him frighten her like this again, she felt stronger now, and she had friends who would help her. Silently she listened for any noises, and then she thought she heard someone at the front door. She had no weapon handy in the bedroom only her high-heeled shoes.

Donning her old dressing gown she picked up one of the shoes lying beneath her bedroom chair by the bedside and held it by the foot then crept downstairs barefooted, only to find that the front and back doors were indeed still bolted and the cat flap in the utility room was still nailed shut. Michael had done that for her. Then despite feeling slightly foolish, she tested the locks on the windows of the kitchen, pulled the long curtains even closer together in the living room and her study.

Before returning to her bedroom, she checked the windows in the two spare bedrooms and the blind in the bathroom, still haunted by the sensation that something was wrong, but determined not to close her bedroom window. I am upstairs she told herself sternly, it's highly unlikely he is going to climb the drainpipe in any case someone would see him.

The temperature had dropped sharply since she went to bed, and her bedroom was quite chilly, she pulled the double-glazed window towards her, but left it slightly ajar on the security catch and pulled the Venetian blind right down this time and then jumped into bed and pulled the duvet tightly around her body. She shivered and moved closer to Picasso who was lying on her bed on his back showing his tummy and snoring gently.

Suddenly her blind rattled, blown by a small breeze that had started up. That's what startled me, she realised and for a moment she considered getting up again and closing the window completely. Instead she slipped further under the duvet and was asleep in a few minutes.

The second time she awoke, she sat bolt upright in the bed, positive that someone was at the window. She looked up at the time projected by her clock, on the ceiling. It was 03.30am.

"Get a grip of yourself woman," she said out aloud, then settled back again.

During the rest of the night, Sarah vaguely remembered stirring in her sleep to an eerie feeling that someone was standing over her and looking at her, but she never actually woke up.

She awoke for the third time around five thirty. Although she'd had some sleep, her mind had been active and she realised that sometime between the interruptions in her sleep her subconscious had been dwelling on the past.

Awake now she realised that there was no hope of going back to sleep, she decided that a coffee would help clear her mind and went downstairs; Picasso followed closely behind. She let him out through the back door and then made herself a cup of coffee and took it back to bed. After all it was Saturday and she didn't really need to get up yet.

Sometime later she heard the morning paper drop through her door and rushed downstairs into the hallway to pick up her newspaper. As she bent down to retrieve it she saw a piece of folded paper on the doormat. Carefully she picked it up and opened it. There were three words written on it.

'QUERIDA, look outside'

"Oh, my God!" She cried out aloud as she dropped it hastily, shocked to the core.

215

So he had been outside during the night watching her house. She wondered how many times he had been stalking her in the daytime as well since she'd left the hospital and how many times at night he had been outside in the darkness, watching and waiting, just waiting in the darkness, like a cobra ready to strike its victim. She felt physically sick and ran to the downstairs bathroom and bathed her face in cold water. She wondered what he would do next, something foul she was sure, like something horrible pushed through her letterbox or death threats, he was starting his mind games again.

She had to do something drastic, she was determined that she was not going to live in fear of him forever.

She went to the small hall window by the front door and cautiously looked out. No one was around, but in her driveway stood her BMW, its black bodywork glittering in the morning sunshine. She opened the door cautiously and then stepped out and looked around tentatively before walking over to her vehicle. As she walked round it to inspect it, she noticed it had obviously had a good clean and then she saw that the damage to it had also been repaired.

There was an envelope under one of the windscreen wipers. With cold trembling fingers she lifted the blade and retrieved the envelope and dashed inside her house and put the chain on the door. In the hallway she opened it carefully; her ignition key fell out together with a snapshot of Julio and her on the beach in Spain taken some time ago. However her face in the picture had been gouged out with something sharp. She dropped it with a small cry. Then she bent down and picked it up and turned it over. On the back of it was written the date and place when it had been taken.

"You bastard," she shouted at the picture and swiftly tore it into several pieces and ran into the kitchen and threw it into her pedal bin under the sink unit. She leaned against the kitchen table her mind churning over, she realised that the time was right. She would start her mission. She was determined that he was not going to haunt her memories forever. She rushed to the back door and called Picasso in, she did not trust Julio not to kill him like Sario her cat in Spain, and she could not go through that trauma again.

About half an hour later she rang Juan, but had to leave a message on his mobile.

"Juan, Julio is still in London, he's stalking me now. Do be careful Juan. Ring me when you get this message please, we need to talk."

BOOK NINE

1 PETER Ch. 5 Verse: 12
Beloved, think it is not strange concerning the fiery trial…

CHAPTER SEVENTEEN

LONDON - 2004

David gazed lovingly at Sarah. They were having a picnic in Hyde Park, it was her birthday and it was one of those lovely sunny Saturday afternoons in late August. He lay on his back for some time, listening to the sound of the park and smelling the soft summer day. The quiet interlude had a calming effect on him. He turned over onto his stomach and stretched out on the tartan rug and looked up at Sarah who was sitting half in the shade and half in the sun, against an old Maple tree.

She was wearing a pretty white cotton top, with thin straps that showed her lightly tanned shoulders off to perfection, tucked into a short pale blue full skirt, which she had pulled up over her thighs, her sunglasses were balanced on the top of her head and she was reading his notes, which he had brought along that day. There was a small frown of concentration on her face. She had kicked off her strappy little white sandals with kitten heels, and every so often she would look up and just stare into space before continuing to read. The sunlight was dappled across her body, caused by the shade of the big tree behind her. He thought she looked so beautiful and he felt so much love for her and he was bursting with happiness.

Where the hot sun touched her bare legs, it highlighted the tawny colour of her smooth limbs and on her hair its light reflected off the strands of pale blonde and a small scattering of freckles showed across her nose and cheeks and her face was slightly flushed from the heat of the sun.

A perfect moment in time, he thought. But they never last, they arrive and then they vanish and we cannot bring them back, we can only make new ones. He thought about his late wife and the wonderful times they'd had together regardless of her MS. He knew she would have approved of Sarah.

David felt so full of love as he watched Sarah, so still and quiet and he marvelled, as he always did, at how beautiful she was. Hair of natural honey blonde and startling blue eyes bright as a clear sky, his heart gave a little jump. He wanted to reach out and touch her, to tell her how he felt. He felt a sudden straightforward desire for her. He saw her as young, sexual and desirable.

He moved closer to her and surreptitiously slid his hands under her skirt and felt the warm skin on the tops of her thighs; she sighed with desire for him and welcomed his touch. But he was still wary and he moved his hands away.

At times she appeared so withdrawn and distant. Yet at other times she was warm and passionate, abandoning herself completely to him. He wondered how much hurt she had endured in the past, had it been from her late husband perhaps? She never said very much about her past, except that she had been married twice before, and he never asked her any questions, he did not like to pry because he knew she would tell all when she was ready to.

Once you have been married to someone he thought they are always in your life, good or bad. The key is to remember the good parts. He wondered what she had to hide. We all have something to hide he reflected, we all have a dark side.

He leaned over and gave her a quick kiss on her lips then rolled over onto his side and reached for a can of cold Budweiser from the icebox next to him on the grass.

Sarah had volunteered to drive his car today, so he was able to have a beer or two. She didn't drink much alcohol, mainly Perrier water or orange juice, occasionally the odd glass of wine. Was that her dark secret? Was she a reformed alcoholic, somehow he didn't think so, or maybe she had been married to an alcoholic? He sensed that inside this lovely woman there was a huge amount of determination to live a normal life. He snapped the ring pull off the can and took a long thirsty gulp of the fizzy amber liquid.

Her eyes he thought were truly fantastic. Big blue eyes were almost turquoise in colour. Eyes that flashed with life, with amusement, but sometimes they were so very sad. He couldn't stop watching her. He loved the way her head tilted to one side whenever she was serious, listening to him or in this case studying his notes with her lips pursed slightly.

Even though they were not touching, he was so aware of her, sitting close by, that he could feel her heat against his bare arm.

They shared the park that afternoon with joggers, cyclists, mothers and nannies pushing the latest style baby strollers. A man with a briefcase hurried past and then paused to stare at them. He smiled at them and slowed his pace. David felt sorry for him obviously having to work and unlike them, being able to enjoy the lovely sunshine.

Sarah paused in her reading to watch a young woman with an even tan, scantily clad in skin-tight red mini Lycra shorts and midi top to match, wearing a white baseball cap. Her long dark ponytail hung out of the back of the cap swaying from side to side as she skated past on her Rollerblades pushing a baby buggy. She had an almost perfect figure, probably not the mother Sarah thought, not with that figure. She was probably the babysitter. She wondered if by some miracle she would ever have a family. If she and David had children one day, she knew they would be beautiful.

She reprimanded herself silently, she was not ready yet to marry again and settle down.

She looked up across at David and smiled one of her secret smiles. Here in the green shadows beneath the trees, she could focus on him. She lowered her gaze once more and studied his notes as she was fully aware he was staring at her. Having him watching her was a little embarrassing, but exciting. She knew she was in love with him and she felt so lucky, it would be a fulfilling love and life. Maybe at last fate was giving her another chance. Julio seemed to have vanished again out of her life. Hopefully it would last forever.

Sarah was looking forward to their evening together. This time she had asked David to pick her up from her house, she felt the time had come for her to invite him inside. Usually she would jump into a taxi and meet him at some other destination, because she was afraid that Julio might be watching her, but not tonight. He seemed to have stopped stalking her for the time being, he had obviously realised that she didn't have any male callers and he had always been rather wary of the Police, so perhaps he had gone away out of her life.

She could only hope he had gone forever and that her threats of calling the Police had sunk into his drug-filled brain. She now felt strong enough to cope with him if he did return and she knew that with Juan's help too that they could handle him.

She returned to David's notes about the killings. There would be no more she promised herself. She felt cleansed now with a bright future to look forward to. One of these days she would confess to David, but the time was not right yet.

***

In the shade of another tree, stood a dark haired man watching them intently behind his black wrap around designer sunglasses as he smoked a cigarette. He was a tall, gaunt man with a stiff, tense stance and a habit of holding his head back unnaturally. He wore a black shirt open at the neck and black designer jeans. His dark hair that was combed back smoothly had a slight grey tinge at the temples that seemed incongruous over his unlined somewhat pale face. His dark piercing eyes watched Sarah's every move.

His bony left wrist tightened as he closed his fingers into a fist. The tension rippled through the muscles in his arm. He raised his right hand to his mouth and inhaled deeply on his cigarette and then threw it down savagely on the pathway and ground it in with the heel of one of his expensive shoes. He turned and walked away, his handsome face black with anger at what he had been witnessing.

CHAPTER EIGHTEEN

LONDON - 2004

At precisely eight thirty that evening, after Sarah had showered and dressed, she stood in front of the full-length mirror in the bedroom and took a good look at herself. She liked what she saw. Her skin seemed to be glowing with the discovery of finding herself again. She clipped a delicate pearl and gold filigree bracelet that had once belonged to her aunt around her right wrist and the diamond and ruby ring that Juan had given her onto the third finger of her right hand, touched her hair again, sprayed a fine mist of Paloma Picasso eau-de-Parfum over her neck and hair; lifted her skirt and sprayed a quick squirt on her thighs; picked up her little Chanel handbag and a small Louis Vuitton overnight bag. She was ready and went downstairs to wait for David.

Very quickly she looked around the lounge, re-arranged some fresh flowers for the umpteenth time that she had placed in an elegant glass vase on the long low coffee table and sprayed air-freshener around again, while Picasso padded after her, purring and wondering what was going on. He followed her from room to room whilst she did a last minute check. Sarah was very nervous; the cat brushed himself against her legs, he knew that something was up and went to find his favourite chair for comfort whilst she hovered in the hallway listening for the taxi. David had told her that he would not be driving that evening.

As soon as Sarah opened the door, David noticed there was something different about her hair. It seemed to float around her. She wore her hair swept up for the evening with several soft strands dangling at her throat, around her face and at the back of her neck. She was wearing a blouse of Victorian cream lace fastened at the neck with a small black velvet bow and a long black skirt with a slit up to her left knee, and a pair of high-heeled black suede pointed shoes with a very thin ankle strap. She looked striking and extremely beautiful. He felt choked with the emotion that arose in his throat. He thought how can a woman look so lovely and alluring and yet so chic.

"Do come in." She smiled invitingly at him and then gave him a small peck on the cheek.

David followed her down the hallway in a cloud of her perfume, towards the large living room. It was the first time that she'd actually allowed him into her domain. Over the last few weeks he'd always picked her up from a place of her choice or dropped her off outside of her house, except on the occasions when she had stayed over at his apartment. For some reason of her own, she had never actually invited him in. He was intrigued.

The house echoed her artistic character. It was clean and cosy, softly lit with elegant wall up-lighters. A large pale Oriental beige and red wine coloured silk rug in the centre of the wooden floor and an antique spinet stood in one corner. There was a mixture of modern Italian beige leather furniture and two elegant antique cherry wood upright chairs.

"That was my aunt's." Sarah explained as his gaze lingered on the spinet.

"She left me the house and the contents. I auctioned off some of the pieces and others I kept that I really loved because they reminded me of her. I remember as a small child I used try and play the spinet and she used to laugh and try and teach me to play properly. She was a fantastic pianist. I wish now I had paid more attention to the lessons that she used to give me. But, I have promised myself that one of these days I will take lessons again and really learn to play it properly. Who knows I might even become a famous '*spinetist*,' if there is such a word," she said laughingly.

There were bookcases filled with all kinds of books. Framed posters of famous artists and it showed her intelligence, good taste, knowledge of what made her comfortable and what didn't. His eyes took in the framed pictures on the walls of her living room.

Well-seasoned Cedar logs waited for winter in a tall round wicker log basket by the large open fireplace in the lounge area. One corner of the large room that was slightly elevated was taken over by her computer on an attractive modern glass and brushed steel workstation. He noticed that a thick black file was neatly placed on one side and several disks were placed in a holder, next to two large dictionaries. A printer also stood on the workstation. He vaguely wondered what she needed it for. Everything was neat and orderly almost to the point of obsession. He actually knew very little about her he realised, she had never really been very forth-coming about her past life.

Sarah noticed him glancing at her computer.

"I write articles and suchlike occasionally for ladies' magazines in my spare time," she explained satisfying his curiosity.

"In fact I am writing a novel at the moment for my new publisher."

A great lump of a blue furred cat was moving on the comfortable modern Italian settee, he had jumped up onto it as David entered the room. Though it was of a modern style, somehow it was not out of place. Everything seemed to blend in so well.

"Let me introduce you to my lovely Picasso," Sarah said pointing to her cat lying lazily on the settee.

Picasso the cat looked suspiciously at David and narrowed his amber eyes and swished his tail and then yawned boringly.

"It would seem that you might have been accepted by him," she said softly.

David in his work had seen many women neurotically attached to their pets. Fat middle-aged women, thin middle-aged women and rich women, who turned to their dogs or cats for the warmth and affection that no lover could ever give them. But he knew this was not the case with Sarah.

As he sat down in an Edwardian chair by the window, the huge cat jumped onto his knees, and immediately started to tread him with his front paws. Then it turned around twice and settled into his lap.

"Well, Picasso certainly likes you, because that is his favourite chair, and he doesn't let just anybody sit in it!" she said teasingly as she leaned over towards David and kissed the tip of his nose affectionately and then lightly stroked his face, making his hairs stand up on end on his arm and ending in a blaze of fire along his skin. Desire hazed her eyes that sent a sensual message, loud and clear to him.

He wanted her there and then as he looked at Sarah and realised he was so very much in love with her, dreaming of some idea of living happily ever after as he liked the feeling of the domesticity around him that he nearly burst with pride at her comment. He wanted to close his eyes and feel her nearness, breathe in her warmth, but his gaze remained riveted upon the passion in her eyes and the softness of her breath as he breathed in her expensive heady perfume and he felt so lightheaded.

"Yes," he smiled awkwardly. "It would seem so. Mind you, I've never really been a cat person myself, but he is rather lovely! Unfortunately with my work load I don't have too much time for pets and I certainly couldn't have one in my apartment. Perhaps when I retire I shall refurbish my father's old house in the New Forest in the small village of Beaulieu and live there. Then I can have cats and dogs and maybe even a horse or two. I quite like parrots as well!"

"Oh, I didn't know you had a house in the country."

Of course she thought I do not really know a lot about him at all. Her interest quickened.

"Yes it was left to me, when dad died, but it is rented out at the moment to an old couple. They want to leave and move in with their daughter very soon in the village. So I was thinking of having it redecorated and using it for weekends. You know, get away from the City and relax a bit. Perhaps one of these days we could go and look at the place." He suggested.

"Yes, I would like that."

She looked at him through her long eyelashes. There was humour in his expression. Indeed, she could see the faint lines that would one day be permanently engraved between his nostrils and mouth. She knew the time was right now to invite him into her life.

She asked suddenly. "Would you like to have dinner with me here, tomorrow night or the night after, or whenever? I'm not a bad cook."

He nodded. "Thank you, I would love to."

She added hastily. "Well you don't have to give me your answer now. I think it is about time we left, don't you. Come on Picasso, David is all mine now!"

She bent over and lifted the large cat off his lap, kissed the top of his head and lowered him back onto the settee.

David smiled at her. "The day after tomorrow would be just fine."

CHAPTER NINETEEN

LONDON - 2004

The taxi driver dropped them off at the restaurant and as usual *Il Mondo*, one of David's favourite restaurants, was busy. The aroma of good food mingled with the cheerful voices of the diners and the romantic background Italian music that was piped through the many hidden speakers and the soft lighting, was so romantic.

The owner of the restaurant, who was very well known to David, smiled at him and escorted them to a table for two in a cosy corner and immediately beckoned to his maître d' to take their order.

"Shall I order for both of us, the food is excellent here?" Questioned David.

Sarah smiled at him and nodded her head. She liked the way he took over, but at the same time consulted her.

Without looking at the wine list or the menu, David ordered a bottle of Italian wine, a good Narkè Nero d'avola-Sirah bottled at Pollara in Sicily, and a bottle of Perrier water, a starter of smoked Gravalax with avocado and mango garnish and a fillet Mignon with baked vegetables and a side salad for both of them.

Sarah studied him across the table as he turned slightly and waved to someone he knew. He was wearing a black open-necked shirt with the cuffs rolled back exposing the corded muscles of his forearms, black trousers and Patrick Cox black leather casual shoes. He wore no jewellery, except a heavy gold Rolex and he looked very attractive and very impressive.

She liked that about him. But she knew that he was the type who tried to maintain a relatively low profile, because while he enjoyed interesting dinner partners and parties, he hated too much personal publicity and ever since his wife's death avoided very large society events, unless it was necessary.

At forty-five, he had lines bracketing his mouth and fanning the corners of his grey-blue eyes, but the years had not faded the faint smattering of freckles that showed beneath the tan on his handsome face. She wanted to reach over and touch his face. She kissed the index finger of her right hand and planted the finger on his lips.

He looked across the table into her deep blue eyes that reflected such genuine concern and reached over, covering her hand and feeling a heated rush to his core.

"Hey, what's all this serious stuff about?" He chided. "We're supposed to be having a romantic dinner; it is your birthday after all. Look, my darling, I have got a little something for you."

Sarah lowered her eyes and looked at his hand covering hers, the warmth from it seeping through her skin. She looked up and blushed, then smiled shyly.

He reached inside one of the pockets of his trousers and drew out a small box, gift wrapped in gold coloured paper and handed it to her.

She opened it carefully. Inside was a small black velvet covered jewellery box and lying inside on the soft cream satin was a brooch. It comprised of two diamond-studded hearts joined together and set in gold and small gold ivy leaves enamelled in green surrounded a fire opal twinkling in the centre where the hearts joined. It had a small gold link between the hearts so that it could also be worn as a pendant on a fine gold chain.

Tears rose in her beautiful eyes.

"Oh thank you." She breathed. "It's so beautiful, thank you David, but I cannot possibly accept this gift." She said putting one hand up to her cheek. She felt as if she was going to explode as the emotion rose in her chest.

"Why not? Of course you can, it is my way of saying that I love you. It was my mother's. I've had it cleaned and reset. My father had it especially made for her on their thirtieth wedding anniversary and she wore it all the time. I know that she would have wanted you to have it. My late wife never wore it. Unfortunately she died, as you know, before my mother could give it to her." He explained as he took her hand once again.

He beckoned to the young woman selling roses from a shallow wicker basket who had entered the restaurant. She came over and he bought all of the long-stemmed roses in the basket and handed them to Sarah.

Tears once more welled up in her eyes as she looked across the table at David and saw love shining from him. It took all her control not to burst out crying. He was such a wonderful man and she too loved him so much. She wanted to tell him about herself, her past and of the killings, but a warning voice inside of her said. *NO*, not yet.

Fortunately their food arrived at that moment and he released her hand, but continued to hold her eyes with his for several seconds.

"There's something I need to tell you." Sarah said earnestly. "I think I'm in love with you too."

"You think. You only think!" He chided as he smiled at her. "Don't you know?"

"Okay, I know," she whispered and they both burst out laughing at her shy reply.

They ate their delicious meal in silence looking up every so often at each other, not quite sure what to say next.

Sarah's eyes flickered away for a moment, by way of an apology. She smiled back blushing again. To make an end is to make a beginning, which is where she would start tonight, she vowed to herself.

David looked around the restaurant and recklessly called the waiter over to bring them a bottle of Veuve Cliquot champagne.

"I would say that we have more than your birthday to celebrate tonight, my darling."

CHAPTER TWENTY

LONDON - 2004

It was just after midnight when David and Sarah returned to his apartment. He held the door open for her and they stepped into the cool air-conditioned room, her high heels clicking loudly on the highly polished parquet flooring.

They stopped in the hallway and she looked at him and shivered with anticipation they both knew what they wanted as he led her to his bedroom and then he gathered her in his arms and folded her to him, holding and touching the fine mass of her blonde hair and gently pulling out the pins that held it up. He heard her murmur against his neck, but the words were lost. He took her face in his hands and his thumbs caressed her cheeks gently, his lips brushed hers with a gentle urgent kiss.

"Are you sure about this?" He asked gently.

She nodded silently as she felt that it would be right this time and her desire for David nearly consumed her as a slight moan formed low in her throat. She had the sudden urge to tear both of their clothes off to feel his hot flesh against her, his bare chest against her breasts. She ached to have him inside of her to fill the gaping emptiness that the desire for him had sparked so intently. She looked at the passion in his blazing blue eyes and knew that he wanted her as much as she wanted him and that their feelings for each other would last.

Gently pushing her away from him, he began to unbutton her lace blouse, easing it off slowly from her smooth shoulders. He pulled her soft hair to one side and bent his head slightly and kissed the curve of her smooth neck. All the time, she watched him through her long lashes and took a deep breath. She felt outside of herself as if the burning sensation of his touch was part of something else; it didn't seem real to her. She exhaled in a rush, her face on fire, her heart thumping wildly with the feelings rushing through her whole being.

He slipped the silk of her underwear down to her waist and the cool air against her warm skin made her shudder. His fingers teased her nipples, sending blinding waves of pleasure through her head, her stomach, and her groin. She watched him bend his head to her breasts, felt his mouth opening then closing, rolling her bare nipples around with his tongue. She touched his cheek and gasped with a surprised little whimper. He continued, his mouth on one breast, then the other, while his hands slowly stroked her smooth thighs, his fingers reaching higher and higher. He released her nipples and looked at her.

"What do you like?" he asked gently. "Tell me. I want to make you feel good. I want to make you feel wanted and loved."

She had no time to answer, his mouth came down on hers, easing it open. Her heart was pounding even more as her arms slipped around him. His tongue slid into her mouth and seemed to go darting right down through the centre of her body. It was unlike any other kiss she'd ever received from him. It was passionate, yet so full of tender feelings for her. Then he released her and stood looking at her, devouring her with his eyes. There was so much love as well as desire written all over his face.

She unfastened the catch of her skirt, letting it fall to the ground, then slithered the black silk thong she was wearing down over her neat hips. She was naked except for her high-heeled shoes and sheer black laced topped hold-up stockings.

Moving to her, he slowly ran his fingers the length of her body, trailing them over her nipples, around the curve of her breasts. He ran them down over her back and she arched slightly, tipping her head back. She was un-ashamed and her nakedness made her feel strong and alive and powerful. He caught her blonde hair at the nape of her neck and wound it around his fingers, pulling her head further back and making her arch her spine even more and press her hips towards him as he bent over slightly and kissed her mouth again. The intensity of their passion knocked them off balance for a moment. Gently he pushed her back against the living room wall, still kissing her, and then unfastened his trousers and released his throbbing manhood from his brief Calvin underpants.

He eased her legs apart and then pressed her hard against the coldness of the wall, lifting her slightly and holding her hips. He pulled her up towards him and plunged deep inside of her. She wrapped her legs around him and then cried out with sheer ecstasy.

Slowly he moved, gripping her thighs and digging his fingers into her flesh. She looked at him, her blue eyes wild and dark, her breath coming in short gasps, and he could feel her tightness and her wetness as one of his hands strayed down to her shaven pudenda, her excitement and the heat of her beautiful body fired his feelings of passion for her.

He pulled her tighter towards him, deeper and deeper, she edged her legs higher, his movements quickening, forcing her spine against the wall and her senses beyond control. Sarah began to moan with ecstasy .

Finally, he felt her shudder inside, her warmth and her release. He let himself go. His climax was almost painful in its intensity and he choked back his cries of ecstasy.

They stayed holding each other for several moments. He stroked her hair and felt her quiet sobs of relief. Eventually she was still and he tilted her chin up to look at her beautiful face. He kissed away her tears, tasting the warm salt of them. Carefully he moved to disentangle their bodies and put his arms around her. Then he picked her up and carried her inside to his bedroom and laid her on his king-size bed and removed her stockings and shoes. He undressed fully and lay down by her side.

Suddenly he felt her arms come around him with surprising muscularity and strength. She reared up over him and put her mouth down on his and kissed him, parting his lips and penetrating his mouth with her tongue.

David felt overcome with love for her again and pulled her towards him, and she came astride him at once, her arms wound tightly around his neck, her body strong and hot against his. As she kissed him, he felt her teeth graze his lips, and he groaned with overwhelming desire. Sarah slipped a hand down his body and grasped his semi-erect manhood, finding it and making it firm again ready to ease it inside her.

She lowered herself slowly onto him with a gasp and then moved, rocking herself faster and faster, making him even harder. The entrance between her legs were wet and, no longer tight.

This hot, sensual woman on top of him was a woman David did not recognise, but he knew, as he instinctively thrust upward, that she was what he wanted forever, he felt almost possessed by her, it was almost as if they were transported to another world as they again made passionate love together. In a blur of sensation he just followed the rapid, movement of her hips. He felt himself drawn in, demanded, and finally consumed.

She moved her weight slightly so their flesh was tantalisingly and irresistibly pressed together with an intimate smoothness and coolness that was turning to an all-consuming heat, as their bodies entwined into one being.

***

In the morning they showered together, laughing and tickling each other. Both knew that they had found their soul mates. They stepped out of the large shower cubicle and they towelled each other down lovingly, giggling like two teenagers.

Neither had ever felt like this before in any relationship and both knew that it would last forever.

"Are you hungry, my darling Sarah?"

"A little," she replied laughingly.

She felt that she didn't want food. She had all she wanted in him.

"I'll make breakfast for us."

"You can cook too! Have I at last found the perfect man?" She teased.

She sat opposite him in one of the brushed steel and mesh dining chairs at the stylish pale turquoise Calligaris glass-topped and brushed steel Italian kitchen table, wearing her short turquoise silk kimono sipping a cup of tea and watching him.

David devoured three eggs, four rashers of bacon, and three pieces of toast with marmalade, a glass of orange juice and two large cups of coffee.

"Do you always eat this much every morning?" Sarah joked.

"No, I hardly ever eat breakfast, it must be all the exercise I've been getting lately and not used to it you know!" He grinned cheekily at her.

She grinned back and blushed.

David stopped eating and looked across at her, he loved the way she blushed when she was embarrassed, he found it very becoming. Like a little girl who has been caught out doing something she shouldn't have.

"Come on, I should like to show you around properly, see if you like it, last time we really didn't get the chance...." He joked as he took her hand and they wandered around his big apartment hand in hand like two children gazing at the latest electronic game in a toyshop.

The enormous living room painted in off white, clearly reflected the fact that an architect and a good interior designer had given the place a makeover.

Narrow fluted columns separated the large room from the entrance, and the room itself had crown mouldings. There was an intricately carved black Carrera marble fireplace with a black glass-fronted gas fire with volcanic rocks carefully arranged inside that gave out convected heat when it was switched on. The floor was a satiny dark brown parquet. A beautiful multi-coloured Persian rug lay in the centre, two comfortable looking soft Italian cream leather sofas and armchairs, two carved Indian tables and brass oriental lamps inset with semi-precious stones. Elegant sliding glass doors separated the hi-tech kitchen from the living area. Both white bedrooms had en-suite bathrooms.

"Do you like it?"

They stood, still hand in hand, at the large double-glazed windows of the living room that were draped artistically with yards and yards of Italian hand woven cream muslin, looking out, and down over London.

"It's wonderful I love it and just look at the views. I love your terrace with all the plants on it as well." She said as she opened the sliding patio doors slightly and looked around at the penthouse terrace.

David put one arm around Sarah's shoulders and pulled her into his body.

"I love you so much, Sarah." He said seriously as he pushed a wayward strand of her hair off her cheek. "Don't ever leave me, will you? I want to take care of you. I want to be with you forever," he said as he pulled her closer to him and kissed her lovingly.

She thought where have I heard that before? Mark and Julio had said those very words to her. Isn't that what we all want though, someone to keep us safe! She had forgotten what it felt like to be watched over.

When her parents had died she was only in her teens, it had left its mark on her. Even when she had been married to her first husband and then to Mark her second, she'd never actually felt really protected. Both had been too self-absorbed in anyone except themselves. Maybe that was another reason that she had been so attracted to Julio, he too had said the same words. But in all fairness he had looked after her in the beginning and now David was telling her the same thing. Could it possibly be true this time, could it possibly last?

BOOK TEN

EXODUS Ch. 20 Verse: 13
Thou shalt not kill.

CHAPTER TWENTY ONE

LONDON - 2004

In the very early hours of the morning, the body of a young Albanian prostitute was found stabbed to death in the small churchyard of St. Anne's in the Soho area. She was discovered by an old wino who stumbled across her body when he was seeking shelter there in the doorway of the small church.

She was a tall, once very beautiful natural blonde girl, of around eighteen years old, dressed in a very short black leather skirt and she wore no panties. Her thin white see-through blouse and white brassiere were covered in blood. It had not been robbery as such, her small black leather shoulder bag lay by her side and the contents spilled out, her bulging wallet untouched. A black patent high-heeled shoe with a thin gold chain ankle strap was on her left foot and the other lay under the bushes nearby with its ankle strap broken. She was sprawled on the overgrown flagstone paved path in front of the entrance to the old church and there was blood all around her. It was a very vicious killing.

Several of the other working girls in the area said that she had probably been cheating on her pimp again by pocketing some of his money to feed her crack habit and that he had cut her up in order to show his other girls what would happen to them if they did the same.

One could tell by the rivers of blood that whoever had attacked her had done so with real anger and hatred. There was a terrible grimace on her once lovely face, and her lips and nose were split, smashed and clotted with coagulated blood. It would seem that she had also been tied up prior to her beating, possibly somewhere else, and then brought to the churchyard and stabbed several times. She had rope burns around her wrists and ankles, but no rope seemed to be lying around. It would also seem that it was not a sexual killing, she had not been raped.

A tall dark-haired man standing by, dressed in black, realized he had nearly been spotted as he watched the scene and just before the police arrived He dropped to the ground quickly and began clinging to the fence, never straying far from the shadows of the overhanging trees. It would be much safer not to be seen. Little tendrils of mist curled on the ground; like it did in the Dracula films he was so fond of watching. The setting was ideal.

Keeping in the shadows of the shrubbery and gravestones he quickly made his way to the front of the churchyard facing the street. A small crowd of curious people coming out of the clubs nearby had gathered near the body all wanting to have a look at her.

By the time the first police car had arrived, the tall man had made his way casually across to the other side. He lingered for a few moments in the dimly lit doorway of a sex shop across the road, cloaked in the semi-darkness and out of sight watching as another police car arrived. He laughed softly to himself and then went on his way, knowing that they would never trace the murder to him.

The police after a cursory investigation that only lasted a few days put it down to the kind of crime common amongst the new band of Albanian asylum seekers who had recently set up prostitution rackets in Soho. It was probably just a warning to the other girls not to play games with their pimps. They also knew that street girls were always being reported missing, they were not regarded as top priority, their lives were so precarious and they often led such transient lives that quite often their disappearance went unnoticed.

The matter would be sorted out in time by whoever was running the racket. It was the usual thing. Of course no one knew anything; there were no witnesses and there was no weapon to be found. The murder report only took up a small space in one of the tabloids four days later.

BOOK ELEVEN

EXODUS Ch. 20 Verse: 17
Thou shalt not covert thy neighbour's wife

CHAPTER TWENTY TWO

LONDON - 2004

Diana Gonzales stepped out of the shower, grabbed a nearby towel and dried herself quickly. Juan was away in America for a few days and she had decided to go and see a film in the West End on her own that started at 8pm and then treat herself to a meal afterwards. She had about an hour and a half to get herself dressed and she hummed softly to herself. She had some very good news to tell her husband and could hardly wait until he returned from New York.

She quickly put on a bra and panties and a cream silk robe and wandered into the kitchen and made herself a cup of coffee, reached for the Evening Standard and had a look at the film adverts. She thought she heard someone trying the lock of the front door and she listened intently for any sound that might suggest someone was in the apartment. Surely Juan hadn't missed his plane and come back early she thought and called out, but there was no reply. She dropped the paper back onto the table and stood up. Pulling her knee length cream silken robe tightly around her slim body, she cautiously made her way into the hallway.

"Hello Diana," said Julio quietly as he leered at her in her state of undress, stripping her naked with his bold stare.

She noticed the raw look of lust in his bright eyes and was suddenly aware of a terrible coldness in her stomach. Diana knew that she must try and stay calm. He looked as if he was high on something and she knew that she had to be very careful how she dealt with him in the kind of mood he was in. She had seen it before in the past.

"What? Why?" She wasn't sure what to say to him. "How did you get in Julio?"

She tried to stop shaking inside and sound pleasant as she stared at him with her pale brown eyes. She noticed he was carrying a large Harrods carrier bag.

"In case you've forgotten bitch, my father gave me a key to this apartment several years ago, before he married *you*. He forgot to ask for it back. I used to stay here when I was in London, but obviously I am not welcome here anymore," he said insolently.

"Oh, yes, I clean forgot that!" She stared straight through him.

How she loathed the tall, good-looking dark haired man standing in front of her leering at her. Try and be nice to him, she told herself again, do not antagonize him, offer him a glass of wine, maybe he was after money, or may be, he'll just go away.

"Uh...can I offer you anything, I'm just getting dressed to go out. We're meeting some friends for dinner. Your father will be back soon to change," she instinctively lied to him.

He came up closer to her and looked at her with his predatory eyes half closed. She knew at once that he did not believe her.

She tried again. "Would you care for a glass of wine, or a coffee? Please help yourself. I'm sure you know where everything is!" She stated somewhat sarcastically trying to feel brave.

He moved towards her and grabbed one arm and then slapped her across her lovely face.

"Liar, my father is not even in this country, I suppose you're going to meet your new lover, aren't you, or is he going to come here, otherwise you wouldn't have that sexy underwear on. Do you really think I don't know about you and your lovers?" He sneered. "Bitch, blonde English whore, I don't want my father's wine or coffee or even money and I have enough anyway!"

He pulled her towards him roughly and thrust his face into hers and hissed menacingly. "I want my father's bitch of a wife. The bitch who caused the death of my mother!"

Cold fear washed over her and she pulled back from him; now she was really scared, how much did he really know? What were the ramblings about his mother; obviously his drug filled mind had her confused with some other woman.

He knew she was frightened of him. He smiled evilly at her and advanced forward again. Her face looked so young and it was blotched with tears, but she looked different he noticed, she looked wiser as she looked at him. She stared hard at him, not as if his handsome face arrested her, but as if she could see into his evil soul and he was completely transparent; there was nothing there at all. He knew how she hated him for all the things he had done to his father over the years.

Diana tried to remain calm. Somehow she had to get rid of him.

"No, no you don't Julio. You don't want me. Besides you have never really liked me, have you?"

She started to back away from him and rushed into the lounge and tried to pull the door closed. She had just pushed it shut when she heard a footfall behind her and she froze, her heart thumping. She knew in that instant that she was not alone; he had come in from the door on the other side of the hall that led into their open plan dining room. She turned, halfway round.

"Slut," he said contemptuously as he approached her and lashed out at her again, his fist smashing against the side of her head.

He felt sexually frustrated as well as angry with her, and also angry with himself for desiring the woman he hated so much. He used to fantasize about screwing her when he was younger and here she was standing half-naked before him. He knew she was teasing him; she was just another whore to his drug filled mind and he had to rid his father of her forever.

Julio had played this game before with other women and had anticipated this time it could be something of a let-down as he did not feel completely in control of the situation. However, it might come as a pleasant surprise to find that it could be more of a thrill than the last time, especially as he was the killer and not just the spectator, and also because it was his father's wife and not one of his own girls! Once again he hit out at her and then laughed insanely.

Diana fell to the floor in a heap. The third blow was to the back of her neck and he hit the hand she had raised to protect her face and head and stunned her, sending her crashing forward.

She scarcely felt the third blow at all. Then she was trying to scratch his face, trying to roll away from him. She pulled and pushed and moaned and howled and fought trying to evade him as he bent over her. She was getting weaker, gritting her teeth, trying to scream out loudly in order that one of the neighbours might hear her.

He hit her again on the side of her head and darkness met her. She was drifting down a long dark corridor. Somehow she instinctively knew that it would be cold when she got there. Cold and safe and yet something was holding her back. There was something she had to do before she died, she had to let people know what Julio was, what a foul beast he was.

She knew she was going to die, she could feel the pain inside her, she was lying on the floor, it was so cold, all these years she'd had fears of dying in hospital of some disease or other not like this. Julio would not let her live she knew this, he had come to kill her, however, there was one last thing to do.

He bent down to pick up the large plastic Harrods carrier bag that he had dropped onto the floor beside her. Just as he had planned, he would follow the same procedure that he'd used before on the other women he had killed.

He would tie her arms and hands to her sides and then bind her legs together and truss her up so that when she came to and realised what was happening, she would be able to move a little, but not enough to save herself.

He did not gag her because as an added little something he had brought a full head black leather mask for her, she would be unable to speak through it. He thought that would be a nice touch, the police would have a field day, trying to understand why he had put a mask on her, when they eventually found her.

While he twisted the rope around her limp body, he explained to her why it was happening.

Julio had explained it to the others that he had killed over the years. After all she deserved to know that she too had become part of a ritual that he had undertaken to expiate the sins of his father, to avenge his biological mother, to pay his father back for what he had done to her.

Had he wanted to, he could have killed Diana there and then, but he wanted her to suffer, he knew he had only stunned her, and already she was beginning to stir. Now she was alert enough to absorb what he had to tell her.

Diana knew that she was utterly helpless and she did not want to listen or answer him, she tried to shut out the sound of his voice, as she knew this would make him angrier and frustrated.

"You do understand Diana," he began in a soft, easy, well-spoken reasoning tone. "I never would have harmed you, but you had to interfere. I know you have never liked me, but in fact I quite liked you. I still do." He lied.

"You are a very interesting and attractive woman, and very smart too. Perhaps you're too smart for your own good. I know you trapped my father into marrying you. I also know you got rid of the baby you told him you were carrying some time ago. You homed in on him when he was very vulnerable, very lonely. I know that you never really loved him; it was just his money and position that you were after. Well now you will have nothing, you'll be alone, dying slowly and painfully." He let out a weird laugh.

Then he explained and talked on about mutual trust, but a hint of irritation had crept into his tone at her failure to respond.

"Speak to me you bitch," he shouted angrily as he started to lose his composure.

She let out a whimper of pain, praying that someone would phone, perhaps even come to the door of the apartment and maybe ring the bell. She tried pleading with him to stop, but it was almost as if he was in a trance as he started to bind her up. He let out one of his manic laughs as he tightened her bonds and then he started humming a dirge as if in a trance.

He was so intent on what he was doing, he did not notice her pull the fine gold chain from his neck and hide it in her left hand.

He began to wind the rope around her upper arms, lifting her body roughly. She tried to kick out, but to no avail. She was lying in the big hallway. He dragged her into the master bedroom. Her silk robe had slid up her legs and over her hips, exposing her lovely scantily clad body in its lacy underwear to him. He looked down at her and felt himself harden. But he was not going to rape her that was not his style anymore. He pulled a pillow from the bed and placed it under her head, then dimmed the overhead chandelier. He liked soft light for his next actions, and whenever possible used candlelight.

He criss-crossed the rope over her upper body and then around her waist down her thighs and around her knees, the he began to tie Diana's legs together at the ankles; they were lovely long legs he thought, a bit like Sarah's. At the thought of Sarah, he became enraged and in his anger and he yanked the rope tighter than he intended as he recalled the months of passion with his precious Sarah. No one else was going to have her he would see to that. The two women seemed to have blended into one being. He was in a trance-like manner, oblivious to Diana's protests. Now he was on his knees beside her, leaning over her. His voice remained quite calm as he once more spoke to her and carried on with his work.

"I became quite a loner at school. You know my father sent me away to public school in England when I was very young, he really never wanted me, only my sister, but I expect you know all that, you slut."

Diana had come to completely now and her head was splitting with pain from the blows he had given her, she opened her eyes. Her brown eyes were full of fear. His face was only inches away

252

from hers. His dark eyes were glittering and shining with a kind of madness. He's mad, were her thoughts, God help me! Please Juan just phone me, please…anybody please ring me, please she pleaded silently.

"I have a shroud for you, very elegant, look, black, very chic."

He stood up, and she could see that he was holding up a long, thick black plastic bag. It was good thick plastic, the kind designed for thorns or garden rubbish in one hand and some kind of black mask in the other.

Oh my God, he's going to suffocate me. She thought.

Then he placed the black leather mask over her head and face and pulled it into place and fastened the zipper and the straps at the back tightly. The black plastic bag that he held came down over the mask and around her throat, hiding her face and neck and then he pulled it over her shoulders and down to her waist and down to her ankles.

She shrieked out her husband's name, but she didn't scream for long. Here in the darkness she was blind to whatever he was doing. She could sense his excitement at what he was doing to her.

He tied a piece of cord tightly around her neck and then at the bottom of the large bag. She was completely encased in the black plastic shroud and could feel herself suffocating. Her ears pounded with her panicked breaths and the thumping of her heart. And that was the point when she lost the will, as well as the means to resist. She struggled desperately for breath and could not find it. The sensation was not too different from having water in your nose and mouth while swimming, except that now she could no longer breathe.

Julio then started the kicking, judging the distance, changing the angle and then stamping on her body, deliberately, ritualistically. It took some time, this relatively quiet death. A pause to catch his breath, to listen, then more kicking; he heard his shoes connect with her bone, sinew and flesh until all her twitching, all her responses ceased. It took some time. In fact it had taken longer than usual. He realised that she was a very strong woman.

He listened again. There was the sound of a hi-fi from downstairs, a TV from upstairs, a door banged somewhere in the hallway, then there was silence.

Finally he knew that she was dead. He must act quickly he had a few more things to do.

As he walked into the hi-tech kitchen he donned a pair of surgical gloves from one of the pockets of the black jeans he was wearing and then searched through some of the kitchen drawers and cupboards until he found what he was looking for. He made his way back to his stepmother's body and finished his fiendish task. He then walked around the apartment and meticulously wiped over all the surfaces that he had touched. He even washed the dirty coffee cup lying on the side that Diana had been drinking out of and put it away. The newspaper that she had thrown to one side on the kitchen table, he threw into the garbage chute. The place was once more clean and tidy. He liked organization in his life. In fact he wondered sometimes if he was paranoid about it.

When he had completed his actions he walked quickly to the door and pulled it quietly behind him and made his way to the fire exit stairs. He descended three levels, and then entered the underground garage.

***

Julio drove off in the old grey metallic Ford Mondeo that he had borrowed and drove to the studio apartment in Soho that he used for some of his deals.

When he arrived back at the place, he disrobed himself and put on a pair of black stretch boxer shorts. He needed to cleanse himself.

He walked into his punishment room, that doubled up for the bathroom and in one hand he held a short heavy wooden handled flagrum - a short handled whip - with six plaited leather braids and small metal balls tied in at intervals and sheep's bones tied on the ends. There were twelve in all, one for each Disciple, and stained with a rust colour stain on the braids. The ninth metal ball symbolised Judas the Traitor. That had been painted black.

He stood in front of the mirror and began to flagellate himself across his back with the leather whip, over his left shoulder and then over the right shoulder. His arms rising and flexing smoothly, his biceps and deltoids began to sweat. Sweat had also broken out on his forehead, his face looked distorted in the long wall mirror as he watched himself.

When the rope struck his already well-scared skin on his back and thighs, the knotted rope made a thwacking sound causing deep stripe lacerations. He had done this many times since Sarah had left him, but never with such force.

He started mumbling as he scourged himself.

"Hear my prayer, oh Lord. I beg forgiveness, I beg for forgiveness. Punish me if you will. I have sinned again. "

Thwack, thwack.

The sting of the rope was like fire, like stinging nettles being whipped across his body. Both agonising and yet satisfying. He paused in his scourging and he felt a warm and comforting trickle down his bare back. Several of the metal balls had turned red with his blood. He turned his face up to the ceiling and cried out again and then fell sideways onto the cold tiled floor and passed out.

Two hours later he came too and picked up the leather whip and put it back into its hiding place behind the bath panel and then showered his tortured body. He knew he had done something to deserve the cleansing, but he had no recollection of what it was.

CHAPTER TWENTY THREE

LONDON - 2004

Paul's mobile phone rang out loud and clear. He groped wearily for it on the passenger seat. He was just on his way home for a light snack and hopefully some sleep. He looked across momentarily at the number on the screen and decided that he had better answer it, as it was his Superintendent. He could ignore it of course and say that he had left his phone in the car or the battery was flat, but his instinct told him that it could be very important, so he pulled into the side of the road.

"Forrest here, yes sir." He said as he glanced at his watch. It was just after 12.45 pm.

"Paul we've got something for you. There's been another killing, but this time it is a very respectable woman in an apartment in Grosvenor Square, owned by the Spanish Embassy, I want you over there as quickly as possible. The body is upstairs. I need you to go there right away. Murdered woman in a mask I believe. Apparently the concierge received an anonymous phone call and he reported it to us after he found the door to her apartment slightly open on his security round. This is an important killing!" His Superintendent informed him. "It will need to be kept under wraps for a while. You know what embassy people are like!"

Paul cradled his phone between his shoulder and his ear and was scribbling furiously on an address pad that he always kept in the glove compartment of his car.

"Mask?" Queried Paul, what kind of mask? He wondered if there was the faintest possibility it could be connected to the other bizarre killings of late.

"Yes, a bondage mask, executioner's type mask, some black leather shit, call it whatever you want. Someone has killed her and left her half naked. It looks like he strangled her and then cut off her left hand. Forensics are at the scene already. Get your own team together and tell them they're on overtime."

He paused.

"Be careful how you treat this one, she is the wife of the Spanish Ambassador, Senor Juan Carlos Gonzales who's away in America at the moment. Obviously he'll have to be told as soon as possible. The new concierge found her about an hour ago when he was doing a security check someone had phoned him anonymously, so he checked it out. As I said, make sure it is kept under wraps for the time being though, no media involvement. Diplomatic immunity! Seems she was wrapped up in a black plastic bin bag, very bizarre. Anyway get over there as quick as you can."

Paul sighed as his Super rang off and dropped his mobile back onto the passenger seat. He wondered what was happening in the World. Life seemed to be so cheap these days he thought as he made a quick U- turn and drove towards the West End of London.

***

Three wide pink marble steps led up to the entrance of the foyer of the luxury block of apartments - Sorrento Towers, in Grosvenor Square and the entrance surrounds were also in the same pale pink Carrera marble with patinated bronze and glass automatic doors.

As Paul entered through the automatic sliding doors he looked around at the opulent foyer. It was decorated in French art deco style, again reflecting the pink and the bronze. The foyer also boasted a long low black Japanese lacquered table with an expensive floral arrangement on it and several up market magazines. The table stood on a large and very expensive decorative Oriental multi-coloured rug. Large potted palm plants were scattered around artistically and two deep black leather sofas were placed nearby unoccupied. A big black marble sign with carved letters in gold leaf on the wall read: –

ALL VISITORS PLEASE REPORT TO THE DESK

The concierge sat behind an attractive black and gold art deco desk with a small, computerised switchboard on the top and two security screens. He was a heavy set man in his late forties, with dark curly hair, scattered with quite a lot grey, a jaw that needed a shave and a greying moustache that covered his top lip and drooped slightly at the ends. He was dressed in a smart maroon uniform with gold epaulets.

He looked Paul over suspiciously.

"Excuse me, to whom are you visiting?" The man's tone was very guarded.

He had a heavily accented voice, possibly Eastern European, perhaps an asylum seeker, who knows Paul, thought? He would certainly check him out later as he seemed to be very nervous.

"I am visiting the murder scene. Was it you who reported it? I'm DCI, Forrest," he stated slowly as he showed him his police ID.

"Ye… ye...yes Sir," he stuttered nervously his eyes darting about. "I received a telephone call from someone and went upstairs and found her dead on the floor. My God, I have never seen a dead person before. She is in number 10, the fourth floor. The lifts are over there." He said pointing with a shaky hand to a bank of three lifts.

He started wringing his hands together as he spoke and Paul felt a bit sorry for him, but he did not wish the man to see that his guard was down and thanked him and walked over to the lift area with its pseudo art deco gold coloured wrought iron and decorative safety glass doors, he entered one of them and pressed number 4. The lift was there in seconds. Part of the fourth floor was already taped off.

Yellow and black Crime Scene Incident tape had been tied across the hallway of the fourth floor cordoning it off and outside of the apartment ten stood a young, pale faced uniformed policeman.

Paul wondered if it was his first murder case from the look of him. He was glad to see that there were no nosey neighbours about, but it would seem that each floor only contained two apartments and the type of people that owned or rented the expensive apartments he guessed were not the kind to want any publicity and preferred to be kept out of the media's eyes. In any case they probably wouldn't have helped in his investigations, the very wealthy did not like anyone encroaching on their territory and privacy and least of all the police.

Paul flashed his ID again and the young policeman looked intently at Paul's identification.

"Good morning, Sir," he said as he handed him a pair of blue latex surgical gloves and disposable blue covers for his shoes from a small collapsible table that had been placed by the door. Paul put the gloves in the right pocket of his dark grey suit and then bent down and pulled the covers over his expensive leather shoes.

"This way please, sir."

The young policeman opened the door of the air-conditioned apartment for his superior. Paul absorbed the feel of the luxury apartment as he entered it. Expensively, but very tastefully decorated, obviously with the help of a very upmarket interior designer and very choicely furnished. He had an acute sense of colour and noticed that nothing clashed. The little comfortable, elegant feminine touches showed that the owners were very fastidious, but certainly had style.

The apartment was also meticulously clean and tidy. Someone has tidied up after the murder, he thought as he pulled on the gloves, the latex making revolting kissing smack noises as he did so.

He nodded a greeting to the few that he knew as he passed them. The Forensic Pathologist and three other people were dressed in the mandatory white forensic suits; pale blue masks around their noses and mouths and also wore blue latex gloves and blue shoe covers.

One of the men was the podgy little photographer, Sean O'Farrell, about Paul's age. He was one of the best in the business. He was clicking the camera and zooming and panning and had shot off thirty-six frames of the apartment within minutes. Another smaller camera also hung from his waist.

Paul patted him on the back with a friendly gesture and exchanged a few words. One of Paul's trademarks was the number of photographs he insisted upon when he was investigating a murder case and the short little Irishman was certainly the person for that. Various pieces of equipment were placed in strategic places in the apartment. Video, still camera tripods, boxes with chemical sprays, masks and long trailing electrical cords for other electronic equipment.

Sean looked across at Paul and winked his left eye. He knew from experience and working with the DCI that he could take one look at a crime scene and tell you things the forensic people would never find with all their fancy equipment. He seemed to have a natural instinct where murder was concerned.

Sean had first met Paul when he was a policeman on the beat working his way up to DCI and they had often worked together over the years. They had seen a lot of crimes in the time they had worked together and had learned a lot during those years.

Paul then headed for the crime scene where a short man with sloping shoulders in a white forensic suit crouched over the body. Although his back was to him, the slightly balding salt and pepper hair gave away the man's identity, Ian McAlistair the pathologist.

The near naked body of the woman was stretched flat on her back on the parquet floor of the luxurious master bedroom, bathed in light from a nearby up-lighter. She had been artistically arranged so it would seem.

She wore a brief pair of white lace panties with a matching bra and her cream silk robe was smoothed out and laid beneath her. Her unseeing pale brown eyes that stared through the slits of the black leather mask that hugged her entire skull were fixed on the ceiling, their gaze lifeless, yet mysterious. He could not see her mouth because it was locked behind a metal zipper.

The mask, with its uncanny power, disturbed him, yet at the same time fascinated Paul. The object suggested absolute evil and perversion. Her body was in good shape, well exercised and slim, the body of a woman in her late thirties, but she was already stiffening with the onslaught of rigor mortis. A large black plastic bag had been folded and bagged up ready for examination at the forensic laboratory and lay near the body.

Paul knelt down for a closer look. The mask still disturbed him even though he was curious. It suggested evil and was obscene. With the stopping of her heart, gravity had pulled the blood to the lower part of her body, causing dark discolorations to the parts lying downside.

Her chest was covered in several cigarette burns, probably done after her death. The victim's left hand had been cut off. From the look of the shear marks on the startlingly white wrist bone a small electric saw or electric knife had been used for the job. Her right hand was is in a tight fist. There were several contusions on her body where it looked like she might have been kicked viciously.

On her right toe a tag had been tied already. The tag was a standard department form with the number **1057/01-2330** on it. The Pathologist had also filled in the time of discovery and other relevant details.

Professor Ian McAlistair, the Pathologist, was a short man in his late forties with receding mousey hair and eye lids that drooped sadly over his brown eyes that caused him to always look mournful, he was kneeling over her as he opened the side zipper on the mask to examine the dead woman's lips. He turned her over slightly and undid the straps and opened the zipper at the back and carefully lifted the grotesque thing from her face and called to Maggie from Forensics and handed it to her to be bagged up for examination later. Then he lowered the victim again onto her back.

"Why the mask Ian? What the hell's that all about? And why has that black plastic bag been bagged up? Is there some significance?" Asked Paul as he looked down at Diana Gonzales, her still waxen face under the fake tan was expressionless and her open eyes were already filmy with the cataracts of death.

"Maybe the killer wanted to protect her face for some reason. Perhaps he wanted her unblemished and recognisable. Maybe he is into that sort of thing. Who knows? What kind of evil person does this to someone so lovely anyway? "He sighed loudly.

The black plastic bag was already folded neatly and laid under her head.

"What a waste for someone to be killed like this," Paul exclaimed as he shook his head in disbelief, more to himself than to anyone else. Then he repeated it once more distinctly.

"What a damned waste, what kind of bastard would do such a thing? Any idea of when she died Ian?"

"At this point in time, it is very difficult to tell the exact time of death, but I would think anywhere from five to twelve hours ago, she's not stiff yet. Certainly not more than twelve," he replied in his soft Scottish voice.

"How was she killed do you think?"

McAlistair looked closely at her slender throat and exclaimed dourly. "Well subject to the autopsy report, I would say at this point in time, fracture of the cervical vertebrae."

"You mean strangled?" Paul asked with a grin at the Pathologist's exacting answer.

"Yes, if you say so!"

"Was she a user?"

"Again subject to the autopsy and a blood test, I haven't the faintest idea! Come and see me tomorrow afternoon. She has no obvious track marks anywhere. My gut feeling is that the person who did this is a psycho. It's all too clean. She was laid out like this. The apartment looks as if it has had a complete spring clean. For certain she has someone that comes in regularly, these are service apartments, but if that was the case she would have been found earlier, more like the killer did it, in my opinion! He could even be the person who rang the desk clerk anonymously."

Paul bit his bottom lip for a moment, his thick eyebrows working like a pair of caterpillars. He nodded in agreement, but said nothing. He had his own ideas. Something triggered a memory he had seen something like this before, a few years ago, when the crime scene had been cleaned up. The case was still unsolved.

Sean, who had quietly approached the dead body, was snapping pictures of the woman from every angle.

Paul walked over to Maggie Ferraro from the Forensic team, with a blue paper mask over her nose and mouth, she was now kneeling down and taking scrapings from the floor, searching for blood and semen using a portable UV lamp and wearing side-shield orange goggles for protection.

Methodically the other member of the team, a serious looking youngster with dark brown erect and thickly gelled hair, whom he had not met before, also wearing a blue mask, dusted for fingerprints and vacuumed for hair and fibres. A powerful ALS lamp hung from the strong leather holster around his waist. He looked like he was just out of school. Paul suddenly felt very old and tired. The young man could almost be his son.

"Are there any signs of forced entry?" Paul asked him.

"No, none that I can see, but these locks are the kind you could open with a credit card anyway. Ridiculous in a high security place like this isn't it!" The young man replied scornfully.

"What's your name son?" Snapped Paul

"Andy, Sir." He replied smartly aware that he might have been too brash with his answer and upset his senior officer.

Paul moved over to the other side of the room without replying. What did he know, he thought, he may have passed all his exams and got his degrees, but he could be a little more polite. The young man would soon learn.

"What have you got Maggie? " He asked quietly as he openly admired her good looks. He knew he was out of her league, but he was really keen on her and would like to have asked her out sometime, he knew that she didn't have a steady boyfriend.

She was half Sicilian and half English, tall and all legs. She had the Mediterranean olive skin colouring, long dark hair tied back, and pushed into her cap, high cheeks bones and her strange green eyes were slightly tilted and just close enough together to give her an odd, yet very arresting feline look.

He visualised her full red lips beneath the blue mask. She was a tall, well-shaped woman of thirty that men watched, even when she was not wearing figure-hugging clothes, she somehow even made the white forensic suit look sexy on her.

He wondered as always, how such an attractive young woman could lose herself in such a job. At times she had an off-putting look about her when she was involved in a case, but she was very, very good at her job and would go far, he was sure. He had heard recently that she was going for a professorship.

"Not a lot sir. As my boss would say, see me tomorrow or later today." She gave him a weary smile.

Paul's eyes darted from side to side as he spoke, taking in every detail of the scene before speaking to the team.

"Okay everybody, may I have your attention, please listen very carefully. I want to ask all of you here not to talk about anything you have seen here today. We want to keep this murder under wraps, out of the media's claws for the time being. Only the killer and the concierge besides us know about this murder. Don't worry about him. I will sort the concierge out. The success of this operation is going to depend on your co-operation. There is a possibility this could be, and I repeat **could** be, in some way connected to our recent murders. Though whoever did this has changed their tactics quite drastically. But I just have this gut feeling. Okay guys and girl, let's finish up now, there's not a lot more we can do here until later today."

He instinctively knew that this case would cause a few ripples and the Home Office wouldn't be too pleased with things especially as the victim was the wife of a very well-known and important foreign Diplomat.

The Forensic Crew nodded their heads in agreement. They were used to this sort of thing, no one spoke, each one absorbed in their own thoughts, all they wanted to do was to get back to their comfortable homes and try and finish their job later. They started to pack up their gear.

There was a staccato knock at the front door of the apartment. Andy opened it to admit two crime scene men, one carrying a portable gurney and the other a folded black zippered body bag. They ducked under the crime scene tapes across the doorway and walked towards the lounge. They opened out the body bag, lifted the body carefully into it and zipped it closed and then onto the stretcher and wheeled it out into the empty corridor towards the garage lifts, to where the Coroner's black vehicle was waiting in the underground parking.

***

Paul stepped out of the lift on the ground floor and made his way quickly to the concierge's desk. His forehead was knitted, with a frown, his thatch of brown hair looked ruffled, his blue-grey eyes were thoughtful, and his shoulders hunched forward as the fingers on his left hand drummed the desk. The concierge looked at him with a frightened look on his face as if he had been could in the act of doing something suspicious.

"Who has the master key to this complex?"

"I have one, sir," mumbled the concierge.

"What's your name?"

"Ayden, sir."

"Okay, Ayden, I am going to ask you again. Where is the master key kept?"

"Here in this drawer, but it is always kept locked."

He looked at Paul with frightened eyes, thinking that perhaps he had forgotten to lock it.

"Do any of the residents have a master key?"

"No sir, maybe, but I do not know for sure."

"Where is the master key now Ayden?" Smiled Paul, as he tried to put the nervous man at ease.

"It is here sir, in this drawer." He fumbled with the lock of the drawer with a short thick key that was chained to his waistcoat and then pulled it open.

Paul started drumming his fingers again as he looked inside, there was a small cash box in the drawer unlocked and open, inside was the master key. So anyone knowing that could have reached over and taken it, or had it copied, unless the intruder had a separate key to the apartment. Did she know her murderer? He wondered.

"Did anyone come to visit her today?" Paul asked.

Ayden shook his head. "I do not know."

"Did you notice any strangers going in or out of the building over the weekend?" He asked.

"Strangers, there are always strangers in the building. You know visitors, maintenance men, etc. Yesterday six or seven people came in and out." He made an expressive movement with his hands as he shrugged. "I do not know."

"Who were they?"

"I tell you. I do not know, maybe residents!"

270

"Which residents?" Paul was really getting annoyed with the man and trying to hold his temper. He reckoned Ayden was obviously trying to hide something from him, but what?

"Sir, I tell you sir, I do not know. The ones who did not go away maybe, it is a weekend you know! I am very busy, there is always something, a water leak, the lifts do not work properly, and these rich people need much looking after. All the time they want something. Anyway nobody could come in without me seeing him or her, but I am new here, I do not know all of them." He complained in a whining voice and ran a hand nervously through his thick black curly hair.

He was beginning to get on Paul's nerves with his whining, but he knew that if he pushed the man too far, he would clam up.

"The garages here? Could you see anyone coming in?" He asked patiently

"Yes, they have electronic remotes to open the doors. Sometimes I can see them."

"How are the garages guarded? What kind of security is there?"

"CCTV, there is a camera on every floor in the hallways. There is one opposite flat 10. The residents can see the garage on their TV sets in the apartments and one down here." He pointed to the wall next to him. "Also there are two monitors on my desk. Also I can see the underground garage."

"I presume that you can give me the tapes. What about fire escape stairs? Any cameras there?"

"No."

271

Again the man looked frightened, he was not sure that the video unit in his small office had even been switched on, let alone had any tapes in it.

"What about a laundry room? The dustbin area?"

"No laundry room here, washing machines in apartments or they use dry cleaning services that I deliver personally. Dustbins, they have garbage chutes. They put everything in thick black plastic bags and in the chutes in their kitchens, then cleaning ladies put garbage in the bins in the room in the garages." The man seemed exasperated with all the questions.

"Where do the bags go?"

"I do not know, there is a private contractor, he collects all the garbage, three or four times a week, is not my job. I am only here one week, please sir, I do not know everything."

Paul studied the swarthy man. He thought he could possibly be from Turkey with his accent and he noticed that his hands were trembling, he would definitely check him out, he seemed to be afraid of the police and he knew the man was lying about something, he seemed so very nervous. He had been a policeman long enough to know that ninety percent of people lied. However, lying did not necessarily make a person a killer.

"Do you have a list of the names of residents?"

"Yes sir, in the drawer, with visitors' book."

He handed a black and gold hardback book to Paul.

Paul studied the book for a few moments and then looked at him.

"Thank you. I will take this with me and return it tomorrow morning. Oh, by the way, have you got a work permit Ayden?" He asked softly as he noticed the man's face flush red. "Also have you got the tapes please, or discs or whatever. Oh! And one last thing, do not, and I repeat do not mention anything to the Press at this point of time if they approach you. It would not be a good idea!" He threatened.

"See you tomorrow morning. Remember do not talk about what has happened. Do you understand? By the way to you want me to sign for this?"

The concierge nodded and his right eye twitched nervously, not missed by Paul before he turned and stepped into his office to fetch the security tapes of the garage and the hallways.

***

As Paul sat in his car he wondered if in fact the killer was still hanging around the apartments watching somewhere. Was he relishing what he had done that evening? Was his blood lust sated, or was his need to kill heightened by the act itself. Quite often killers would hang around or even come back to the scene later on or the next day out of curiosity to see what was going on. He pushed the visitors' book under the front seat and decided that he'd had enough for the time being.

Frustrated and melancholy Paul finally gave up for the night and went home to his small flat in Hammersmith. It was around nearly five thirty in the morning and he realised that he had not eaten all day. He ate a Chinese microwave meal from his freezer, took a beer from the refrigerator and opened it and then settled down on the floppy old settee in his tidy lounge. He clicked the remote control on the coffee table in front of him and chose an old black and white film on channel five, one he had seen several times before. He took a long swig of his beer and lay back on the settee.

Closing his eyes he drifted exhausted into a deep sleep. It was almost seven in the morning, when he awoke feeling cold and crawled into his bed. He set the alarm for eight am and turned out the light. After a few moments he gave up trying to sleep, got out of bed and made a cup of coffee and took it back to bed with him. He would speak to McAlistair again, he would go to the apartment again, and have a good look around. There was something, but what? What had he missed? It worried him.

He reset the alarm for eight forty five. At last sleep came and he dreamed of Diana's twisted and mutilated body.

CHAPTER TWENTY FOUR

LONDON - 2004

At exactly ten thirty the next morning, Paul entered the bedroom of the diplomat's murdered wife with Detective John Rivers and Detective Tony Smith hoping to find some evidence that he might have missed the night before.

John Rivers was a big redheaded paunchy man; around six foot four with florid colouring, small pale blue eyes and a thin mouth. He was a very outspoken Scotsman at times who had missed out on promotion because of it. But nevertheless he was a very good detective. People often felt intimidated in the tall man's presence and this helped him to get results. The detective walked through into the living room.

Paul stood alone in the bedroom, the sunlight glaring through the large triple-glazed window as he pulled on his blue latex gloves. He was working now, stirred by the sense of something secret waiting to be found, a sense that was tantalizing and almost sexual, in its excitement. He thought he could detect the slight smell of stale cigarette smoke, being a reformed smoker his sense of smell was very acute and he thought the smell was probably from a Marlboro' red cigarette. He shrugged his shoulders, maybe the diplomat smoked cigarettes, but he had not seen any ashtrays around the apartment.

He looked around the luxuriously furnished bedroom, seeking some object, some detail that bore the imprint of what had happened the night before. The chalked outline of the woman's body stood out on the dark brown parquet floor. It was strange there was no blood on the wooden floor. Blood was very difficult to wash away, he thought. There was usually some sort of trace of it. Maybe he had put something under her. But why? That was one of the things that had worried him during the night. Why had the killer cleaned up after him? So far he'd not got the Forensic report. He could find nothing untoward. Then his eyes turned towards the ornate wooden door, something had caught his attention.

Paul swung the door open. In the crack just below the bottom hinge something small and dark was glistening in the sunlight. He put on a pair of latex gloves and took a ballpoint pen from his jacket pocket and bent down, using the tip of his pen he gently poked the dark thing. A tiny piece of black plastic fell to the floor. He picked up the fragment, turned it over in his hands and tested the thickness between his thumb and forefinger. It was a piece of a very thick plastic dustbin bag. He dropped it into a clear plastic evidence bag and sealed it and put it in one of the pockets of his jacket.

"Have you found anything yet John?" He shouted through.

"No, but I'm going to have a good look around," he stated as he made his way through the kitchen towards the fire exit.

John entered the room a few moments later, also holding two small evidence plastic bags.

"I found this caught on the rail of the fire exit stairs opposite the lifts. What d'you think?" He asked as he waved a small piece of black plastic in the air. "Also a butt end of a Marlboro' cigarette, could be the killer's, should get some DNA off of it." He said as he handed the bags to Paul.

"Snap, I found a small piece of black plastic too," said Paul. "It's probably a bit of heavy duty plastic dustbin bag. I reckon the killer suffocated her in the big plastic bag after he had beaten her up and she was probably unconscious at the time. She probably gained consciousness at some point, possibly still in the bag and then he cut off her hand later in the bag, before taking her out and arranging her body on the floor."

"Presumably he wrapped the missing hand in another smaller plastic bag. Also another reason for no blood around, because he killed her first and then later sliced her hand off when she was dead, hence also not too much blood. There should be a lot of blood in the folded bag that we found, but that will belong to the victim; he probably put the saw in the bag too. So the killer didn't hide the body, but hid the saw, or whatever he used, what kind of mind does he have? I really don't like this case; there are too many unknowns in this one." He shook his head with disbelief. "I don't know. There are certainly some *nutters* walking around out there! That's great about the cigarette end, well done. Let's hope it was his. Could be anyone's though and hopefully there is some known DNA on it."

"Sir, we have a very bizarre killing here, but it is almost theatrical, what do you think? The person was probably drugged up to the eyeballs anyway!" John said with a grimace of distaste on his unsmiling face. "As you say there are certainly some nutters around."

"Yes, you're right. But I don't think it was just a random killing, I have the feeling that she knew her killer and let him in. Maybe they were having an affair. Maybe she was into kinky sex. Who knows? There are going to be a lot of maybes and ifs and buts in this case."

Paul told him what he had seen the night before. Describing the mutilation to the lovely woman, reviewed what he had found and walked John Rivers through the apartment.

"I want you to canvass the area. Go around the residents of the block, probe a bit deeper, but do it as tactfully as you can, you know what the rich and powerful are like. Take that MP for instance who lives downstairs, I bet he's got a thing or two to hide from his wife."

"Cover the neighbourhood and see if any of the local toms and perverts, winos, storekeepers noticed anything. Choose whom you like to assist you, but I want to know as soon as you have any information. Young Tony Smith might be a good one to go around the gay bars. You never know the killer could be gay, might have a thing against pretty women. Who knows? Okay then on your way, see you later."

Paul paused as he remembered something.

"Oh! By the way, check out the concierge's office and cameras, and see if there were any newer films hidden away somewhere that he didn't give me. The couple that he gave me probably won't be of much use. You know what these places are like. I

278

think he is hiding something from us. Maybe there weren't even any up to date films. Maybe he didn't even have a video cassette in the machine. Could be some of the cameras have even been disabled. He doesn't seem to have any record of anything, I am also very sure that he is an illegal. Can you check through your connections, I don't think our records are very up to date? I don't trust the other concierge either. I want you to run a Home Office check on both of them as well."

Paul took the see-through plastic bags from Rivers and put them with the other in his jacket pocket to give to Forensics.

***

Paul felt he had been poking through the kitchen cupboards for ages, but his eyes kept going back to the dishwasher. It was in fact only ten minutes when he looked at his watch.

A coat of grey fingerprint powder lay on the tops of the door handles in the kitchen as well as the refrigerator, sink and cabinets and the dishwater. He studied the stainless steel fronted dishwasher and on impulse pulled down the door and searched through the dishwasher, then he gave the upper tray a forward tug; it glided out easily and he set it on the floor. He pulled on the lower basket that held plates and the like. It slid almost all the way out and then it got stuck although it was empty. He pulled at it again and this time felt a firm resistance, then he reached a hand in and probed about and came out with a small neatly coiled bundle of black insulated electric cord that was jamming the lower tray. He gave it a good tug and pulled out the lower basket completely and set it on the floor as well, then knelt down in front of the machine.

The water sprinkler, shaped like a small propeller sat in a recess on the floor of the machine. He peered closely at it and then it hit him, only two of the blades belonged to the machine the third that was wedged into the hollow beneath was part of a blade from an electric knife.

The other detective, Tony, young very good looking, effeminate man, had just entered the kitchen and stood to one side and bent over for a better view. He had short blond spiky gelled hair, and a lean-cut tanned face, quite a pretty face in fact for a man, intelligent dark brown eyes and long sensitive fingers. He wore a discreet gold earring in his left lobe.

"Here, have a look at this Tony," exclaimed Paul.

"Umm…Braun, one of the best electric knives. That was rather careless of someone, sir!" He commented as he took the broken blade in his thin-gloved hands. "This will cut bone, all right. Strange thing to have in a dishwasher though! I always wash mine by hand so that it will not get blunt. I wonder where the rest of it is?"

"Probably in one of the drawers of the kitchen units," Paul commented as he took the blade and the coil of insulated cord from him and bagged them up individually.

Tony looked in a couple of the kitchen drawers and came out with the rest of the electric knife with only one cutting blade in it. He shuffled the kitchen tools around but could not find the other part of the blade.

"Well look what I've found." He stated and handed it to Paul, who bagged it as well.

"By the way sir, I've got a couple of plainclothes guys outside, they're doing the rounds. So far we've managed to keep the Press out of this one."

Paul nodded his head. "Good thinking Tony, thanks."

As a final step the police rang the doorbells of all the apartments in the block. The questions were simple. Had anyone noticed anything unusual or any strangers in the building on Friday night or Saturday morning? They had not really expected any success from the kind of people that lived in the exclusive apartments. They led their own private lives and did not want any interference from the police or any publicity. They knew they would not get much information from them. Friday night had been dark and cold. High shrubbery around the building would have made it possible for anyone who did not want to be seen to stay waiting in the shadows.

CHAPTER TWENTY FIVE

LONDON - 2004

Paul paced up and down while he waited in the V.I.P. lounge at London Heathrow Airport for Senor Juan Gonzales. This was the part of his job that he hated, telling people that their loved ones had been murdered and needed to be identified.

He saw a tall man with dark curly hair greying at the temples, come through the barrier carrying a laptop bag in one hand and in the other a very expensive designer overnight bag. He had an arrestingly handsome tanned face and dark penetrating eyes. He knew instinctively that he was the husband of the deceased. He didn't need to hold up his idiot board that had the Diplomat's name on it that had been given to him, so he tore it in half and discreetly dropped it into a nearby waste bin.

"DCI Paul Forrest, sir," He said quietly to Juan as he stepped forward with his right hand extended.

"I have been sent by New Scotland Yard to escort you to the mortuary. I am so sorry, but we do need you to give us a positive identification. I hate to press you Senor Gonzales but I have a car waiting outside. Do you have any other luggage?' He noticed the strong grip of the Diplomat as they shook hands.

"No, I don't, this is it. Shall we go?' Juan said quietly.

Paul thought how tired the poor man looked. His handsome face now appeared haggard and grey under the harsh airport lighting.

Even though Paul had a gift for getting on well with people, it was always difficult in the face of an investigation, especially in the death of a loved one and even more difficult when it involved foreign diplomats and it was a murder case. They always kept a low profile when it came to police matters and this man he knew was no exception.

***

The mortuary attendant slowly raised the white sheet and pulled it off Diana's face down to her neck and folded it back neatly.

Juan's face looked thin and sallow under the stark mortuary lights and he could feel the waves of shock hit him as every atom of colour was driven from his face. He felt nauseated and swayed and thought he would pass out.

Death always caught people unawares. Those moments when one knew life was not forever, Paul thought, as he steadied the shocked man. He looked distraught, sick, and nervous. He looked like a man whose life had been completely shattered in a matter of seconds. Which of course it had!

The look on Juan's face was the same if not worse that Paul had seen on countless people who had to identify a victim close to them. It was filled with pain and confusion about how someone they had loved so fiercely could have been ripped away from them through no fault of their own. The last time Paul had seen anyone so grief-stricken was when he was a much younger policeman and had to tell his friend David Myers that his wife was dead.

Since then he had seen countless deaths, but he had never really got used to it. Paul was pleased to note that the diplomat's wife's arms were well tucked in under the sheet that covered her bruised body. At some point he knew he would have to mention the missing hand to the husband.

As Juan looked down at his dead wife he smiled weakly. The overhead light shone down squarely on her face, even in death she was beautiful, and she just looked as if she was asleep. He choked back a sob. He could not speak and he gasped at her smooth skin, her drawn back blonde hair. He had always liked it done that way. Her full lips were slightly parted as though in surprise. He reeled backward as he felt his limbs suddenly boneless and he had the dizzying sense that he was floating away, his body felt as if it was no longer anchored to the tiled floor.

Paul Forrest standing by his side reached out and with a strong hand grasped his arm, steadying him.

Juan had forgotten he was there. Looking down at Diana was surreal, like a bad dream. He saw everything through a haze of exhaustion. His body was still functioning on New York time where it was now about eight hours behind. He thought. I was only walking down the busy streets of New York several hours ago, towards Saks to get a present for her. Less than twenty-four hours ago when I got the call from London. How did I manage to be here looking down on my dead wife now? This is really and truly surreal, I'm asleep in a jet somewhere, and I've been working too hard. I'm having a bad dream, I'll wake up and find that the plane has landed and none of this has happened. He blinked his eyes several times and shook his head as he cleared the thoughts from it and slowly came back to reality.

Paul watched him intently and felt for the handsome man and swallowed the emotion that welled up in him. Death was always just around the corner. The Bible told one so, and life itself also told these things too. But still it was not easy to accept, especially when it was such a violent death and when it was someone very special that death claimed.

Juan knew instinctively that it was his son's doing. He wondered if he had done it, or got one of his henchmen to do the evil deed. Sarah had been right when she had said he would not rest until he had killed her or his wife.

He would find him; he would make sure that Julio would suffer for what he had done; he would even face being jailed for life if necessary. What would his life be without her? Somehow he would avenge her death and he would not rest until he found his evil son and rid the world of him forever. He stared at Diana's lovely face above the sheet with his head bowed in deadly silence. All these thoughts ran through his brain. He muttered a small prayer and made the sign of the cross, then bent to kiss the lips of his dead wife. The tears of his loss flowed freely down his cheeks. He was not ashamed to show his emotions.

As Paul watched Juan grieve in dumbstruck silence and bewilderment, he knew he was a broken-hearted husband. This was genuine grief and once more Paul felt an overwhelming sorrow for the sad Diplomat. He didn't really want to add to his grief by questioning him yet, however, it was his duty and no time should be lost for the investigation.

Suddenly Juan let out a cry, like a wounded animal. His diplomatic persona had vanished in seconds, leaving him to cope with the stark reality that she was dead, gone from his life, forever. He would never touch her again, never make love to her, and never hear her singing in the kitchen while she invented a new dish for him. All these thoughts ran through Juan's mind and he was trying to come to grips with them.

"WHY GOD? Not again!" He shouted at the ceiling his hands in tight fists of anger beating on his chest.

He swayed and Paul steadied him once again. He wondered what the man meant by, *not again!*

"If you would like to come with me, sir, into the office a little way down the corridor I need to ask you some questions, off the record of course. I know it is a very difficult time for you at the moment..." His voice trailed off.

He really did not want to ask him too many questions at this point in time while the man was grieving, but it was his duty, it had to be done. This was the part of his work that he hated.

Juan took his gaze away from his wife's lifeless body and once more became the Diplomat. He shrugged resignedly.

"If you must." He said as he followed Paul towards an empty room along the corridor that was kept for this purpose.

The attendant covered the woman's beautiful face and pushed the drawer back into the stainless steel body locker. What a bloody waste he thought, that such a beautiful woman had been slaughtered so brutally. What was the world coming to?

**

Paul gave Juan a few minutes to collect his thoughts while he poured him a glass of cold water from the large water cooler standing in one corner of the room.

"Can I ask you where you were on the night of your wife's murder sir?" He asked quietly.

"I flew in from New York via Rome, it was a long flight. The only one I could find. You can check with the airline if you like."

"That will not be necessary sir, we already have. However, when was the last time that you saw your wife alive?" He asked gently.

"Just a few days ago, two and a half days to be exact. I was leaving for New York. She drove me to the airport. I was going away for about a week, but your people phoned the Embassy and I came straight back."

"What was your wife's mental state when you left?"

"She was her usual self, bright, cheerful, giving me a list of make-up and perfumes and other goodies that she wanted brought back. The sales were on in the States you know, she always liked a bargain." He choked on a sob as he recalled the memory.

"Do you know of anyone with a grudge against you or your wife? Do you have any enemies?"

"I don't think so. But you never know these days," he replied wearily.

Paul cleared his throat.

"Umm…I'm very sorry to have to ask you this, sir, but do you happen to know or suspect that your wife was having an affair?"

Paul could see raw emotion in the expression on Juan's face at the question. He could sense that he did not want to comment. Was there some connection between the killer and his late wife he wondered? The thought kept gnawing at him. Quite often in a murder case, the killer was often nearer home than anyone ever suspected.

Juan's tone was controlled when he answered. "No, definitely not, I would have known."

Paul found him interesting, intelligent and pleasant. With his good looks he was a very appealing man and was sure that the ladies found him so and he knew that the man was away from his wife on diplomatic call quite often, travelling in the United States and in Europe.

"Just one more rather personal question, sir. Were you, or are you having an affair?" He asked, slightly embarrassed by the question.

"No." Juan shook his head slowly in disbelieve at the question. "We are, we were an idyllic couple, as anyone who knew us would tell you, and we often travelled together. I was very proud of my beautiful wife, she was such an asset to my position and everyone who met her adored her." He sighed.

"Why would I need to have an affair when I had such a lovely wife as Diana? I just wish we'd had children."

"Thank you, Sir. Er...just a couple more questions. You said, not again, when you were identifying your wife! Did that have any special meaning?"

"Yes and no. You see Diana was my second wife. My first died quite young of a heart attack. I just can't believe I've lost another woman that I love."

"Do you own a gun, sir?"

Juan looked him straight in the eyes.

"I have a permit for a handgun in Spain. Most of the time especially when I am in America, a bodyguard usually accompanies me. I don't really need one in England do I? Why?"

"Just asking."

Paul did not want to antagonize the poor man in his grief. But he had noticed a fair sized safe in the diplomat's apartment and wondered what it contained. But that was on Spanish ground the man had diplomatic immunity and he couldn't force him to open it. He knew though that many of the foreign diplomats often owned a firearm.

"Thank you sir, I have no more questions for the time being. I'm so sorry. I did not wish to offend you. I will be in touch over the next couple of days for a formal interview, I am extremely sorry for your loss. If you think of anything please call me on this number," he said as he handed his card to the man in front of him.

Paul felt truly sorry for the intrusion into Juan's private life. But first and foremost he was a policeman and he had certain duties to perform.

"If you don't mind I should like to go, perhaps you could give me a lift to the Lansborough Hotel now. My secretary has booked a room there for me. I need to get some rest and I assume that my apartment is still off limits and sealed?" Juan asked.

In the morning Juan thought I will wake up and think I have imagined the whole thing.

"Yes, of course sir, I'll take you there myself," said Paul courteously.

***

Once settled in his suite at the hotel, Juan made three calls on his Spanish - pay as you go - mobile phone because he knew that calls could not be traced. He also knew the time had come to rectify the injustices that Julio had performed over the years. By nature he was forgiving, but now he would no longer forgive, he was full of rage and he was ready to rid himself of his violent psychotic son.

CHAPTER TWENTY SIX

LONDON - 2004

The Coroner's office and the mortuary were located in Islington. It was a large complex building, the offices were quite old, but the basement and the new extension that served as the new mortuary, had recently been refurbished and was extremely high tech.

A very pretty, tall and young dark-haired woman of Asian origin was in charge of the old lower level of the building, which served as an anteroom to the new mortuary and she was talking to a policeman who nodded in acknowledgement when he saw DCI Forrest.

Paul thought she looked very young to be in charge and working in such a place. Or was he just getting too old for the job he wondered again?

The room contained several glass fronted cabinets that held supplies of pre-packed scrub suits for autopsies, masks, plastic aprons, paper caps and shoe covers done up in parcels.

"The Professor is expecting you sir, please follow the officer in charge." The young woman said in a well-educated voice as she handed him a pre-packed package and then nodded to the young policeman who was to accompany Paul to the autopsy room.

They took the stairway to the basement with its depressingly familiar overhead fluorescent lights and walls of locked stainless-steel body lockers.

Several drains dotted the white tiled floor at approximately six-foot intervals.

This level was full of figures in white lab coats, hurrying along. Many of them, Paul noticed from their ID badges, were medical students.

Through a large viewing window they could see into the autopsy room, where Professor Ian McAlistair was at work, his eyebrows pinched into a frown of concentration through his plastic face shield. His assistant spotted the detective through the glass and beckoned Paul to come in.

The policeman pushed open a doorway with heavy transparent rubber lips that snapped back closed behind Paul. The automatic glass doors had not been fitted yet, as the place was still undergoing refurbishment. Paul's nose was immediately assaulted by a sudden smell of formaldehyde as well as decaying human flesh. He knew he should have rubbed some Vicks around his nose to stop him breathing the familiar smell.

He saw at a glance that three of the tables in the new cutting room were being used. One white male and one black female had their rib cages split open, exposing lungs and viscera. The third body was Diana Gonzales that had not been cut yet and was partially covered. Beside each table stood scales for weighing the internal organs. Each table had a microphone hanging above it, which had retracted back into the ceiling slightly ready to be used.

Another young male assistant with a large camera stood nearby ready to photograph Diana Gonzales as she lay peacefully on the autopsy table.

My God thought Paul, the assistants get younger and younger. He disliked having to come to the pathology room, but it was part of his duty. Violent death plunders one's dignity as surely as it has taken one's life. The body is handled, photographed, scrutinised and cut up with someone taking numbers and writing comments, step by step. The victim becomes an exhibit and loses all sense of dignity. At least this victim had a name.

He made his way over to the professor and tried to smile a greeting.

"Hi, Paul." Professor Ian McAlistair the Pathologist crossed the room towards him. He was wearing a dark blue surgical smock, a light blue rubber apron and pale blue latex gloves. He had pushed his transparent plastic face shield up over his thinning hairline revealing the disposable mask that covered his nose and mouth.

"We have just finished draining your Jane Doe, she is ready for you. Right over here," he said in his soft Scots voice a question in his eyes. "Are you sure you want to be here Paul?"

Paul nodded his head and then looked around.

"Yes I certainly do. By the way, where's Maggie?"

"She's on another case." McAlistair explained. "Would you like to get gowned and masked, please"

Paul ripped open the plastic package he was carrying and within seconds was ready.

McAlistair led Paul to the stainless steel necropsy table where Diana Gonzales's body lay beneath a white sheet. Her one arm with the hand was jutting out at an angle. McAlistair twitched the sheet covering her and it fell to the floor revealing her nakedness.

Paul looked down upon the woman on the table with her identification tag, with case number 2330, hanging on one toe and experienced his usual wave of anger, at the site of her dead body. He saw the clipboard hanging by the side of the mortuary table with the police report number, the mortuary number and the name of the laboratory, his anger arose again at the arrogant indifference of the system. Violent deaths were allowed no privacy. At least she was given a name; she was not just a number.

Death in its anonymity could not be added to the list of violations that she had suffered at some psychopath's hand. He knew that her body would be handled, scrutinised and photographed and finally plundered as the pathologist went about his work. It was something that he could never get to grips with when someone as lovely as her was murdered. Her face was undamaged, but he noticed there were fresh puncture marks in the neck and groin where the other morgue assistant had drawn blood for lab tests, but the torso was otherwise untouched, except for the bruise marks where she had been kicked many times and the cigarette burns.

Ian's scalpel had not yet made a single slice.

Had her chest been already opened, the cavity exposed, she would have struck him as a more disturbing sight. He didn't very often attend autopsies, but he wanted to see for himself the full damage that had been inflicted upon her by some maniac. What a terrible way to die he thought. How much fear had she endured before she was finally released to death. He thought about her poor husband and his grief at her death. He knew that Juan would not rest until he nailed her murderer. He wondered how he would feel if he was looking at his wife in this situation. A shudder ran through Paul's body.

McAlistair pointed with a gloved finger at her body and Paul hoped she had been dead and escaped her tormentor before he had tortured her so much.

"The burns on the chest are superficial; don't take any notice of them. They were most probably done after she died for some reason or other. The skin colouring and contusions on the front of the neck, probably thumb imprints, indicate asphyxia. Like I said before, she was strangled. The other contusions on her body were from someone kicking savagely at her whilst she was still alive. A rash is also visible around the neck, of course we will know for sure once we get to the lungs. I think she was dead for some time before the mask was put on her, there don't seem to be any pressure marks on her face. Just a theory at this point though."

One of the assistants took several shots of her naked body from different angles and then stepped aside. The other assistant stepped forward ready to take notes.

The Pathologist angled the light further down the body.

"There is also a rash around the waist and ankles, probably from being tied up as well. The cigarette burns on her chest were done just after she was murdered as I mentioned before. Strange, they are normally done whilst the victim is still alive. In my opinion, I think we have a real psychopathic killing, could be wrong but my gut feeling tells me so. I suppose it could be some kind of a ritual killing." He tutted and made a *phewing* noise through his lips.

The lightly closed fingers on her right hand were long and slender and had well-manicured soft pink coloured nail extensions. Her fingertips had not been inked up yet.

"Her left hand was probably cut off after her heart stopped beating as well. The shear marks on the wrist bone were definitely made by a small electric knife blade. It is a good clean cut though!" He said as he lifted her hand.

"Her dental X-rays have not yet been completed, but we have already identified her, so that is a mere formality."

Paul noticed that the ends of her creamy white tendons jutting out slightly from the wrist looked as if they had been cut through like electric cords and his gut recoiled as he felt the bile rising into his throat, he swallowed hard before speaking.

"But Ian, what I don't understand is, why take her hand off? Why not just… oh! I don't know."

Paul shook his head in disbelief as to how someone could have butchered the lovely woman lying on the table. He noticed a thin white line tracing near her right hip showing through her expensive fake tanned skin, probably an appendectomy scar he thought.

"Well, maybe she or he was wearing something, a piece of jewellery perhaps that might have identified her killer, a ring perhaps. Or maybe she scratched her killer. Under those long nails of hers were some particles of his skin that could identify him, we shall know more when the DNA tests come back. Maybe this killing was some ritual thing or maybe he just did it for kicks, I don't know either, that's your department, Paul." Ian gave a tight smile.

"I only cut'em up, find out how and when, not why and then sew'em back up again!"

"Yes, I was thinking out aloud, I think we can rule her husband out. He wasn't even in the country! Hey, what are the scars under each breast?" Paul asked as he bent forward.

"She's had breast implants, probably within the last couple of years." Ian explained as he pulled each breast up to show him. Nice job, surprised you noticed them."

With a stab of remorse Paul noticed that her toenails were painted the same colour as her right hand, he wanted to scream out for all of them to leave her alone. Instead he just stood and watched, waiting for more information.

The pathologist's assistant removed the suction catheters from the dead woman's ankles and then he angled the bright overhead light over her body for the pathologist, as he began speaking into a microphone suspended over the table.

"The body is that of a pre-menopausal, well-nourished Caucasian female, 30 to 35 years old. Height approximately five foot ten inches, body weight prior to drainage one hundred and forty one pounds. Absence of left hand severed at the wrist joint."

The Forensic Pathologist opened her mouth and peered inside.

"No upper fillings evident, however upper row of teeth consistent with expensive crowning, bottom row two white fillings. No evidence of ejaculative fluids or obstructions."

Once more the young man, who was photographing the body, took some more close-up shots and when he had finished stepped back again. The pathologist assistant came forward with his clipboard and made some final notes.

"We've taken vaginal swabs. There is no evidence of her having had intercourse within the last forty eight hours. However, she is approximately eight weeks pregnant!" Said Ian quietly.

The assistant added this information to his notes.

Paul thought that Ian looked like a vulture hovering overhead, ready to swoop any moment on the women and tear her to pieces. The information about her pregnancy surprised him. He wondered how her husband would take the news when he heard it or perhaps he knew already. If he was aware why did he not mention it before?

Ian moved to the foot of the table, took hold of her right ankle and rotated it slowly, repeated the same thing with her other leg and then he walked to the other end of the long table and lifted her head, testing the resistance of the neck muscles.

"Rigor mortis is not too pronounced at this point in time, indicating that death could have occurred at least twenty to thirty hours before examination. This can be verified later after the autopsy has taken place."

He lifted each eyelid of the woman on the table that had started to open slightly in turn and gazed down into the unseeing pale blue eyeballs. He then studied her throat.

"Contusions on front of the neck, probably thumb imprints. Red abrasions around the neck." His assistant angled the light further down her body. "There are also abrasions around the waist."

The detective watched wordlessly, as the professor completed his surface examination and spoke softly into the overhead microphone. The young man alongside marked his new comments on a pre-printed diagram of a human body for his records.

Paul felt himself slip into a numb void, watching McAlistair at work, he felt he was floating in the air and looking down at the scene unfolding on the table.

Why did he feel like this, he questioned himself? I don't even know the woman. She is just a body on the table, no connection to me. But he could not get the image of her distraught husband out of his mind and the wave of pity he had felt for him. I am certainly getting too old for this job, he thought for the third time that day. I'm getting too sentimental. I have got to change my career. I go home to an empty house every night because of my work. He shook his head to clear it and tried to concentrate on the surroundings with their steel tables and sharp instruments and to what Ian was talking about.

"She was tied up first." He slowly examined her arms and wrists. "No needle marks, she was not a user," he commented matter-of-factly as he frowned.

Her right hand that was closed before seemed to have opened up a little. McAlistair pulled at each finger in turn trying to open the hand more. "Well, I'll be damned, Paul, she's holding onto something I hadn't noticed before, I missed that. It's like she is trying to tell us something. I'm afraid I'm going to have to break her fingers."

Another photo was taken.

McAlistair took a pair of surgical pliers from a small stainless steel trolley next to the mortuary table, adjusted the grip around the dead woman's index finger and gave a quick twist. The finger flapped loose with a sickening crack, like a chicken's wishbone being snapped in two. With three more cracks he was able to bend the hand open almost completely.

Paul felt sick at the sound, but managed to swallow his bile. He was able to see something small and golden, wedged into the pulpy heel of the palm.

McAlistair probed the object free with a pair of long tweezers. It was a gold charm, in the shape of half a heart pendant.

He handed it to Paul.

"I wonder who wears the matching half." He said softly. "Find the other half or the chain that goes with it and you might find your killer!"

Ian spoke softly into the overhanging microphone. "End of notes, mortuary number 1057/01-2330 and case number 175."

His assistant pushed the button on the microphone and it slowly retracted upwards.

CHAPTER TWENTY SEVEN

LONDON - 2004

Paul and David entered the incident room together. There was a lot of noise in the room of people talking, some were sitting down, others standing and shuffling about, a couple leaning against one of the desks; Paul's team was already waiting for him and as David closed the door, the babble of voices soon ceased.

The room was crammed with a large metal desk, three filing cabinets and two old wooden tables as well as several uncomfortable plastic chairs. There were also four large whiteboards around the room with a wooden table in front of one of them that contained the only forensic evidence that had been collected so far. David looked around, the room was badly in need of a makeover, but it sufficed. There was a wide-screen monitor on one of the walls with a video and DVD player beneath it on a shelf.

Paul Forrest walked over to one of the whiteboards. He took a black dry-marker from the jacket pocket of his dark grey suit and studied the words already written on two of them:

LOCUS: VICTIMS: EVIDENCE: SUSPECTS: MOTIVE:

In large bold letters. Then under each heading several details, some also in bold letters.

He added to the comments and wrote: - **Wounds to the genitals by eight inch custom-**

made crossbow bolts. This information has not been released to the media yet.

On another whiteboard were more details and pictures of the four murdered young men.

David looked at the boards as well and then turned to Paul and said loudly for all to hear.

"The assassin will probably commit another murder, to show you up, you know. He or she is most certainly laughing at you. What we have to do is to get inside of the mind of this killer. This is not your classic serial offender. But one thing I must say is that this new murder of Diana Gonzales does not seem to be part of it. Whether it is connected or not at this moment in time, I cannot say for sure."

On the fourth board was written: - **DIANA GONZALES** in large bold capitals - along with her Mortuary ID and case number and other relevant information that had been obtained.

Spouse of Spanish Ambassador, Juan Carlos Gonzales. Estimated time of death - before midnight - location - Sorrento Towers, London, West End. Body discovered approximately twelve fifteen pm by the concierge. He had drawn a diagram of the apartment, putting an outline with a stick figure to show where the body had been found in the bedroom.

Also on the board Paul had listed the evidence that had been found so far. A Marlboro' cigarette end, the two bits of a black plastic bag and a black leather mask, standard SM gear, a bondage mask bought from any bondage shop in the Soho area, the broken electric knife blade that he had found in the dishwasher, and finally the gold charm. These items lay on the wooden table in front of the board in plastic evidence bags and tagged. This so far constituted the only physical evidence in the case so far. Paul followed these with their corresponding tag numbers and some of the details of the Coroner's report.

Strangled, left hand cut off. Ritual killing? No signs of RAPE. On the right he had written in bold letters the words **WITNESSES? SECURITY VIDEOTAPES?**

Paul turned to face his team.

"Now regarding Diana Gonzales. This recent one is a very male killing. Looks like a typical pay back crime. Nothing was disturbed or stolen according to her husband. So far we have not had many productive leads. It does not seem to have been a sexual killing, not that sort of crime, she was not raped. Could be ritual or a vendetta, or even an execution. Maybe the murderer was in love with her sometime ago. You know there is a kind of love that never lets go, no matter what happens. It sounds almost romantic, doesn't it?" He asked his team.

"But remember that kind of love is often very evil."

Several nodded their heads in agreement.

"It is a black love," he continued. "A terrible thing. Think about how many people have been killed because a lover won't let go, will not give up! Mr. Myers will confirm this. Not so David?"

David turned to him and nodded in agreement.

"Then we have the binding of the hands and feet, this I think has some connection with this woman. Did he know who she was? The killer obviously wanted to exercise his power over her, perhaps to deliver justice, or so he thought in his warped mind."

He paused and looked around him.

"Mr Myers and I have worked on the principle that the killer is male and knew his victim, there is no forced entry. There is the possibility he might have had a key. So, what have we got so far? Our Crime Scene Crew has come up with four partial prints that do not match Mr and Mrs Gonzales prints that of course were all over the place. They could be the concierge or the cleaner's. More like the killer wore gloves. Let's hope the Lab comes up with something. If so we shall pass them on to Interpol as well. The killer was very meticulous; he made sure there would be no bloodstains. The floor was well covered; he must have worn shoe protectors too. He's probably done something like this before and knows how to cover his tracks. We are up against a very, very professional, clever killer. He too may have been a serial killer in the past. Many serial killers fool the world for a long time before they are caught."

He paused for a moment to see the reaction of his audience came up with.

"I'm not a psychologist that is pure speculation though. Forensics are giving the apartment the once over again, it's almost impossible to kill without leaving some trace behind, unless he was a ghost or a superhuman being. The partial prints we're still trying to identify as I said before, and we're in the process of matching these against the prints of all the residents and the concierge who discovered her body. It would seem that the killer made his exit by the fire escape stairs. The stairs were clean, no footprints, only a small piece of black plastic bag caught on the bottom of the stair rail and a cigarette end. I reckon it could be his. There was a slight smell in the apartment. To reiterate I say, his, because this is not the sort of crime that was done by another woman. Diana Gonzales was young and fit and it would take a very strong woman to tie her up. So if we work on the assumption it was a man, he probably had some kind of protective clothing on his body as well as the shoe protectors on his feet. Hopefully in time they will turn up, in a skip perhaps or similar."

He drew breath again and looked around at his team again. Once more there was silence but several heads nodded and waited for him to continue before asking their questions.

"We have the security tape from the garage, but it is a bit blurred and the hallway tapes don't show much either. The Lab is still working on them and should bring them through any moment now. Finally there is the neatly coiled black insulated electric cord that was probably used to tie her hands and feet together and the broken piece of blade from a Braun electric carving knife found in the dishwasher that he used to cut her hand off. The blood on it is human, but too small an amount to be typed yet. The dishwasher did a good job, but not quite good enough. No matter how thorough the investigation, some doubts inevitably remain; rarely will you encounter a case, where all the questions are answered. Remember nobody really sees, they are blind, especially when it comes to the police questioning them."

He paused and looked around for some reaction from his team. There were murmurings but no questions at this point.

"Okay. Now I would like to hand you over to David Myers our Forensic Psychiatrist, whom several of you know already."

David looked around at the earnest faces watching him, some were new to him and others he recognised and he smiled as he acknowledged them before speaking.

"As most of you are aware I am a Forensic Psychiatrist, and I deal with the criminal mind, with the criminally insane, the mentally abnormal whose acts of violence, often murder cannot be presented to the courts in the usual manner. I look into the mind of the murderer; call me a Profiler if you wish. I find out what makes him or her in certain cases tick. Especially Serial Killers. Therefore, I should like to deal first of all with the four cases of the young men, so I will tell you some of the things I have learnt about Serial Killers, especially for those present who are new to me. Several people in the room may have heard some of this before, but please bear with me."

He looked around the room at their eager faces and smiled as one of them let out a nervous laugh.

"There are four kinds of serial killer. The Pleasure Seeker. The Visionary. The Purger and lastly the Controller. I would say in this particular case that the killer of the four young men is a Purger, trying to rid society of scum. The

307

compulsion to kill becomes stronger with killings becoming more frequent. Perhaps craving celebrity status sometimes for their killings and feeling no remorse. This Serial Killer, who in my mind is undoubtedly a woman, seems to keep to the same pattern and she could become bolder. But she is definitely not the killer of Diana Gonzales. I'm pretty sure that a man did that. From the way she was killed and then tied up, he is a Controller. Perhaps there is a connection somewhere, who knows? We'll find out as we go along. I also think that the killer staged the body making a mockery of her death. He wanted her to be found, I think he phoned the concierge, again he was in control."

He looked around again at their intent faces and noticed that no women were present. The words were chilling and several of them shuffled their feet and looked around the room as he stared at them trying to avoid his piercing look.

"Now let me ask you all something gentlemen, what turns you on? What really turns you on? A pert backside perhaps, a glimpse of full breasts, a woman's legs, a man's body even?"

He looked around him again at his audience for a reaction. There were a few embarrassed coughs.

"Why do you think these men were killed by a woman, sir?" Queried young Tony Smith.

"Because in my opinion this is not your classic kind of male Serial Killer though, I could be wrong. In fact very wrong. "

"Okay, then what really turns on the classic Serial Killer, sir?" Smith once more asked.

"Well, it is the suffering in death of another human being. The screams of the victim deaden the pent up frustration of the killer. The act of killing makes the killer feel intensely alive. What he or she feels next is not guilt, but often disappointment. It was not as wonderful as the killer hoped. Maybe next time it will be perfect and as his or her determination builds and as he or she takes another life, they plan in obsessive detail what they will do next, how to kill the next victim, will it be the same way or perhaps another way. Is the killer trying to drive the demons from his or her head? One thing I have learnt, Serial Killers are often quiet, unassuming people. They often make good neighbours and quite often in some cases, they are even known to their victims."

He looked around once more. "Has anyone any questions at this point?"

"Yes sir. Would this be the same in the case of the Gonzales killing? Do you think it could have been a random drug addict, or indeed someone she knew? I know I'm jumping the gun a bit sir, but I just wondered if they are actually connected in any way! I can't see her letting a stranger into her apartment!" Commented DC. Rivers.

David Myers smiled and tilted his head to one side before he spoke.

"It would seem that she could have been killed by someone she possibly knew. Someone, who could have been under the influence of drugs or drink at the time, or even just high on the thrill of the action of death, it is a very bizarre and evil killing indeed and points almost definitely to a

Controller. Fortunately with our knowledge of Forensic Science, we are able to tell that evil does not come from monsters, but from men. It offers us the methodology to find these men and women. This is the textbook explanation, but we are not dealing with textbook murders, this is something else. Any more questions?"

There was a shaking of heads and a few murmurs. They wanted to know more before they asked any other questions.

"Right, now onto drug addiction. Separately drugs and sex go either way, good or evil. But put them together, use them for kicks and there's no limit to the evil they can cause."

David paused allowing what he had said to sink in and reached for the glass of water on the table nearby. He drank deeply from it and then set his drink down and was silent for a few moments as he watched his audience taking it all in.

"I have seen what drug addiction does to addicts. It's an impulse - **a what if?** You can't imagine that under normal circumstances the impulse wouldn't be there, but it is under control. You take a drug, the drug freezes that moment, that impulse and the what if - turns into a - **why not** and then you're doing it and the drug is telling you that it's not doing it." He paused, watching, seeing if they were taking it on board.

"I am also here today to provide a psychological profile, a characterization if you like of the killer of the young men as well of Diana Gonzales. In my mind I am clear that someone who uses drugs killed the Ambassador's wife, it was a very male type of killing, but not like the murders of the four young men as I mentioned before. That was different; it was too calculated, dramatic perhaps, but done for a reason. Drug addicts do not reason. You see, a drug addict cannot always differentiate the truth from fiction when he is high. I have seen someone change around in less than one hour, it was a psychotic break brought on by cocaine. The killer of Diana Gonzales is ruthless. He's psychopathic, cunning, yet very sure of himself. It was a holiday weekend. No one was going to be around, he must have known this; he turned on the air-conditioning so the body wouldn't deteriorate too much. So he is also very intelligent. The way the apartment was cleaned up shows he is also at times very meticulous, probably verging on OCD. But he made one big mistake. He forgot to shut the front door securely or left it open on purpose so she would be found by the concierge. Maybe it was him that made the anonymous call to the concierge. I think he knew she was married and wanted her husband to find her or somebody else. He probably didn't know her husband was out of the country for a while or did he? He could have suffered in the past from psychosexual disorders that could have been harboured from adolescence or some other sexual deviations, hence the mask."

Tony Smith's shot up.

"Excuse me sir, is it your conjecture that he reasons this way?" He queried.

"Maybe he wasn't under the influence of drugs at the time. I have spent some time with drug addicts and because they often have sane moments and they are also very devious, occasionally sanity breaks through and they can act normally, but as one so rightly says, what is normal?"

David looked at him for a few seconds before continuing.

"Yes that is true sometimes, and as you say, what is normal. If he takes **coke** it can lead to some pretty off-the-wall thinking and we don't know what other drugs he has or was doing. People who use drugs long term often find it very difficult to identify the truth from the imaginary. We can only hope that he will be careless if and when he kills again. Now I'll hand you back to Paul." David said as he pointed to him before sitting down and letting Paul get on with his job.

Paul handed out photos of Diana Gonzales taken when she was alive.

"I want you all to find out whatever you can about the murdered woman. Some door to door questioning in the apartment block to start with! I've already briefed Rivers on this, especially on how to handle the residents."

The Incident Room door opened slowly and a bright young, fresh-faced Lab assistant entered and handed Paul a large brown envelope with a note attached to the back of it and left as quietly as he had appeared.

Paul extracted two security tapes from it and walked over to the video player and picked up the remote control.

"Right, let's see what we have got on the first tape of the fourth floor where apartment floor 10 is situated," he commented as he hit the play button.

On the flat screen monitor there came up a view of the corridor of the fourth floor. As the concierge had explained most of the residents were away that weekend and the corridor was empty. He let the black and white tape play for several more minutes and then pressed fast forward. Nothing! Then a tall smart woman of around forty years old he reckoned, wearing big dark sunglasses and a smart baseball cap that partially obscured her face, with a ponytail of fairish hair swinging out of the back of the baseball cap. She was carrying a small dog under her right arm, and then disappeared down the hallway and around a corner. They had no chance to see which apartment she entered, then again nothing.

Paul fast-forwarded again until the end of the tape. There was nothing else of relevance.

He ejected the tape and pushed the other one into the machine and hit play once more. A view of the underground garage appeared. There were only two cars in the large garage, but their number plates were not in view. Then a Saab convertible with hood up swung into view and disappeared. The Lab had managed to identify the number plate. It belonged to a prominent Member of Parliament. He had an alibi. He was visiting his mother that day, or so he said.

The security camera obviously did not work properly, or hadn't been set properly; it did not swing around the garage. Paul knew that the kind of people that lived in the block were very private and did not want anyone knowing their business. Most probably it had been set like that from day one. A rubbish collection lorry entered and disappeared. That too had been checked on. The detectives in the Incident Room listened to the whirring of the video machine and watched the screen intently. Then there was nothing. Paul pressed rewind and the digital pixels briefly scrambled on the monitor, then re-formed into the image of the rubbish collection truck, he thought he had seen something. He paused. He zoomed in on it. They all peered at the screen at a blur behind the truck. There was nothing else. He pressed re-wind once more to the beginning and ejected that tape too.

He turned the brown envelope over and looked at the note attached to the back. It read: - **SORRY NOTHING MUCH!**

Damn he thought, this person is very clever and I must insist that the Management Committee of the apartment complex, if there is one, takes more care of their residents and updates their security equipment. Sometimes he despised the rich for the chances they took. It always made his job so much more difficult.

"Well, that's it for today folks, any more questions?" He asked turning to the men in the room once more.

Several members of the team shot up their hands and Paul and David answered some more pertinent questions relating to the Serial Killer and Diana's death for around an hour and a half, before dismissing them all.

CHAPTER TWENTY EIGHT

LONDON - 2004

It was a Sunday evening. Paul got himself a coffee from the old coffee machine in the corridor of the Police Station and entered his private office. He sat at his desk and stared at it wondering where to begin. He hated all the paperwork that went with the job.

He took a sip of the bitter coffee and then he started to tackle the stack of transcribed dictations and lab reports in his tray together with some of the other case notes that were piled up on his desk so far. He preferred hard copies than trying to read them off the computer in front of him. In fact he very rarely switched it on, he hated the thing, he left that to one of the others of his team who were more computer literate than him to print things out.

For a change nobody else was around, his office was quiet and he was able to study the report of the Pathologist in front of him and the crime photos of the Gonzales case. The serial killings he had turned over to DC Rivers for the time being as they had not continued and he was running out of ideas. Right now they had no witnesses and very little physical evidence to speak of, in that case it might have to be put to bed for the time being, he thought.

Forensics had got nothing more useful from the living room at the Gonzales apartment. He seemed to be hitting his head against a brick wall and started to shake it with exasperation as he read the statements from some of the residents of the block, some other notes, and a pencil drawn plan of the exclusive apartments. Twenty in all, surely someone must have seen something. On he worked, trying to put the pieces together, looking, searching for the elusive piece that did not fit. Why did he have the gut feeling that somehow Sarah Lawson was involved? What was the missing link? As usual Paul was concentrating so hard he was not aware that his door had quietly opened and David Myers was standing just inside the doorway.

Paul was frozen in his usual work pose, his left elbow on the desk, forehead resting on his palm, and his right hand poised to turn the pages of the file that was spread out in front of him. His thick brown curly hair was already rumpled from running his fingers through it. There were two slight sweat marks under the arms of his pale blue shirt. His jacket was neatly draped over a chair nearby.

David stood in the open doorway of the office and watched Paul drumming his fingers as he sat at his untidy desk. Copies of the crime scene photos littered it, along with some other papers.

Suddenly sensing someone's presence in his doorway Paul looked up, his smile brief, but warm.

"Well look who's here! Good weekend, or shouldn't I ask?" Joked David.

"Don't ask, David." Paul retorted wearily and yawned.

Paul Forrest took a sip of his lukewarm coffee, he was going to be forty-nine next birthday and wondered if he was getting too slow. He had been a policeman for nearly thirty one years. He had joined at the age of eighteen and worked his way up through the ranks and two years ago he was promoted to DCI. He was a bit of a maverick, but certainly not a bent copper.

He was a good policeman, an experienced homicide detective and trained in crime scene and death investigation. He was also very well-liked and respected by everyone, but most of the team he worked with nowadays were much younger and fitter. He felt the pressure was getting at him. He seemed to be getting pressure from every side these days. His bitch of an ex-wife, who was always asking him for more money, his daughter was mixed up with a junkie, his sick old father was losing his faculties and he needed to find a daily carer to help out because the old man would not move into a private sheltered housing apartment. His Superintendent was on his back all of the time, he badly needed a holiday. He needed to get away somewhere and rethink about his future.

Maybe he could get a job in security or perhaps he could even be a bodyguard to some diplomat. He was well trained in armoury, one of his friends who had recently retired early, had gone over to Saudi Arabia as a bodyguard to one of the Princes and was earning mega bucks and had contacted him recently to see if he was interested.

Paul knew he was missing something in the cases, but couldn't quite put his finger on it. Things were going badly, no witnesses, very little evidence on the serial killings and now this latest murder, Diana Gonzales. He knew somehow they were linked but what was he missing, who was keeping the answers from him?

"I don't know David, something is staring me straight in the face, but what? I'm sorry to say this, but I think your Sarah knows more than she has told you, but I don't want to hassle her. What is the connection between her and Juan Gonzales, do you know? Is there any chance that you might find out something for me? Oh! By the way Diana Gonzales was a couple of months pregnant, when she died."

"Good God. That must have hit Senor Gonzales very hard. I'll do my best, Paul, but I can assure you Sarah has nothing to do with the murders. As far as Juan is concerned, I don't know very much, they go way back. She used to live in Spain. She knows his family very well, and she was a friend of his present wife."

"Was there any sort of a romantic relationship between Juan and Sarah at some time?"

"Not that I am aware of."

Paul sighed and then stood up from his desk, stretched his back and walked over to the window. He gazed out into the night. His fingers drummed on the top of a filing cabinet near the window.

"I have a good idea why Diana Gonzales's hand was cut off? I think she probably made a grab at him when she was struggling and could have scratched him and got some of his skin under her long nails, he would be worried about DNA results or maybe she had a piece of jewellery on a finger or around her wrist that could be traced to him. The killer obviously didn't realise that she had a gold charm in her other hand, could have been hers of course, but I don't think so. Funny that, could have been a necklace, I wonder where the chain is! What do you think David? I wonder who has got the other piece of the broken gold heart. I wonder if there are any others worn by women or even men. I also noticed that Senor Gonzales smokes a lot, the first two fingers of his right hand are badly stained with nicotine, the cigarette end we found could even be his and there was a faint smell of tobacco in the apartment. I couldn't see any ashtrays around though!"

On Paul's desk in a small clear plastic evidence bag was the piece of gold. The two black plastic fragments he had found in the apartment had also been placed on his desk in separate evidence bags, and the cigarette end in another bag, each bearing its own tag.

David looked at the piece of jewellery intently for several seconds. Something bugged him about it. He had seen something like it before. He remembered seeing something glistening through Sarah's fine blouse at the dinner table. No he told himself. No, it must be purely coincidence, charms like that were quite common. The cigarette end could have belonged to anyone.

Paul sat down again at his desk and gestured to David to take the chair nearby and join him. He opened the case file and skimmed through the pages of the report.

Two photographs of the dead woman were stapled to the first page. One with the mask on her face and one without the mask which had been removed from her face at the apartment before her body had been taken away. She looked so tranquil in death almost contentedly dreaming. There followed the time and place of the murder and a description of the scene of the crime etc. There was also a big brown envelope that contained other photographs of her as well, given to him by her husband. Paul passed the envelope to his friend.

David carefully slipped the glossies out of the manila envelope that Paul handed him. There was two of her before her death at a diplomatic party with her husband and another, a large portrait photo. She had been a very, very beautiful woman. It surprised him how young the dead woman looked. Though he knew that she was in her late thirties; very blonde, with shoulder length shiny hair and deep brown eyes. Her eyes were long-lashed, her lips full and pouting, possibly collagen filled he thought momentarily. Her chin was very firm.

"She was so beautiful," Paul sighed. "Such a waste, what a dreadful way to die. What kind of bastard would do such a thing to her like that?"

Paul never ceased to wonder about death and the people who caused it. Even though he was used to death in the course of his work, he constantly saw vivid and gory pictures of crime victims. Usually he was able to separate himself from the emotional aspect and concentrate on the legal side of wrongful death. But sometimes it was difficult and he was finding it harder to be impartial lately. He felt very sorry for her husband and he really liked the man.

David looked at two full body shots of the victim and the bruising on her body.

"I wonder too what type of evil person did this to her! But we'll find him, I promise you, he will not get away with it! How has her husband taken it?"

"Oh, not very well I'm afraid, he's absolutely devastated. He flew back day before yesterday early in the morning, from the States and identified her. I thought he was going to pass out when he saw her. He is staying in a hotel at the moment. We have sent a couple of plainclothes detectives over to keep an eye on him as a precaution in view of his status."

David looked intently at the shots of Diana with the mask on her face. "Any prints on it?"

"No, leather can be very difficult sometimes to print. Anyway I'm sure the killer wore latex gloves. The only lead we have on it is that it is custom-made and there are only three sex-shops in the Soho area that specialize in this kind of hand-made S&M gear, not one shop owner recognised it of course. Personally I think they are lying, but what evidence do I have of that? Young Tony Smith is making other enquiries this morning on the *net*. Amazing what you can buy through the net anonymously!"

He paused to clear his throat.

"Oh, by the way, I had some information sent to me this morning through Interpol and I am sure there is some connection with the original four murders of the men. There is a South African guy-Jacko von Jonge who came on the London drug scene in late 2002. He was living in America in 2001. In the early part of 2002 he was spotted in Spain and then turned up in Amsterdam in late 2003 for a short while. Then he arrived in England in early 2004 again. It would seem he could have supplied all the dead men with drugs, he also runs several girls here in London and Manchester. He has several apartments and there were rumours that he was also a partner in a gay nightclub. The killings started around the early part of 2004, I've also checked with the Manchester Police, apparently he was cautioned a little while ago, two of his girls, a Croatian and an Albanian were badly beaten up, and he denied any knowledge of it. They think he might also be involved with a gang who are bringing over Eastern European girls to London. They had him under surveillance for a while, but they came to a dead end. He seems to have disappeared. We've also had another murder, a prostitute, it happened a few nights ago, I thought nothing of it at first, but there could be a connection with this Von Jonge I think, but the Super wants me to concentrate on the Diana Gonzales murder. I've turned everything else over to Rivers."

Paul stood up and stretched his body, leaned over and picked his jacket up from the chair.

"I can't concentrate anymore. I am going to have a break. Will you join me for a coffee over the road? But let's talk about something else. How is it going with Sarah?" He asked as they left his office.

BOOK TWELVE

CHAPTER TWENTY NINE

LONDON - 2004

"So, did you see anything on the night of the murder? Did you see any cars driving around or hanging about? Or did you see anything going on in that apartment?" Asked Paul, slightly exasperated, pointing to the block of flats opposite. His unruly brown hair ruffled even more in the cold late afternoon breeze as he questioned the old wino standing nearby.

The old man's bleary eyes narrowed with suspicion beneath a shock of dirty grey matted hair. A varicose bulbous nose dominated his thin face. He knew the man was a copper. He shrugged. Not bothering to lift himself from the pavement where he had made himself a pallet of newspapers and old rags to keep warm from the autumnal wind. A strong smell of stale urine emanated from him.

Paul moved downwind from the disgusting old man, reached inside his jacket for his wallet and pulled a ten-pound note from it and dangled it in front of him.

The old wino reached up a dirty trembling hand and took the money. He hastily stuffed it into one of the pockets of the filthy old army trench coat that was wrapped around him and tied at the waist with an equally filthy old piece of rope.

"Yeah, I've seen things," he said sniffing and wiping his nose with a frayed cuff.

"What sort of things?" Prompted Paul patiently.

The old man scratched his thick grey cheek stubble with a filthy long fingernail.

"Things. Y'know. People goin' in an' owt. You know, gays, foreign birds."

He coughed, hawked and spat on the pavement just missing Paul's black Patrick Cox's shoes.

"There's a tall blonde sometimes, around here, a classy looking dame with a small dog. There's also some old fat guy that visits his bit o' stuff. There's an old biddy too whose chauffeur drops her off when she has been shopping."

"What does the classy dame look like?" Paul prompted him

"I told yer! Tall, blonde usually wears black leather clothing. Never seen her face properly, she always wears big dark glasses and a baseball cap pulled down over her face. Y'know, but what an arse! Cor! Could be a tranny though, she's quite tall, walks a bit like one, if yer know what I mean!"

He spat again at the pavement and once again Paul had to jump out of the way to avoid the slimy green jet from hitting his shoes.

"Anything else? Can you remember anything else?" Paul asked slowly, starting to lose his patience with the old man.

"Shame ain't it about the nice lady. She sometimes stops and gives me a few bob to buy some food. I saw her husband a couple of times too.

He gave me a packet of fags once. Well, I dunno, do I? Anyway, I'm tired now. The place around here's not safe anymore for decent folk." The old tramp started mumbling and moaning and licking his lips.

Paul opened his wallet again, he suddenly felt a bit of sorry for the old man.

"Okay, you could earn yourself twenty if you could remember some more things about what went on up there!" He pointed to the large building again.

A middle-aged prostitute wobbled past on shabby white high-heeled shoes, slowing down to stare at the £10.00 note Paul was waving about. Her short skirt was a bottom hugging cyclamen pink Lycra pelmet, and her blonde wig looked as if it had been stolen from an old mannequin that had been dumped into a Euro bin outside of one of the big department stores.

The note disappeared quickly. The prostitute gave the old man a contemptuous stare and she immediately picked up speed as she saw a prospective punter curb crawling.

"Well, let me think. There's been a strange foreign looking, Spanish or Arab type, tall dark-haired man hanging about for some time. Very nervy guy, y'know, walking up and down, fidgety, smokes one cigarette after another, but the bastard didn't offer me one though when I tapped him up."

The old man had a pretty good impression of what the dark-haired man looked like, even though he had only seen him the once close up, he had not actually stared at him, but he had noticed the tall, good looking, well-dressed young man standing on the pavement looking up at the windows of the

Sorrento Towers apartment block on several occasions and that morning even, just before the police had arrived, then he'd moved on. He had worn black wrap-around sunglasses, looked like he was in his thirties. Perhaps he could get more money out of him than the policeman, if he could locate him.

"Okay old man, when was this?" Demanded Paul now fed up with the slowness of the wino's retorts.

"Well, a few nights ago, looked like there was a party up there." He pointed at the same building as Paul had a few moments ago, with a dirty finger then picked his nose before continuing and wiped it on his old coat.

"The end window I fink. It was the weekend y' know."

"Any idea what was going on?"

"I dunno." The old man broke into wheezy laughter.

His breath was an explosive mixture of stale beer, cigarettes and tooth decay in Paul's face.

"They never invited me!" He let out a raucous laugh and then had a fit of coughing.

"Come on, earn your twenty. You must've seen or heard something from here, if you don't co-operate, I'll have you up for vagrancy," threatened Paul.

"I got me rights y'know. I ain't doing any 'arm to anyone. Well I couldn't see noffin anyway, he closed the curtains. Heard some loud music though and screamin'. Lots of screamin'."

"Who's **HE**?"

"Y'know, the one I told you abat, the dark 'aired foreign bloke."

"What screaming?"

"I told you, I dunno, screamin' like someone was being hurt or summit. I'm too tired now, I can't remember and I need a drink."

Paul knew he would not get any more information for the time being from the old man until he'd had a drink, he might come back later and question him again and try to trace the dark haired man, maybe one of the other layabouts had seen something.

"Okay, old man, that's all for now. I will see you later that's if you want to earn yourself some more money. Maybe some of your friends have seen something. Ask around, will you?"

The old man grunted and shambled away, he was feeling good, he'd got twenty quid and he was going to make a night of it.

Paul walked towards the block of flats. He would have another word with the concierge. He had done a check on him and it seemed he was an illegal; there was no trace of him at the Home Office having entered the UK.

Then he would call on Mrs. Sarah Lawson the next day.

***

The tall rather heavily made up red headed woman with dark glasses, watched the detective walk away from the dirty tramp. She was dressed in a tight black lycra skirt that clung to her body, emphasising her shapely figure, pulling it in and around the curve of her tight buttocks, sticking

327

closely to the outside of the top of her thighs and stopping halfway down them to show her long legs to great effect. She also wore a very short black top that revealed her naked waist with a plunging neckline and thin shoulder straps. She took her mobile phone out of the small handbag she was carrying and made a quick phone call. She shivered slightly as she was not used to the cold wind.

CHAPTER THIRTY

LONDON - 2004

Two confident rings sounded on Sarah's doorbell. They shook her out of her trance as she sipped her morning cup of tea.

Sarah somehow knew it was Paul Forrest. She had been expecting him and she knew that he would come to see her unannounced. She looked at the kitchen clock, it was 8.45 am. She went nervously to the door carrying her large mug of tea. She was wearing an old white T-shirt and a faded pair of Calvin Klein jeans and on her feet was a pair of old white Adidas trainers.

Paul had the feeling she had thrown the clothes on some time ago, he could have sworn that she was almost expecting him. Her shoulder length blonde hair was pulled back into a neat ponytail.

Her body was trim and her beautiful face unlined without makeup, except a touch of pale lip-gloss, completely belying her age. He could see why his friend David was so besotted by her and he felt a small pang of something almost like jealousy sweep through his body.

"Good morning Mrs Lawson. Not disturbing you, am I? Not too early I hope. My name is DCI Paul Forrest, I am the officer in charge of the case of Diana Gonzales. I have a few questions that you might be able to help me with. I understand that you knew Mrs Gonzales and her husband. May I come in?" He asked as he showed her his ID card and stepped forward with a smile and offered her his hand.

She had not met him before, but knew of him from the newspapers and from David. He was quite tall and broad, not overweight exactly, but solidly built of thick muscle. His good-looking face was rugged. She shook his hand firmly.

"Of course, shall we go into the sitting room?" She smiled back at him, her composure slowly coming back.

He followed her slowly and seated himself on the settee, whilst she positioned herself in an armchair with a small table by the side and placed her mug of tea on it. Her throat felt dry, the kind of dryness not to be quenched by tea, coffee or water.

"Can I offer you something? Coffee, tea…?"

He smiled at her. "No thank you, I had a coffee a little while ago." He took out a small notebook and pen from a pocket of his jacket and flipped the cover back ready to take down the details of the questions he was going to ask her.

She noticed that he was darkly handsome with his high cheekbones. Charcoal brown eyes and thick brown unruly hair very slightly tinged with grey that was in need of a good trim. She also noticed that he wore an expensive dark grey designer pinstriped suit. It was accentuated by a light blue shirt and darker silk tie in muted tones of blue and grey and expensive shoes. She had known that he would come and see her sooner or later, she was prepared and she was now the actress in the story that she had read whilst in hospital.

With a broad smile she waited for him to ask his questions. Her heart was pounding furiously, yet outwardly she presented a calm exterior.

He kept his questions brief and to the point and carefully watched her re-actions.

Sarah answered the same way and stared back at him.

Yes, she did understand the concerns of their mutual friends. Yes, she was a good friend of David Myers. Yes, earlier she had gone shopping. But what had that to do with Diana? Yes, she knew Diana and her husband; they had been friends of hers for some time. Yes, she and her second husband knew him in Spain. Yes, she had been with David the night of the murder as she was sure Paul was fully aware of the fact.

"But surely you know that without asking me, he is such a good friend of yours!" She commented with a cheeky smile even though her stomach was fluttering with apprehension and she took a long sip of tea from her mug.

Sarah could feel the atmosphere of fear that hung in the air like gas, invisible but suffocating. The air in her sitting room became clammier and edgier with tension, making it hard to breathe. She felt a line of perspiration forming on her top lip, waiting, knowing there was more to come. She was at his mercy and could feel her stomach churning over, even though she was smiling at Paul.

The detective hesitated, and then leaned forward, his manner confidential. He knew the best way to steer a conversation to where you want it to be, is to disarm the other person, he told himself. He closed his notebook and put it together with the pen back into his pocket, crossed his legs and leaned back into the comfortable settee.

"What is it about you, that makes me so convinced that you are somehow involved in some way with all of this and possibly more, yet makes me also want to believe that you are not."

He noticed that her knuckles were clenched and white, as if she were forcing herself to sit in her chair and not to get up and run away. There was something else too, was it anger or fear that flashed in her lovely blue eyes? It came back to the basic questions, who, when, where and why?

Sarah stared straight back at him matching his gaze. She unclenched her hands knowing that he had noticed, her expression was set, portraying nothing even though her heart was nearly jumping out of her body it was beating so fast. A slow river of sweat trickled down her back.

His dark brown eyes were like granite now as he stared at hard her.

Then came the question that nearly took the floor from under her!

"I think you better start working with me instead of working against me! Why do you think those young men were killed in that manner, Mrs. Lawson?"

"What young men? Uh, manner? What manner?" She stuttered.

"I am sure you must have read about the young men who have been killed over the past few months. Being shot in the genital area, it was all over the newspapers?" He explained.

Fear filled Sarah's head like a cloud of swirling mist.

"Oh yes, I remember now, but I didn't know that. I read only that they had been shot, but what has that to do with me or the murder of Diana Gonzales?"

WHY? WHY? She wanted to shout at him. **Why** was she killed? Because of Julio! She wanted to tell him, to let him know what kind of evil man she had once lived with, how he was to blame, how he was capable of such cruelty.

She reached over still outwardly calm, for her mug of tea. The contents were cold now. But she gratefully gulped them down her dry throat and then replaced the mug slowly. The dryness had come back. The thirst, the sweating hands, the quickened pulse, it was all the same reflex which the mind and the body was preparing itself for the imminent threat of Paul that he was trying to trick her into answering or accidentally let something out. Relax she told herself, he is reasonably sure that I have some connection with the serial killings but he has no absolute proof at this point. There were no clues left.

"I'm sure I don't know. The whole thing is so terrible, she was such a lovely lady and they were both such good friends to me when I lived in Spain and we continued seeing each other when I moved back to England."

Sarah looked at him and tears of fear filled her eyes. She wondered how much he knew about her. Did he know that Julio had been her lover? How could he, who would have told him, or had he figured it out for himself? He was a very astute man. Did he know she had something to do with the killings of the young men? She burst into tears.

Paul looked at her and realized he had upset this beautiful woman sitting opposite him. Of course he'd upset her, he knew she'd been a friend of Diana's, he had found her name, address and phone numbers in the dead woman's address book. How friendly had she been with the husband though, he wondered?

All at once he was so gentle that she grew even more nervous, after all he was a policeman and policemen do not like to be wrong.

He spoke briefly again. "I'm so sorry if I've upset you, Mrs. Lawson, or may I call you Sarah, but of course we have to explore every channel in an investigation such as this. I wonder if you would just take a look at this photo."

He put his hand into the inside pocket of his jacket and pulled out an A4 envelope and took out a photo of Diana and handed it to her. Sarah looked distant, isolated, sitting there, her skin paled as she looked at the photo of the upper half of Diana lying on the mortuary slab. She wondered if he was going to try shock tactics on her now.

"Did you know her well?" Paul asked softly in his professional manner.

Sarah came back to the present. She thought knowing someone doesn't automatically make me an accomplice.

"Yes, I knew her, quite well in fact. I met her sometime ago in Spain and then we struck up a good friendship just after I arrived back from Spain,

I know them both; I met her husband originally in Spain, when I lived there. He is a diplomat as you are probably aware and travels around quite a lot. I originally met Senor Gonzales at several cocktail parties that I attended with my previous husband and then twice more when his wife accompanied him. He also helped me find some work when I was in Spain. Of course I was very upset when he rang me. But, I don't know why she was killed, any more than I know anything about the young men who were killed. I'm sorry officer, I cannot help you, however, Michael Akaro at the drug Re-hab Centre might. He deals with a lot of drug addicts and such people. Maybe you should contact him!"

She smiled more confidently now.

"I expect you probably know that I do voluntary work at the Centre as well," she added. She knew she sounded a bit cocky. But she felt she was once more in control of the situation.

He looked at her as if he resented her attempts to play detective and pursed his lips before answering.

"Just two more questions. Do you think Senora Gonzales was having an affair? Also did you know that she was eight weeks pregnant?"

"Oh, my God! Oh no, they always wanted to have a child. I really don't know. Oh dear, oh dear, poor Juan, I know he wanted a child with her so desperately, she'd already had one miscarriage last year. No, I do not think she was having an affair. Diana was such a lovely woman and they were very happily married." She said sympathetically.

She wondered if Julio had in fact forced himself upon Diana, it wouldn't surprise her, knowing how evil he could be. Or had she had an affair with him sometime previously? But Sarah knew that Diana hated him with a vengeance. No, the child would have been Juan's.

She looked Paul straight in the eyes. "I really don't know. What I do know is that she loved her husband very much, they were a perfect match for each other."

"Thank you, I think that is all for now, Sarah, if you can think of anything that might be relevant to the Gonzales case or..."

He left the end of his sentence suspended in mid-air.

"Please let me know," he said as he handed her his card. "You can reach me on this number, day or night."

Sarah knew he was playing with her, as a cat does with a mouse. She accepted his card with a smile.

"Of course I shall. It was nice to meet you at last, I have heard a lot about you from David I'll let him know that you called on me!"

"No don't get up, I will show myself to the door, thank you for your co-operation. I will keep you informed about the proceedings. I presume you will be attending Diana Gonzales's funeral as you knew her so well!" He added somewhat sarcastically as he held out his hand.

"Thank you I appreciate your concern. Yes I will be at the funeral, they were both Catholic you know and so am I."

She answered him in the same tone as she looked him in the eye and once again shook his hand and then watched him leave the room.

Paul's gut feeling as he made his way to the front door was that Sarah knew more than she would let on and it ate away at him. He knew David was completely infatuated by her and could lose sight of all reality and he did not want to offend or hurt his old friend. He would go back to his office and check her out.

As the door of her house closed, she felt her breath was still trapped in her lungs, she didn't realize that she had been holding her breath and she gave a long sigh of relief.

Sarah suddenly felt very alone and vulnerable. She felt that somehow he knew it was she who was involved with the young men's demises. He'd asked her no more questions after showing her the photo of Juan's wife. Why? She thought was he testing her? Was he hoping that she might make a mistake and blurt something out?

She had smiled sweetly at him trying to make out that she was in command of the situation, even though for one wild moment she felt like running after him and confessing about her part in the other killings. But the only way she was going to survive was to keep silent.

Fear slithered through her body like a poisonous snake. Somehow she managed to get through the rest of the day as she kept reliving her conversation with Juan.

***

She had already known about Diana because Juan had rung her up after he had made a positive identification of her body and he was absolutely distraught with grief.

"It's Diana, she has been murdered, murdered by that evil son of mine, I know it was him. You were right, she was in danger and I didn't see it. I left her alone. What am I going to do Sarah?" He blurted out as he'd sobbed down the phone.

"It's all my fault!"

"She was what Juan? Oh! My God!"

She felt as if she had been punched in the stomach, as if someone had slammed into her with his or her full weight. She clutched the side of the hall telephone table and sat down in the small chair by the side of it, she thought she was going to pass out with the shock of his bad news. She was completely speechless.

"Sarah… Sarah, are you still there?" He cried down the phone.

"Yes, Juan," she had replied quietly, completely and utterly shocked by the news; she had to help him and do something for him, but what?

"You hadn't heard then yet? Diana was killed, murdered two nights ago. My lovely Diana."

Again he sobbed into the phone.

"Why didn't you tell me before, Juan, do you want me to come over to you, or better still, come over here. But drive carefully."

"Yes, I'm already on my way to you, Sarah, I'm in the car, I won't be long. I'll take care."

About half an hour later he met her on her doorstep looking absolutely devastated and ready to drop. She ushered him inside quickly and closed the door behind them.

"I'm sorry I didn't phone before, but I couldn't take it all in, I had to identify her and the police have been questioning me. I know it is Julio, I will not rest until I find him and kill him, myself with my own bare hands."

He'd shouted waving his arms about, he was so distraught.

"What shall I do, what shall we do? I'm sure he killed that prostitute in the churchyard that I read about in the paper as well. I know his trademark. Or if he didn't do it himself, he got someone else to do it and watched while it was happening. He likes that sort of thing. Goodness knows how many more women he's' killed, or had killed. He doesn't need to dirty his hands anymore. He can pay people to do his evil deeds for him instead. I told you he was evil! But I know it is he who has killed Diana; he has done it to show you and I that he is all-powerful. I know that he will come after you too. But I will have him stopped."

He ranted on waving his hands about and pacing the room.

Sarah knew there was no comforting him; he had to deal with his tragedy in his own time. No one knew his son better than him.

Juan sat down again, but not for long. He had been wandering between the chairs and the settee smoking heavily, as if he was trapped in a lonely game of musical chairs almost unaware that she was there.

She left the room and brought back a bottle of scotch and two glasses from one of her kitchen cupboards, placed them on the coffee table and poured two generous measures.

"Where did you stay last night Juan? I hope it was not at the apartment. You could have stayed here you know, you should have rung me immediately."

"I'm sorry, I wasn't thinking straight and I didn't want to get you involved in case the police were watching me. I stayed in a hotel last night, the apartment is off limits of course to everyone and anyway I never want to go back there, I tried to read a book last night, but I couldn't get into it, I tried to watch some TV but I just kept remembering Diana. I don't know what to do Sarah. I feel so guilty if only she had come to America with me, I begged and begged her to you know, but she said she could not because of her mother, whom as you know is not at all well." He said dismally, then gulped his scotch down nervously and poured himself another large one before lighting a cigarette.

"If only I had persuaded her more, if only I had organised a live in nurse for her mother. I keep on thinking, *if only*. Thank you for the invitation Sarah, but I think it is better not to stay here, as Julio might think we are having an affair, he is obviously so paranoid and probably having hallucinations about us now. He could even be watching us now. Who knows?"

He started pacing the room again.

"What's the point in saying if only? It is not going to bring her or my baby back."

"Your baby!" She had gasped. "Oh I am so sorry Juan."

"Yes she was eight weeks pregnant. I expect she had not told me, because we had already lost two when she was three months pregnant. I suppose she didn't want to tell me until she was sure this time. As you know, we've been trying ever since for another baby."

He broke off as he burst into tears.

She watched as a look of pain flickered across his handsome face.

"Sometimes I think the world's going mad! All these people on drugs; all this aggression, what in God's name do they think they're doing, what are they looking for?"

His restlessness and incessant smoking was making her very edgy. She was very frightened. Was Juan right? Was his son somewhere around watching them? Would he try and kill her also? She had to tell David or better still Michael about her involvement with his son and let him decide whether to tell the police or not.

Sarah knew how Juan felt. He was suspended in a limbo of futility, beyond comforting or help. Only he could help himself, time would eventually heal him. At least his busy life would give him less time to succumb to his loss. He'd suffered so much in his life, due to Julio's wickedness and now he had lost his beloved Diana.

"Of course once the police have sorted everything out, I shall sell the contents of the apartment, if there is anything that you would like, please take it. I had thought vaguely about having it refurbished anyway, but I could not bear to look at the things that Diana and I bought together. The Embassy has already told me that they will find me another appointment abroad when I am ready to move from the UK. At the moment I'm on compassionate leave for a month, which is a very good thing because it will give me time to think about sorting out the problem of my son. I'll probably take the transfer somewhere else. Maybe go back to the States or even Mexico. At the moment I just want to go away as far as possible. Thank heavens I have my work. Oh dear, I keep going on, don't I? I'm sorry Sarah, but I will get my head together once her funeral is over. I remember when I first met you, I was apologising for my son, and now I'm doing it again."

"Juan you know you can stay here as long as you wish. Both you and Diana helped me over a very bad patch and now I want to help you. I have plenty of room here."

She pleaded with him to stay, but he had refused.

"No, you will not be safe, Julio will come after me, and he will not rest now until he's destroyed me too. Then he will hunt you down. Well, maybe I will stay a few more days just to make sure that you are safe. I should be alright in the hotel. Beside I have a few things to do, the funeral arrangements, when they release Diana's body. There is so much to do. I have to go and see her mother too. God forbid! This news will probably give her a heart attack. You and I need to have a serious talk as well about Julio and what has to be done about him. I'll stay a couple of days with you and then we can come up with a plan regarding Julio."

He sat down in the Edwardian chair and placed his drink on the small table by the side of it and was silent for a few moments. He knew just the right person whom he could trust to help him without leaving any traces.

***

Sarah's phone in the hall rang out sharply and broke the silence as she came back to the present. She glanced up too quickly, and then tried to pretend to herself that she wasn't nervous after her interrogation of Paul's. Her instincts told her it was probably David. She couldn't tell him yet, thank heavens he was too busy on the case to see her for a few days, but she knew that Michael would understand, she would talk to him and ask him for his advice. She wondered if Paul was having her house watched. She wondered if it was Julio, gloating. She let the phone ring and then she could hear David leaving a message that he would call her back later.

***

During Juan's stay at her place, they discussed what they were to do about his son, but there was no consoling him regarding his wife. On the third morning he booked himself into a hotel in the West End in case Julio was watching him.

He was left with the stark reality to cope with his wife's death, also the reality that he could be jailed for life if he went through with his plans for Julio. But he knew what he had to do. Two phone calls were all that it would take. When he had learnt

343

from the Pathologist's report that Diana had been eight weeks pregnant, and that his bastard of a son had also killed his unborn child, he had decided that Julio would pay for his heinous crime.

**

Sarah did not try to contact him and she was scared that her telephone was being tapped by the police and also she knew Juan would prefer to grieve alone. He said he would ring her on her mobile when he was ready to let her know when Diana's body was released and sent to a funeral parlour and when the funeral took place. They would talk then.

CHAPTER THIRTY ONE

LONDON - 2004

At last Diana's body was released from the Mortuary and was sent to a funeral parlour nearby ready for her burial service at the Catholic Church in the West End.

It seemed to Paul that several weeks had passed since he had walked into the nightmare scene that was actually only just two weeks ago.

Juan looked old, tired and shattered with grief as he looked down upon his wife's decorative coffin covered with a mass of beautiful flowers.

Paul stood waiting for him to return to his seat in the front pew.

Juan was numbly acknowledging the sympathetic utterances of the few friends and colleagues that attended the funeral service at the Catholic Church. Sarah stood by his side and he almost seemed to be leaning on her in his grief as she stood by him looking very pale and sad.

Paul knew there was a strong bond between them and he felt that there was more to their friendship than either one was telling him.

Diana's mother had been unable to attend the funeral as she was still in hospital recovering from her cancer operation.

It was a very small and private service.

As one of the mourners at Diana Gonzales funeral, Paul was eager to see that her murderer was brought to justice.

What stranger he reasoned, would she have admitted to her apartment that fatal evening? It had to be someone she knew, or was she, unbeknown to her husband, having an affair with someone? After all he was away a lot. He thought that the latter was unlikely. But who was the Spanish type man who'd been hanging around, that the old wino had mentioned? Perhaps her husband knew him. He knew there was a connection. He would do a full check on Juan and his background. Also on Sarah Lawson and whether her story was true about originally meeting him in Spain. But why would they both lie? He would find out the truth anyway!

Paul bowed his head reverently as the priest led the mourners in prayer.

CHAPTER THIRTY TWO

LONDON - 2004

The intercom buzzed on David's desk.

"Excuse me," David stabbed the talk button with his pen. "Yes Samantha?"

"Sorry to bother you, sir. Your 12.00 o'clock appointment is on the line, she wants to know if she can come a little bit earlier."

"No, reschedule her for tomorrow, make my apologies and then cancel the rest of my appointments for the afternoon. Please Samantha." He pleaded with his secretary.

***

Michael sat in David's office and looked around him. It was a large room, with tall double glazed windows artistically draped with cream muslin curtains and dark mahogany bookcases and furnished with a large mahogany leather-topped desk. There were also two comfortable leather armchairs and a leather couch. The floor that was stained natural pine and polished was softened by a large well-preserved multi-coloured Oriental rug in front of the desk. Two pedestals topped with bronze Roman heads stood in the corners by the windows. A big healthy Parlour Palm stood in another corner and a water cooler in the last corner. On the desk was an artistic display of cream and salmon pink orchids and bright orange lilies and a carved ebony pen and pencil holder.

The walls were adorned with diplomas and pictures of David at Public School and later at

Medical School at Cambridge. There were several pictures with Michael in them. There was one special photo of both men and they had their arms around each other's shoulders and looked very seriously at the camera in their cap and gowns on their graduation day.

"I remember that photo," laughed Michael. "Gosh weren't we slim then!"

"Hey, speak for yourself," joked David. "I'm still in good shape!"

They started to reminisce about the old days, while they sipped the delicious coffee that Samantha had made for them.

Suddenly the sunlight, which only moments before had been streaming through his office windows vanished and cooled as heavy black clouds rolled in from the west. A bright flash of lightening could be seen.

"It's been raining a lot lately." Michael commented as he looked thoughtfully at David.

David ran a finger along the side of his nose. A gesture Michael had seen him do whenever he was puzzled or anxious. "Yes, it's that time of year isn't it?"

"There's something bothering you old chap, can I help?" Queried Michael.

"Well, yes and no, it's about Sarah, Paul Forrest seems to think that somehow she is involved with the murders of the drug addicts that happened a while ago. How could she be? They stopped ages ago, didn't they? So how could she possibly be the murderer? And I know that she's certainly not involved in the Gonzales case."

"Yes, the killings did stop sometime ago, in fact shortly after she met you David. I think you should have a serious word with her and clear the air. She is a very private person, but she loves you, very much, I can tell you that now. She has been very brave and gone through a lot in her life, especially the latter years."

Michael commented not wishing to break his promise that he had made to Sarah regarding confidentiality. He admired Sarah, she was a person who was not afraid to pick up the pieces and continue with her life.

"Coincidence, purely coincidence I'm sure, and she definitely cannot be accused of the recent murder of her friend, especially as she was with me that night! That was very sad, Michael." David commented.

"I know she was very friendly with both of them. Come on, enough of this, I'm taking the rest of the day off. Let's go to my club for lunch. It's just around the corner and we can have a drink and talk there.

David refused to imagine that his Sarah could be involved in something like the murder of the young men.

***

David did not see Sarah for three days after his meeting with Michael and had taken a rain check on her invite to dinner, as he was so tied up with the Gonzales case as well as his own patients. But he called her each day. He thought about what Michael had said about Sarah, but Paul's comments still worried him. Of course she was innocent, how could she be otherwise.

When he arrived back at his apartment at around six thirty pm, he checked the refrigerator. His housekeeper had left him a bowl of her excellent homemade asparagus soup, ready for the microwave, also a mixed green salad with several thin slices of tomato and pieces of cold chicken thinly sliced topped with flakes of fresh Parmesan cheese and a small side dish of her very special homemade mayonnaise with chives. He selected a well-chilled bottle of Chenin Blanc from the door of his refrigerator and poured himself a glass. He would eat first before he set to work on the two cases.

He wanted to satisfy himself that Sarah was not connected in anyway to them so he could eliminate her from his records. So, she worked at the Rehabilitation Centre! She knew Juan Gonzales and his wife, so what? That didn't necessarily make her a murderer, just because she knew Diana and her husband.

He knew that people were not always what they seemed, but he was in love with Sarah, dreaming of some kind of happily ever after future. How could he be wrong about her? If, and it was a very big **IF**, she was the killer of the four young men, she must have had a very good reason for doing so. The thoughts started tormenting him. He had to find out. Was she perhaps insane and he had been sadly wrong in his choice of her.

Had she fooled him into thinking that she was in love with him? He didn't think so. As far as

Diana Gonzales and her husband were concerned they had just been good friends. But he was in love with Sarah and he remembered the old saying about love being blind. Was he blind to her faults? Was he becoming too soft? These thoughts worried him. He had to get to the bottom of it. Whatever the reason he would protect her.

David remembered a case that he was on some years ago. The man stabbed his wife almost two hundred times and slept with her body for several days, bringing her breakfast in bed, watching TV with her, talking about old times. Even when he was finally caught, he refused to acknowledge the fact that she was dead. He kept saying he loved her. Many people get killed in the guise of love, because a lover will not let go, won't give up even when there is nothing there anymore.

He also knew for a fact that on a farm in the north, a woman killed her husband with an axe, because he was unfaithful to her, and then she ground him up in a wood-chipper and came back two days later to burn up his pieces in the wood burner in the cottage. A neighbour got suspicious about the husband's disappearance and called the police. People did strange things under stress. He knew that Sarah had gone through a lot in the past, but surely, nothing bad enough to become a Serial Killer?

He picked up the phone and gave her a call.

CHAPTER THIRTY THREE

LONDON - 2004

The following evening Sarah went to dinner at David's apartment. He wanted her on his territory instead of on hers, as she would be less likely to lie to him if she was out of her comfort zone.

They sat at his dining room table. He had not sent out for food this time, he had cooked the supper himself. Two juicy sirloin steaks, perfectly cooked running with meat juices, a bowl of crisp mixed green salad and jacket potatoes with sour cream and chive dressing. They shared a bottle of fine Sicilian red wine. His life-like gas log fire warmed his elegant dining room and the soothing light of scented candles created dancing shadows around the room. Soft classical music was piped through his Bang & Olufsen stereo system.

He looked across the table at her lovingly.

"Sarah there's something I have to tell you, I need to talk to you very seriously. Paul Forrest stopped by yesterday, he was asking about you, how I met you, etc? He seems to think that in some way you have something to do with the previous serial killings of the four drug addicts, or at least that you know something about them. Do you, my darling? Or is it something you have picked up from your work at the Rehab centre?" He prompted.

David's questions took her by surprise and she carefully considered her reply as she sipped her wine and then she placed the exquisite crystal glass back onto the table and paused before answering.

"Darling, I'm not quite sure what you're saying. How can he tie me in with the serial killings, as you call them? I thought they had been solved and the case was closed, or put on the shelf or whatever the police do. You told me that there was so little evidence that the police had dropped it for the time being and were concentrating on the Gonzales case."

"Well it would seem that the case is still open even though they have not got any more evidence. He also knows you were a friend of Diana and Juan Gonzales and seems to think that you might possibly have some idea who her killer was. Of course I told him that was rubbish, just because you knew the two of them. But how well did you know both of them, and what do you know about a person called Jacko von Jonge?"

She could feel perspiration running down her back. She felt he was cross-examining her in a very subtle way. She looked at him, her blue eyes dark and feral. She felt the blood draining from her face as she picked up the glass of wine again and sipped it before answering his question.

"Yes, Juan and Diana were my friends. Very good friends to me in fact when I needed them. No I don't know who killed her actually.'"

She was not really lying, because how could she be sure that Julio had killed Diana, maybe Juan was having a nervous breakdown. But was it a lie? She couldn't really be sure that Julio had actually done it, even though she felt inside of her that he did. Her hand trembled as she put the glass down once again and her eyes filled with fear.

"Do you think I'm crazy, I've thought so much about Diana these last few days, do you think the killer will come after me too, if he knows that I was her friend?" She asked trying to steer the conversation in another direction.

"I've been so worried the last few days. Who is this Jacko von Jonge? I certainly do not know anyone of that name."

In that instant David saw that she was close to the edge of breaking down and crying and he was experiencing a mind-numbing epiphany. She was very upset. She wasn't crazy at all; she was just very frightened of what might happen to her. In spite of his intellect and training telling him she was lying about something, he almost believed every single thing she was telling him, but the 'actually' on the end of a sentence often denoted it was not the complete truth.

"I am sorry Sarah, but I was only asking, I was upset myself when Paul said that you might be involved. Forget about it. How would you like a little of the dessert I brought in? It's a lovely Tiramisu." He said changing the conversation to give her time to think.

He left the table and brought back from the fridge two large portions of Tiramisu that he had had sent over from Selfridges and placed them on the table.

She licked her dry lips and cleared her throat nervously. "I don't know what you mean." She said as she looked away from him, trying to think of something else to say while she slowly tasted the delicious dessert.

"Okay, just tell me one thing, were you having an affair with Juan Gonzales, or have you ever had an affair with him?"

She burst out laughing.

"No, David my love definitely not. He has always been a wonderful friend, almost a father figure. I can never thank him enough for what he has done in the past for me. When I lived in Spain, as you know, I used to go to several parties with Mark my second husband. His parents knew a lot of influential people over the years and Juan was one of them. When Mark left me on my own, I turned to Mr. Gonzales - Juan - for help. He tried to trace Mark for me, I had very little money and I needed help. After all I was a single woman, on my own and I needed some advice on Spanish law. I'd never felt so scared and helpless before and I was in a strange country. Also he was my landlord and I was running out of money, I was frantic at the time, he helped me, and he got me some work."

She sighed before continuing.

"Hell, it would seem that all the men in my life that I've got involved with have been weak and I have been left to pick up the pieces. You don't understand. I've been married twice to two men who let me down, I needed someone to help me, and he did. Without his help I would not be here today."

She smiled weakly at him, though her eyes were glistening with tears.

"I do understand, would you like to tell me more about it then?" He saw the tears run down her cheeks and felt he had maybe pushed her too far.

All at once she wanted to tell him, to tell him everything. Perhaps he would understand after all. She swallowed hard as she nearly gave into the temptation. She knew how the guilt scenario went. She was growing hollow, her nerves felt exposed and she was on edge. Her nerves were twisted, pulled taut like a violin string. There was only one reason why she did not feel completely helpless and that was her love for David.

She took another sip of her wine, before continuing, playing for time and placed her wine glass carefully back onto the table and looked at him wide-eyed.

"That's all there is to tell really. We kept in touch when I came back to England and I got to know his wife better. She and I became such good friends. I miss her too."

Somehow she guessed what he was thinking and reached up and touched his cheek.

"You do believe me, don't you?"

"Of course I do Sarah. I told Paul that he was mistaken. He has to do his duty you know."

David got up from the table and came around to her and took her in his arms.

"I do love you so much Sarah, I never thought I would love anyone so much again. After my wife died, it was very difficult for me too. I don't think you ever stop loving someone you cared for very deeply about. I also think you should try not to erase any part of your past, because in fact you can't anyhow, no matter how hard you try. The difference is to let go, let go of pain and get on with your life."

"That's very philosophical. Have you done that David?"

"Yes, I think so now, and you must do the same. I want you Sarah, I want to take care of you and perhaps one day we'll get married and even start a family. But I want us both to be sure. If there is someone else you're seeing, tell him he's got stiff competition, because whoever he is, he's not looking out for you. If it's the past you are holding onto, I'm going to break that hold." He said very seriously as he pulled her into his strong body and kissed her long and hard.

She thought about her aunt and knew she would have definitely approved of David. She knew the time had come when she had to come clean with him, or at least tell him something more about herself and Julio.

Where shall I begin she wondered? Her mind was a tangle of contradictory emotions, the foremost of which was fear. Would David leave her if she told him the truth? Would he turn her over to the police? She had to put an end to it. She had to rid herself of Julio.

She knew where he hung out. Juan had told her. Between them they had devised a plan. Julio deserved to be killed. He would pose no problem at all. She would go to him and tell him she wanted to come back. In his drugged condition he would believe her. His ego would do that for him anyway. Then she would let Juan know, he would know what to do, then perhaps she could relax. David had got too tangled up in her dilemma. She had to tell him something.

"I need to tell you something though." She said quietly.

"Take your time," he said gently as they moved to the comfortable sitting area.

"I don't really know where to begin," she said. The emotion in her voice sounded real enough.

"It all started in Spain a long while ago."

David listened thoughtfully as she began to carefully unravel her story. She told him how she had met Julio, how he had stalked her in England, how Michael had helped her recover. She left out the fact that Juan was Julio's father at this point. Also that Julio was known in England as Jacko von Jonge and last of all that she knew who the serial killer was. That would come later, if necessary. She hadn't actually lied to David, just embroidered the truth a little.

"I want you to forget about Paul now and your past, let's enjoy the rest of the evening." David exclaimed after he had heard her story.

He knew she was still keeping something from him. But for the moment that was her prerogative, he felt sure she would tell him the rest when the time was right and he knew more than ever now that he had to protect her. He too had certain things in his past that he had never told her. Everyone has a right to their privacy. He remembered what his father had always told him, that *confession was good for one's soul but not for one's reputation.*

Sarah knew deep down that Paul Forrest was too smart not to connect the murders somehow to her. She wasn't too worried because she knew by the time that happened Julio would not be around and she would never see him again and most probably Juan would be out of the country and he did have diplomatic immunity.

She knew what had to be done.

CHAPTER THIRTY FOUR

LONDON - 2004

Michael was sitting behind a confusion of letters and dog-eared medical journals when Sarah arrived. His large black face beamed at her, the smile reached his eyes and the corners crinkled. When he stood up to greet her, he accidentally knocked his worn jacket from the back of the chair. His desk seemed to shrink to a classroom size, as he towered above it.

"Hello Sarah, what can I do for you?" He asked as she entered his office.

She stood in the doorway. Behind her dark glasses and the jeans and T-shirt she wore, like a camouflage, she seemed scared and vulnerable.

"There is something I need your advice on, I have spoken to David as you suggested. Now I need to tell you something Michael, again confidentially, as a patient of yours."

BOOK THIRTEEN

JOSHUA Ch. 10 Verse 25
And Joshua said unto them, Fear not, nor be
dismayed.
be strong and of good courage...

CHAPTER THIRTY FIVE

LONDON - 2004

As she drove along after her meeting with
Michael having unburdened her guilt, she felt
strangely drained and oddly depressed, she had
decided to come clean with him and he had assured
her of complete confidentiality.

"The reason I got involved with the killings in
the first place was because I was trying to exorcise
Julio out of my life, they were not frenzied attacks
as the police imagined, they were very well planned
and organised. The victims had all been associated
with him, it was him who influenced them and
made them what they were."

He'd just listened patiently and done nothing.
He understood her actions and had told her it was
now up to her. Maybe her feeling that the whole
thing had been a weird game caused her depression.
A game in which she was the expert player, but she
felt somehow that she was no longer in command.

She made her way towards Hyde Park. She
needed some solitude to think things out.

In the park Sarah walked beneath the tall trees. The clear blue sky held the heat as the sun beat down, even though it was the third week of October. Everyone was calling it an Indian summer. But it was cooler beneath the umbrella of leaves. Several striped deck chairs lay back on the dried grass, silvery pigeons scavenged the grass, looking for anything that was easy to satisfy their greedy hunger. She too felt hungry as well as thirsty as she made her way towards a burger stand, pausing only to direct a couple of tourists towards Piccadilly Circus.

CHAPTER THIRTY SIX

HEATHROW AIRPORT - 2004

The tall, thin, sun-tanned man with the shaven head made his way through Immigration and Customs at Heathrow Airport. Then once outside, he took a taxi into Central London where the hotel had been previously booked for him. He made a short phone call from his mobile and met his client at the agreed meeting place again.

CHAPTER THIRTY SEVEN

LONDON - 2004

Pinkies gay club was full of people. It smelt of a mixture of cigarette smoke, perfume, after-shave and sex. The multicoloured strobes gave the place a weird glow. The club was all chrome and tinted mirrors and booths with glass tables. On the pocketsize dance floor, many bodies were rubbing up against each other in a pretext of dancing as a build up to something more intimate later.

The bar was busy and the padded chrome stools were occupied by mainly young, very good-looking gay men looking for sex. A few sleek women wearing - *fuck-me* - high heeled shoes and other women in designer trouser suits and expensively cropped hair were in hot pursuit of same. Most of the action was in the booths, men kissing men and women kissing women.

Young Tony Smith casually looked round him at the some of the people in the club. As he strolled up to the bar he noticed a tall, slender, woman with long red-hair, startlingly made up and colourfully dressed in Armani jeans and a scarlet D&G off the shoulder blouse, with jangling chains around her neck and a wide gold cuff bracelet on her left wrist, standing at the bar watching the action, sipping a colourful cocktail and watching the entrance. He thought she was probably a *trannie* and smiled at her.

She stared at him, but did not acknowledge him. She just drained her glass and then picked up her DKNY black patent handbag and made her way towards the rear fire door. She had seen enough, her plan was ready to be executed.

Tony ordered a beer from a beautiful looking young barman of about twenty with blond curly hair who had a diamond earring in each ear. He sported a St. Tropez tan and a black leather waistcoat, and a very brief pair of skin-tight black leather shorts with cutaways at the back and they hugged his pert muscular backside and left very little to the imagination at the front.

This was the fourth Gay bar that Tony had visited that night, as ordered by John Rivers. His training told him to follow orders and trawl yet another Gay bar, but his gut instincts told him that this could be his chance to shine. Tony had the feeling that he was in the right place.

"Hi, my name is All…a…an, can I help you?"

The barman lisped and gave Tony a big smile, showing off his perfectly capped white teeth as he looked him over and flirted with him.

"New here? What's y…ou...r name?" He asked as he pursed his lips in a suggestive gesture.

"Yeah, Tony, just moved to London, a friend of mine in Manchester recommended this place. Told me I could find some action here, if you know what I mean!"

He said, holding out two twenty-pound notes, aware that he was being watched and probably listened to on one of the discreetly placed security systems and cameras he had noticed when he'd entered the bar area.

"Ye...ea...ah, I know what you mean." The bartender mewed with affectation as he pocketed the money in his waistcoat and then pushed a button under the bar.

"Just down the corridor, first door on the right. Just press the red button. See you later?"

Tony walked down the narrow corridor and pressed the red button on the wall. The black leather padded door opened to reveal a large room at the back of the club. It was like something out of a Hollywood set.

There were four people sitting around a big smoked glass and chrome circular table. The walls were covered with real tiger and zebra skins, carved African masks and Assagai spears. In the four corners of the room stood four African tribal drums each one with a tall thin stereo speaker fixed to it. There was a 5' x 5' TV screen on one wall, and a fifty-inch security screen showing ten different areas of the club on another wall. A gay blue movie was showing, on the large screen of the TV and there were two young men on the film fucking each other. He wondered how many other rooms there were in the club being used at the moment for similar activities.

A tall, good-looking rather gaunt man with dark hair sleeked back off his face, arose from the glass table nearby.

"Welcome Tony," he said with a heavy affected Afrikaans accent. "Would you like a drink, or something else?"

He held out a hand to welcome him. "My name's Jacko von Jonge, welcome to my club."

As Tony had thought there were hidden microphones in the bar and he had been watched and listened too. As he shook the outstretched hand, he had the weirdest feeling that somehow he had either met him before or seen a photo of him somewhere and the name definitely rang a bell in his mind from a case that he had read about the year before. He knew he was on the right track

The tall man moved over to one of the tribal drums, removed the top with the loudspeaker on it and took out a four by five inch plastic bag half-full of white powder. The large well-cut diamond in the ring on his left little finger sparkled with fire as he did so, catching the glow from the wall uplighters.

He walked over to Tony.

"How about a quick snort!" He smiled wickedly. "A little Something to put you in the mood, perhaps!" He exclaimed as he placed the bag on the table.

"Well maybe just a little." Tony mewed as he pursed his full lips.

He carefully scooped up a few grains between his thumb and fore finger on his right hand and took a quick sniff, closed his eyes and sighed.

"I don't do it all the time, you understand! Just now and then to relax." He rubbed his fore finger over his gums and then grinned.

A good looking young blond man at the table moved his chair back and ran his hand over his crotch suggestively.

"Go on, take a proper hit, you'll feel better, Tony," said Von Jonge smiling charmingly and watching him with his dark predatory eyes.

The horrible part was that the dark haired man was so right. Cocaine always made him feel better, infinitely better. At least for a few hours, but he was working and only occasionally indulged when he was off duty.

The other young man with gelled erect dark hair at the table picked up the plastic bag and held it to his nose.

"Umm. That smell. That tingle, nothing like it, do you mind if I have a hit too?"

Tony ran his tongue over his lips. "Yeah, sure you can."

Von Jonge's expression was contemptuous as he looked at Tony, his dark eyes huge and deep, swirling like pools of muddy water beneath the surface, watching and waiting. His instinct made him suspicious of the stranger. Suddenly his mobile phone rang; he answered it and left the room leaving the three men to their own devices.

Tony Smith, although only slightly befuddled from testing the cocaine suddenly recalled the investigation in the Drug Squad to find the man Von Jonge. His own task of seeking information about Diana Gonzales was going nowhere; could this be the chance for him to gain some brownie points with the Drugs Squad though and see where Von Jonge was going?

Hesitating momentarily and silently uttering the eponymous bollocks, he quickly left the room to follow the tall dark haired man hoping to catch up, but at the same time not to be seen.

***

Outside the rain was coming down in sheets, overflowing the blocked gutters and turning the streets into long waterways.

The tall, slender redheaded, heavily made-up woman sheltering in a doorway opposite Pinkies watched the tall dark haired man leave the club and get into a parked midnight blue Porsche and drive away. The rest of the street was empty. The woman knew exactly where he was going, having seen him do the same thing over the past two nights. She made a quick phone call and a black SUV came around the corner and stopped. She hitched up her skirt and jumped in, in a most unlady like manner.

CHAPTER THIRTY EIGHT

LONDON - 2004

Paul bedside telephone shrilled him awake. For a millisecond, he thought about not answering it, but the fantasy passed and he reached for the receiver. As he grabbed it from the side of his bed he also managed to focus on his radio alarm clock. 05.30 am was projected on the face.

"Paul, it's Tony."

"Tony who?" He asked sleepily.

"Tony Smith, look, get over to 92 Dean Street, Soho, a small rundown apartment block, now? It looks like there's been another murder. Could be connected to the Von Jonge case."

Paul bristled with a surge of anger.

"This had better be good, and at five in the morning and I'm DCI Forrest to you," he admonished. "Wait there for me."

***

Paul, leaving Tony Smith outside, peered into the dingy room. A naked dark-haired man was lying on the floor face down in a pool of blood that was beginning to set; his clothes had been thrown to one side in the room. Paul stepped over the doorway and looked down at him.

A tall very thin young man of about twenty five old, also with dark hair, appeared and hovered in the doorway, then entered the room and rushed over to the man to try and turn him over.

"Come on help me," he shouted at Paul as he pulled the body over onto its back and held him.

Paul stood in shocked silence staring down at the body. He recognised him instantly from some new photos he had in his office from the Drugs Squad. The man's face was partially covered by a curtain of blood-stained black hair. He looked like something out of a B - horror film or snuff movie.

He realised that he ought to call Forensics, but what the hell; perhaps the death of the once very good-looking man was retribution in itself. Forensics could wait a little longer. He knew he shouldn't feel like this, but what the hell, the man was beyond all help now. He suddenly smelt cigarette smoke and he recalled that he had smelt the same brand of cigarette in the apartment of Diana Gonzales and he knew immediately that there was some connection to the killing of the beautiful diplomat's wife.

As Paul peered closer at the body man, he noticed that there was a gunshot wound through the left temple of the dead man, possibly a 9mm bullet. Looking further down the body he saw more blood seeping from the man's groin. He carefully knelt at the side of the body and could see a short stainless steel crossbow bolt protruding from his genitals. But why the shot to the head as well, he thought to himself. So, the killer had shot him first in the head and then finished him off with a small crossbow? Or the other way round perhaps? What did that signify he asked himself? What was the link between the killing of a known drug dealer and the previous four deaths of drug users, Paul wondered? None of the earlier murders had involved the use of firearms. Only the crossbow bolts symbolised the possibility of the perpetrator being the same person. He reluctantly pushed the thoughts to the back of his mind; his innermost feelings would remain secret. Drug dealer or user, so what! They were all scum and did it matter if a few died? This murder would ultimately go down as another unsolved drug death. He sighed deeply and rose to his feet.

As Paul stared at the scene before him, a smell other than fresh blood assailed his nostrils and his attention was turned to one corner of the untidy room. Something lay there, half-wrapped in a small plastic bag. It smelt like rotting meat. He closed his eyes feeling sick to his stomach and waited until the room stopped spinning around and then nudged it with the toe of his right shoe and something fell out.

"Oh, dear God!" He exclaimed aloud.

It was a hand! It was a woman's severed left hand with a pink long polished nail extension on it.

He knew instinctively to whom it belonged. It had to be the Diplomat's wife. It lay on the floor like a discarded old toy, neatly cut through. Its fingers had curled inward and were starting to putrefy. A piece of fine broken gold chain was hanging from one of the curled fingers. Seeing the gold chain Paul knew that the dead man on the floor was definitely the killer of Diana Gonzales. He discreetly took his handkerchief from one of his trouser pockets and bent down and carefully pulled the chain from the finger, wrapped it up and put it into one of the pockets of his jacket.

Now he knew the significance of the gold charm, somehow Diana Gonzales must have, whilst she was dying made sure that somehow she was going to leave a clue to whoever found her, by separating the charm from the chain. The killer must have only seen the one hand holding the broken chain. But who had killed the man on the floor and what was he doing in this filthy room with two beds and a shabby dressing table in it? Perhaps he kept the girls he imported as prostitutes or he dealt drugs from it. The minute he had seen the severed hand he had a bad feeling that this was possibly one of those crimes that would haunt him for the rest of his life. Paul sighed deeply and rose to his feet once more.

"You can't do that, you're destroying valuable evidence. The Forensic team will be here soon, they'll do that," Paul said quietly to the distraught young man holding the lifeless body of Jacko von Jonge.

"I don't care. I have to clean him up or something. I can't just leave him naked on the floor," he replied distraughtly.

The dead man's body was losing its heat. The young man took the body in his arms and began to cry and cover him with kisses regardless of the fact that the man was dead. Some blood began to suddenly flow again from his wounds having been moved and smeared the young man. At that moment a pretty young Oriental girl, who could be a prostitute, from the way she was dressed, entered the room and between them they managed to lay the body on a bed in one corner of the room.

Paul looked on horrified. He couldn't believe what he was seeing; yet he didn't have the heart to stop them.

"Please leave us alone," begged the young woman. "We want to clean him up."

"No, you can't do that," shouted Paul. "I   have to call the coroner. This is a crime scene and both of you should not be interfering with it." He shouted at them again trying to get them to understand what he was saying to them.

"Well at least let me cover him up." The young man pleaded as he pulled a dirty thin sheet from the other bed nearby over the lower half of the dark-haired man's body, as a gesture of decency.

A small bunch of people had collected by the door. Tony Smith was amongst them.

Paul pulled himself together and shouted at Tony.

"For God's sake, get these bloody people out of here and secure the scene. I'll phone McAlistair and you get some backup."

Tony looked at the chaotic scene before him and recognised the young dark haired man from Pinkies, holding the body.

"Does anyone know who the dead man is?" Paul shouted to the people standing nearby.

With a start Tony recognised the body as being the owner of the gay club, whom he had just been following. Regaining his power of speech, Tony confirmed to Paul that the victim was indeed Jacko von Jonge.

"His name is Jacko von Jonge, "re-iterated an attractive tall black girl with a shoulder length blonde wig and an extremely short black skirt and red sequinned top who suddenly appeared in the doorway.

"Why don't you ask **him** about Jacko?" She inclined her head towards the young man.

"They were very close," she sneered contemptuously as she looked at him crying over the body. "Very, very close!" Then she spat on the floor, with disgust, and muttered something in a foreign language and turned and left.

Like the pieces of a jig-saw falling into place, Paul knew instinctively that the dead man was the person he'd been looking for in connection with the prostitute killings as well as the murder of Diana Gonzales. Maybe the case could now be closed or could it? This was not just another gay, drug related murder, although there were plenty of those in the Soho area. The media would have a field day. He knew who the victim was. He had recognised the family likeness, and he knew who his father was. He sighed, now he had the duty to tell Juan Gonzales about his son. Somehow he had to keep the Diplomat's name out of the newspapers.

***

When eventually questioned by the police no one who had been at the crime scene said anything, they had heard nothing, and they had seen nothing. It would seem there were no witnesses.

***

A tall, thin, redheaded woman, watched from a doorway across the road, clinging to the shadows near the scene of the crime as she waited for the rain to cease. Her thick make-up hid her tanned skin and had run slightly in the rain. Her wig had fallen a little askew. She was cold; she had been there for some time and she pulled her thin raincoat around her slim body.

The street was empty. The rain was still coming down, but not as hard as before. Gradually the rain began to diminish as the police left. She bent down and picked up the sports bag on the ground by her feet and stepped out and walked over to the approaching Black Mercedes with heavily tinted glass and got in. The big black car drove swiftly away as she relaxed on the back seat.

The man sitting beside her handed her a large brown envelope. She looked inside and smiled.

"I would appreciate it if you would drop me off about 100 yards from my hotel. I need to change out of these clothes before I go in."

Her companion pressed a button on the arm of the back seat and spoke into the hidden microphone and gave the instructions to the driver.

As they approached the hotel she got out of the Mercedes, nothing and nobody else was about.

The man in the back of the black car did not bother to look back. The deed was done. He had other things on his mind as he lit himself a cigarette.

CHAPTER THIRTY NINE

HEATHROW AIRPORT - 2004

The tall, thin suntanned man with the shaven head boarded the plane for New Orleans. Once on board he ordered champagne, after all he was five hundred thousand dollars richer! He had been called in once again to clean up another one of Julio's messes and he had also finally sought revenge for his niece's death in New Orleans - another murder committed by Julio several years ago.

He had more than enough money put away to start a new life. He could also now afford to have the final medical procedures that would allow him to lead the rest of his life as a woman. All these years of doing dirty work for Senor Gonzales and others like him were nearly over. He had achieved his goal.

He had enjoyed his long stay in London, dressed to kill - make-up and all. He had in fact really enjoyed dispatching the drug addicted low lives.

One of his particular pleasures had been in being chauffeured around several times by a lady who called herself... Sarah.

CHAPTER FORTY

LONDON - 2004

Juan slept fitfully, awakening several times during the night.

The deed was done. He knew from previous experience the police could not trace the killing to himself. Every day there were murders in London. The real danger lay in the fact that they might suspect him though and find out eventually that Jacko Von Jonge was his son. He would deal with that when it happened, he would leave the country. After all he had Diplomatic Immunity.

He turned on the TV in the hotel where he was staying to listen to the mid-morning news. It was announced that a well-known drug-dealer whom the Drug Squad had been after for a long time had been murdered in the Soho area the previous night. Investigations were in progress. So far there were no witnesses. A picture of the man flashed up on the screen, probably taken some years ago when he looked young and handsome, not like the last time when Juan had seen his son, pale and haggard.

The newsreader referred to him as Jacko von Jonge.

Juan's eyes filled with tears for the son he had fathered and once loved.

***

Sarah and David were sitting in her lounge in Richmond watching the mid-morning news. As the picture of a good looking dark-haired young man was shown on the screen, she shivered inwardly, but she knew she was finally free of Julio. He was laid to rest forever.

She smiled at David, her eyes held a secret look as she kissed him. He kissed her back lovingly. Of course he had guessed all along that Sarah had been involved with the mysterious killings of the young men. He also knew that the man on the screen was Juan's son and that Juan would be protected from the media by his Diplomatic Immunity. He also knew that the police had ways and means of putting certain cases to bed!

***

David recalled the day when Juan had visited him in his office and told him his plan to get rid of his son. Justice had prevailed after all. Sarah would now be free to marry him, once her decree absolute, from Mark, came through and there would be no need for any more secrecy and they would get on with their lives, perhaps move to another country. He could sell his practise and he had plenty of money invested and also put aside, perhaps they would travel around the World for a while until things blew over.

Michael had said he would look after Picasso. The two men had had a serious talk after Julio's death and David had told him, he too would have killed for her. He too would have rid the world of such scum. Michael had just nodded with agreement.

CHAPTER FORTY ONE

LONDON - 2004

A dark haired young man in a beat-up metallic grey Ford Mondeo, wearing wrap around dark glasses and a black baseball cap covering his gelled hair, watched Sarah's house as he had done so religiously for two weeks as he planned his movements.

She came rushing out unaware of his presence and jumped into her BMW parked in her driveway.

He followed her at a discreet distance to David's office. His obsession still very much alive, how could Sarah have betrayed his lover for another man? Jacko in his drug-fuelled state had often told him of the evil that Sarah had caused. In his warped and twisted mind he blamed her for what he had become, like all psychopaths nothing was his fault the blame must lay at her door, at his father's door and at Diana's door. He had taken no responsibility for his own actions. Sarah must be got rid of first. They had made a pact.

The young man saw her black car parked outside the consulting rooms of David Myers, in the permit zone and parked about twenty-five yards away.

No one was about. He opened the driver's door, looked around him and walked casually around to the boot of his car, he lifted out a small backpack and walked up to Sarah's car and carefully placed it underneath it. The twin exhausts hid it from sight.

He returned to his car and moved away from the BMW behind some trees in Grosvenor Square, just far away enough to keep an eye on it; he would sit and wait until Sarah came out and then detonate the bomb from his mobile telephone. He had watched her for several days and knew her routine by heart.

He lay back against the driver's seat, exhausted and closed his eyes and dozed off for a few minutes, he knew he was sick and that he needed to see a doctor for treatment.

The sound of a car door closing awoke him. It was the black BMW just about to drive away. He pressed the button on his mobile as the car quickly pulled out. From where he was parked he saw the blast and he was temporarily deafened.

The young man shouted aloud through his windscreen. "This is my Retaliation."

He opened the door of his car and made his way towards the wreckage of the black car as if to help. He noticed several cars had stopped, one car had been blown onto the pavement with the force of the blast and drivers were getting out also to try and help and he saw a woman's black high-heeled shoe lying on the pavement near the burning vehicle and knew that it belonged to Sarah. He walked back slowly to his car.

David also heard the blast of the bomb and ran to his office window and looked up the road. Sarah's car was almost unrecognisable.

A tall dark-haired young man dressed in black jeans, black bomber jacket and a black baseball cap was slowly walking towards the old Ford Mondeo that he had noticed about half an hour ago parked almost on the pavement, when he had looked out of his window to see if Sarah had arrived. Somehow he knew instinctively he was the culprit of the bomb explosion.

"Oh my God," he screamed through the closed window. "No, not Sarah, no, no," he again screamed in torment.

She had said that she was going to pop out and bring in a snack lunch for them both.

He would hunt down whoever had done this; he could not go through the torture of losing another person whom he dearly loved.

Suddenly he noticed Sarah's handbag lying open on his desk, she had forgotten to take it with her and the handle of a small gun peeped out. He pulled it from the large handbag. It was the nickel-plated Beretta that she had told him about that Juan had given her for protection some time ago in Spain. He would kill this bastard with her gun. Justice would prevail after all.

He returned to the double-glazed window and opened it. He watched the dark haired man approach the railings just under his office window and carefully took aim with small gun. The man dropped to the ground. It was over in seconds.

That's all it took one shot to the head. No one had seen him. It was so easy thought David as he carefully closed the window.

David heard a slight noise behind him and Sarah stepped into the room.

"What happened darling? What was that noise?" She asked.

He stared at her in disbelief. "I thought, I thought...you... your car...?"

"What David?" She stared at him, horrified.

"No your secretary took it, she offered to pick up a couple of baguettes for us on her way back from lunch, I gave her the key to my car. I hope you don't mind. I wanted some quiet time with you."

"Oh my God, it was Samantha! I thought it was you. Your car has just been blown up. I must call the Police. Oh thank God it wasn't you." He looked out of the window as he heard the sound of Police sirens approaching. Obviously someone had already called the authorities.

He sat down in his office chair and let out a long sigh of relief. No one would know now that Sarah had any connections to the previous killings. His Sarah was safe. He now had the unpleasant role of telling Samantha's parents about her death. But he knew that he would never be able to tell them he had already avenged their daughter's death.

At that moment David had a flash of understanding of exactly how Sarah had been driven to do what she had. He knew then that his life's work to look into the minds of killers would have to be revised, but he would never be able to explain the reasons why.

David shook his head in disbelief as he picked up his phone and dialled Samantha's parents in France.

***

The young dark haired man managed to crawl towards his car, a bullet had caught him in the throat, not his head as David had thought, but he was bleeding badly. He managed to open the car door and slumped into the driver's seat his blood and saliva bubbling out of his mouth. Another bullet had gone clean through his shoulder and imbedded itself into a tree although David had only fired one shot from Sarah's gun.

The effort of getting back into his car caused more blood to pour out and as he leaned back the last thing that the man thought about before he died was Jacko and how he had found his lover dead in the dingy room of the flat that he had shared with the girls, but he had got his revenge. A half smile formed on his lips, as he knew they would be united once and for all, they had often spoken about it.

EPILOGUE

Juan walked slowly to his black Mercedes parked just off Grosvenor Square. His Spanish bodyguard stood outside of the Embassy car with one of the rear doors open ready for him to get. He settled back into the comfortable rear seat and sighed deeply, he knew now that Sarah would be safe and sound.

He was flying that evening to New York, with his bodyguard, to the Spanish Embassy and would not be returning for at least a couple of years. He knew that no one could connect him to the death of his son and his lover or the others for that matter.

The bullet from his gun could not be traced to him, there was no serial number on the gun and he had already packed the little crossbow away that Sarah had given him some time ago, in the rest of his personal belongings that were due to be shipped to America in a container. His *associate* would dispose of the weapons when they caught up with each other in New York at a later date.

He suddenly had a fit of coughing and put his white handkerchief to his mouth and wiped his lips. Several specks of blood were on it, he knew that he probably had no more than a year to live anyway. His many years of heavy smoking had finally taken their toll.

***

DCI Forrest completed his reports on the murders of Diana Gonzales, Jacko von Jonge, the Albanian prostitute and the last killing of the young man involved in the car bombing at Grosvenor Square.

Although Paul had strong suspicions about the involvement of Sarah in the earlier deaths of the four young men, he would never be able to prove that they were part of a serial killing or anything to do with Sarah and Juan Gonzales. Probably the case would be put into the unsolved file, for regular review by the cold case squad.

***

At the Rehabilitation Centre, Michael Akaro opened his mail the following morning. There was a short note from Sarah expressing her regret that she could no longer help out at the Centre. In another envelope there was a cheque for £350,000.00 from David with a short note.

This should help towards your new clinic.

Michael chuckled to himself. His match-making skills were still active and so successful that the Centre would be able to stay open for a lot longer thanks to the generosity of David, presumably in gratitude for the introduction to the beautiful Sarah. There was still some of the witch-doctor in him, which he had inherited from his ancestors.

THE END